MW00593204

SHAKING HER ASSETS

SHAKING HER ASSETS

ROBIN EPSTEIN AND
RENÉE KAPLAN

BERKLEY BOOKS, NEW YORK

THE BERKLEY PUBLISHING GROUP
Published by the Penguin Group
Penguin Group (USA) Inc.
375 Hudson Street, New York, New York 10014, USA
Penguin Group (Canada), 10 Alcorn Avenue, Toronto, Ontario M4V 3B2, Canada
(a division of Pearson Penguin Canada Inc.)
Penguin Books Ltd., 80 Strand, London WC2R 0RL, England
Penguin Group Ireland, 25 St. Stephen's Green, Dublin 2, Ireland (a division of Penguin Books Ltd.)
Penguin Group (Australia), 250 Camberwell Road, Camberwell, Victoria 3124, Australia
(a division of Pearson Australia Group Pty. Ltd.)
Penguin Books India Pvt. Ltd., 11 Community Centre, Panchsheel Park, New Delhi—110 017, India
Penguin Group (NZ), Cnr. Airborne and Rosedale Roads, Albany, Auckland 1310, New Zealand
(a division of Pearson New Zealand Ltd.)
Penguin Books (South Africa) (Pty.) Ltd., 24 Sturdee Avenue, Rosebank, Johannesburg 2196,
South Africa

Penguin Books Ltd., Registered Offices: 80 Strand, London WC2R 0RL, England

This is an original publication of The Berkley Publishing Group.

This is a work of fiction. Names, characters, places, and incidents either are the product of the authors' imagination or are used fictitiously, and any resemblance to actual persons, living or dead, business establishments, events, or locales is entirely coincidental.

Copyright © 2005 by Robin Epstein and Renée Kaplan.
Cover design by Steven Ferlauto.
Text design by Tiffany Estreicher.
Cover and interior art by Evil Kid.

All rights reserved.
No part of this book may be reproduced, scanned, or distributed in any printed or electronic form without permission. Please do not participate in or encourage piracy of copyrighted materials in violation of the authors' rights. Purchase only authorized editions.
BERKLEY is a registered trademark of Penguin Group (USA) Inc.
The "B" design is a trademark belonging to Penguin Group (USA) Inc.

PRINTING HISTORY
Berkley trade paperback edition / May 2005

Library of Congress Cataloging-in-Publication Data

Epstein, Robin.
   Shaking her assets / by Robin Epstein and Renée Kaplan.
      p. cm.
   ISBN 0-425-20240-2
   1. Essay—Examinations—Authorship—Fiction. 2. Unemployed women workers—Fiction.
3. Self-employed women—Fiction. 4. Women editors—Fiction. 5. Businesswomen—Fiction.
I. Kaplan, Renée. II. Title.

PS3605.P65S47 2005
813'.6—dc22

                                                                        2004062674

PRINTED IN THE UNITED STATES OF AMERICA

10   9   8   7   6   5   4   3   2   1

ACKNOWLEDGMENTS

First and foremost, thank you to our editor, Allison McCabe, for taking a chance, making it happen, and then making it better. Thank you to Nina Collins, our agent, for her encouragement and remarkable responsiveness.

We are extremely grateful to Dr. Paul Epstein for his great expertise, great humor, and paying for college (where Robin got to meet Renée). Thank you to our moms, for the good examples and all the love. Thanks to Laurence Kaplan, for his supersolid common sense, and to Marlorie Stinfil, our first reader. Linda Blumberg-Smith and Cory Smith, thank you for making us interactive.

We are indebted to Alex Blumberg, for the story that started it all. And to Alex "Essay" Edge, and the start-up that started it all. Thank you to Louise Brockett and Lynn Goldberg for the priceless crisis management, to Diane Tarshis, for your business savvy, and to the Good Samaritans of Tigernet. And thank you to Alia Phibes, for drawing Marilyn to perfection.

Finally, thanks to Matthew Elblonk, Michael Cantwell, Pam Perrell, Emmanuelle Chiche, Connecticut, and Chief Running Feather, for all their help. And thank you to *all* of our friends for their endless and touching enthusiasm.

Everyone is a potential winner.
Some people are disguised as losers; don't let their
appearances fool you.

—Kenneth Blanchard, author of *The Leadership Pill*

PROLOGUE

I wonder what's worth holding on to. Do I keep the stress ball? Do I steal the stapler? Can I line the *whole* bottom of the box with Post-it notepads? I'll toss the company pens: They're cheap, and they bleed, and they suck.

I can hear people walking by. I can feel their pity, and I can smell their fear. If it can happen to me, it can happen to them. Ultimately, the most important question that remains is whether I should bother packing my three cartons of unused business cards. I take two and leave one, just to give them something to remember me by: RACHEL CHAMBERS, EDITOR, *The Byzantium Catalog.*

The large document box is full, and I want to get out of the office before I start crying. I would like to retrieve my picture from the wall of company Polaroids. It was taken at our Summer Solstice Party in the Hamptons. In the photo, I'm wearing an orchid lei on my head and I look dangerously close to falling out of my gingham bustier as I bear-hug Alan, everybody's favorite C.F.O. But that would mean walking by Byzantium employees deemed *not* disposable. I top off the box with my pilled office cardigan, because I know if I don't hurry up I'll be using it as a hanky.

Rob had called me into the conference room to let me know the luxury goods market was hitting a really tough spot. Though they "esteemed my work," and I had made "invaluable contributions to developing the unique identity of the catalog," they were going to have to let me go.

"So . . . I'm fired?"

"No, Rachel," he had replied, realigning some papers on his desk. "Unfortunately, in the interest of cost-cutting, the company has been compelled to do a lot of consolidation, and much of the editorial work is in the process of redistribution."

What Rob was saying was that I had been laid off, not fired—an important corporate distinction between being run over by a Mack truck and being run over by a Mack truck with malice.

After pushing the "down" elevator button, I run my fingers over the deep grooves of the company's embossed brass nameplate that hangs on the wall. I turn around to stare at the lush flower arrangement sitting on the receptionist's desk, behind which Suzie the receptionist is hiding. The bouquet of bird-of-paradise is essential Byzantium. As a luxury-goods catalog selling high-end housewares, the company's currency is the rare and overpriced. The bound catalog's deluxe ivory paper features pen-and-ink illustrations selling everything from sculpted cherry-wood end tables to Chinese lacquerware. My job until ten minutes ago consisted of creating all the product descriptions and the boldface copy scattered throughout the catalog. I had been the mistress of prose, responsible for generating countless synonyms for "superior," "distinctively crafted," and "one of a kind."

As I wait for the elevator, I hear the muffled ring of my cellphone at the bottom of my shoulder bag. I balance the box between my hip and the wall, and dig around, desperate to make the chiming stop. I find the phone and flip it open. "Hello?"

"Hey, baby!" It's Andy. "You are not going to believe the sweet Pumas I just picked up! Buttery-brown nubuck suede. They're awesome!"

"Andy—"

"So we're on for tonight, right? It should be really fun. Bradley has no idea we're surprising him."

"Andy—"

"I think we're going to Bond Street, the SoHo sushi place—"

"Andy, Andy, listen to me. I just got laid off."

"Wait—what?"

"The fuckers fired me!" I hiss as the elevator doors open.

Rob and Alan are now standing in front of me. They look at me looking at them, then look down. After all, they are the fuckers in question. I want to vanish in a puff of acrid smoke. Instead, I step aside to let them off the elevator. Alan gives me a hang-in-there punch on the arm, causing me to drop the cellphone. I resist the urge to kick it into the elevator. Rob bends down, picks it up, and hands it to me. Andy continues chattering through the phone as my now-former bosses step aside and I walk into the elevator. The endless pause before the doors close could possibly be the most mortifying moment of my life.

1

For the second time in less than a month I find myself standing on the street, holding a collection of my personal effects, trying to catch a cab at rush hour. But today, instead of juggling a box of coffee mugs and pilfered office supplies, my big paper shopping bag overflows with the contents of my two-year relationship with my now ex-boyfriend Andy.

It's been a shitty month.

When I finally hail a cab, I give the driver the address of Ben's office. It's the only place I want to go. He's been my best friend since college, and when something's wrong I always travel in his direction. I know that no matter what he's doing, he'll stop, give me a hug, tell me what I need to hear, and make me feel better. Like, "Don't worry, Rach, there is always a spot for you in my harem."

I walk into his midtown building's granite lobby and rest the bursting bag on the security guard's desk. I tell him I'm here to see Ben Seidman on the eighth floor. He dials the number and waits.

"That's a big bag. Watcha got in there?"

"A few parting gifts from my ex-boyfriend," I say, peering into the box. "Some of my CDs, my Minnesota Twins baseball cap, and oh look! He accidentally included a bottle of Chanel Number 5 perfume that must belong to the girl he cheated with. Here." I plunk the bottle down on the security desk. "You married? Got a girlfriend? For her."

The security guard raises his finger to his lips and points to the phone. "Mr. Seidman, uh, there's a young lady here to see you . . . No, it's not an Olsen twin—what's your name?"

"Rachel Chambers."

"It's a Ms. Chambers. Okay, I'll send her up." He replaces the receiver and picks up the bottle. "Well, hey, thanks!"

*   *   *

Ben is the promotions director for *DesignLab,* a lifestyle magazine for the wannabe hipster professional. He started six years ago as an assistant to the publisher and made his way up the ranks; four months ago he was promoted to director. As Ben explains it, his job now consists of organizing sponsored parties, having long expense-account lunches, and upgrading his working wardrobe from Banana Republic to Emporio Armani. When the elevator doors open on the eighth floor, he is waiting for me.

"Chambers . . . are you okay?"

He takes the bag and starts leading me down the hall.

We walk in silence until we get to his office, a small, cluttered space overlooking a busy stretch of Madison Avenue. The shelves are loaded with piles of books, CDs, and other promotional stuff—a twelve-inch plastic statue of Captain Morgan, a miniature Eames chair, a clear lucite ashtray. His large desk eats up most of the space, like a king-size bed in a starter apartment. Ben refuses to turn on the overhead fluorescent lights, so the office has a comfy, messy-bedroom feel.

I sit down in a chair with my back to his window and look at the framed pictures on his desk. There's one of us from junior year spring formals, me wearing the same flowery Ann Taylor dress every other junior girl wore that year; we had gone together because we'd both been dateless. As Ben shuts the door, I pick up a silver-framed picture of his girlfriend, Leigh. "Is this picture new?" I ask.

He ignores my question, hands me a can of Dr Pepper, and sits down behind his desk. "Tell me."

"Leigh is so pretty. Is this from the summer at the beach?"

"Rach, c'mon. What happened?"

The tears I've been fighting since Andy handed back all my possessions finally start sliding down my cheeks. I can't talk yet. I take a swig of the Dr Pepper, and I swallow hard. I hate Dr Pepper. "Andy and I met for lunch today. It's the first time we've seen each other since things ended. He gave me back all my stuff."

Ben is looking at me sympathetically but says nothing.

"You know I've been temping for the past week in an office near his downtown, so I e-mailed him yesterday and suggested we get together for lunch. We really hadn't *talked* since the breakup. And I don't know, I just needed—"

The phone rings. Ben leans forward to check the caller ID. I point to the phone and nod. "Take it."

Ben waves his hand dismissively, leaning back in his chair.

"Anyway, the first thing he does when he walks into the restaurant—before he even sits down—he hands me this bag. Tells me it's all my stuff from his apartment, thought I'd want it back, then pulls out the chair, opens the menu, and he's like 'So, what's good here?' "

"That's shitty, Rach."

"We were together for two years, Ben," I shout, grabbing the Captain Morgan doll from the shelf, looking to do him some harm. "Two years! You'd think there'd be something to talk about. You'd think he'd have something to say about us. Or, I don't know, something like, 'Sorry you found out I was fucking my co-worker when I accidentally sent you an e-mail intended for her.' But no. He says nothing, just like we never even happened. Done."

"Saying I never thought he was good enough for you probably won't make you feel better right now. But that he could treat my best friend like this," Ben says, shaking his head, "someone as awesome, funny, and kind as you—not to mention voluptuous and smokin' hot. I mean look at you, you're gorgeous! Who wouldn't want to go out with Bettie Page's younger sister? Well, it just tells me that, like always, I'm a damn fine judge of character. And, you know, at least that makes *me* feel better." Ben smiles and winks, trying to make me laugh.

But just thinking about it makes me want to cry, and I'm tired of crying. I reach for a tissue in my purse to blot under my lashes, hoping the extra lash-lengthening mascara I applied this morning isn't now coating my cheeks. I'd made an extra effort with the makeup this morning. And under my suit jacket, I'd put on a plunging V-neck sweater—one that I knew highlighted my cleavage—that I knew Andy liked. I was also wearing my hair pulled back in a ponytail, which I almost never do, because I knew he liked that, too. I feel so stupid now.

"He always was an asshole." Ben nods. "And now you can find someone better."

"Sure, and another temp job, too. I was supposed to go back to work after my 'doctor's appointment,' but I just couldn't. I just started wandering around the city with my bag of crap. So I'm sure I've screwed myself with this temp agency also."

"Well, I have the perfect solution," Ben says. "Daytime drinking on my expense account!" He takes Captain Morgan away from me and reattaches his head.

I envision myself doing an Esther Williams dive off the lip of a pool-sized martini glass into the clear liquid of a vodka gimlet. "That sounds great," I nod.

"Just one second," Ben says, throwing on his coat and reaching for the phone. He dials his assistant's extension. "Abby, hi, Ben. Listen, it turns out I have to go to this last-minute meeting at the Publicis agency, so I can't make it to Madeline's shower. Can you swing by on your way and grab this gift I have for her? I'll leave it on my desk. Thanks."

"What did you get?" I ask, as Ben hangs up the phone and takes a wrapped package out of his desk.

"I have no idea—baby's first power tool? Leigh picked it up for me."

I reach for my shopping bag on the floor, and we head out of his office.

"So what's in there anyway?" he asks.

"Everything I kept in Andy's apartment or left there over the years. Clothes, hair-dryer, makeup."

He peers into the bag. "Did you ever really wear this?" he asks, holding up a U Penn college T-shirt Andy had given me. "Hope not," he says, leaving it on a desk we're passing. He looks in the bag again as we keep walking. "Nooo! Please tell me you didn't buy this for yourself?" Ben exclaims, wrinkling his nose and holding up a purple silk teddy that I've always liked. He drapes it over the side of a cubicle as we pass. By the time we get to the elevators, there's a trail behind us: all the pieces of my daily life that had intermingled with Andy's, all the evidence that we'd once shared a bed and a dresser and a relationship.

*   *   *

We walk into the Whiskey Bar at the Paramount Hotel and slide onto leather-upholstered barstools. "So, big guy," I say, reaching for the drinks menu and scanning it quickly, "give me some details on the dimensions of your expense account. Will it cover the $14 Plum Saketini? Because that seems like a nice early afternoon drink."

"Ask me something about the magazine."

"Will you go with white pages and black ink for this next issue?"

"Yes. And now I can expense this."

"Genius! Pass those mixed nuts."

"So shouldn't you call in to the temp agency and invent some excuse about hemorrhaging and hospitals that explains why you couldn't go back to work?"

"Nah . . . what could I possibly come up with? This job is over Friday, anyway, why bother for just a few more days? I'll just go to another temp agency tomorrow."

"You know," Ben says, "*DesignLab* has an in-house temp department."

I sip my drink.

"Most of our full-time editors started out working free-lance as temps. I think getting you an interview would not be a problem."

I don't want any handouts from Ben. "No thanks." I reach for the swizzle stick in my drink and stir.

"Why?"

"I got laid off from a job I loved a few weeks ago. The wound is still fresh. I want to wallow a bit."

"I think it could be a good opportunity for you."

I look at him out of the corner of my eye without turning my face, and raise my eyebrows.

"You've been in lots of different jobs, Rach," he says. "This could be a good opportunity for you to finally get some focus."

I feel an inspirational get-on-track talk coming on.

"I've seen people at *DesignLab* come in who didn't know

what they really wanted to do, who are now at the top of the masthead."

"I'll keep it in mind," I say, with an affirmative nod. "I really will. And you're a great friend, man." I try leaning over to give him a hug, but his saketini glass gets in the direct flight path of my elbow. His drink spills in a plum-colored puddle on the bar.

"You're a great friend, too. And you're right, I didn't need any more of that drink," Ben says, mopping up the mess with a wad of paper napkins. He leans over the bar and tosses the sodden napkins into a trash can.

*   *   *

When I get to my apartment in Hell's Kitchen, I can hear Carlos's Middle Eastern house music blaring from Christy's stereo. I inherited Christy as a roommate when my former roommate, Debra—Christy's older sister—moved to San Francisco. Christy was moving to New York, so at the time it seemed like a good swap. Since then, I've tolerated Christy, but I've come to hate her too-often-undressed boyfriend, Carlos, who really should go home more often. As I walk down the hall to my bedroom, I rap on the door twice. I hear Carlos sigh loudly, and the music goes down.

I walk into my room, peel off my clothes, throw them into the growing pile on my butterfly chair, and put on last night's T-shirt and boxer shorts. Then I plop down in front of my computer and prepare to log on to eBay.

Covering the entire surface of my glass-topped dressing table is my collection of vintage compacts. I vividly remember my mother opening her gold-plated Estée Lauder one to double-check her lipstick before getting out of any car. She'd been a beautiful woman who loved to dress up, but at the time of her death I was eleven and didn't appreciate the tailored skirts and the Ferragamo shoes she wore. The compact with her initials engraved on the lid in delicate script was the only object of hers I'd wanted to keep.

I started using my mother's compact in junior high school and then started collecting them with baby-sitting money. The advent of eBay changed vintage-compact collecting forever, introducing me to a global community of compact junkies and a selection of colors and clasp designs I'd never imagined. It became my paradise and my purgatory, as I discovered how easy it was to spend a healthy chunk of change on a little shiny object. I was going to find one right now that would more than compensate for being unceremoniously handed my relationship in a "Big Brown Bag" from Bloomingdale's.

Two and half hours of clicking and scrolling later, I come upon a conch-shaped specimen circa 1940 with sterling silver plating and a mother-of-pearl clasp. At $95, the collector in me knows it is a bargain; as a now-unemployed person with no savings and no more banker boyfriend to pick up the bar tabs, I momentarily question the wisdom of the potential purchase.

Then I place my bid.

2

When people ask my father what he does, he loves to joke that he's the lawyer who patents the honey and the nuts in the Cheerios. He owns a small law firm in Minneapolis specializing in intellectual property, and his business, almost all relating to General Mills, is mostly local. He doesn't particularly like New York—or the East Coast—so it has always puzzled him that both of his daughters have found a home here. Every time he visits, he asks us when we we're moving back to Minnesota and pretends to believe it will happen one day.

He's in town briefly for some business, and we're having an early breakfast before he flies home. I walk into the lobby of the Park Avenue Winchester Hotel to meet him Saturday morning, enjoying the echo of my clicking heels on the polished marble floor. I'm wearing a cotton polka-dot sundress and high-heeled slides and carrying a white vintage leather handbag, just big enough for cash and keys (eBay acquisition: $36). We'd agreed to meet in the lobby restaurant, and as I approach, I can see that he's already seated at one of the mostly empty room's tables. He's studying the menu, even though I'm certain he'll order an egg-white omelet and a glass of orange juice, then encourage me to order the waffles or French toast so he can steal a bite. Dad is tall and a little paunchy with giant, gentle Bambi eyes that make you feel terribly guilty when you describe him as paunchy. I walk up behind him quietly, lean over, and put my chin on his shoulder, as though I'm trying to read the menu.

"Rach!" he says, turning around with a big grin on his face. He pulls back his chair, stands up, and gives me a big hug. "It's too bad Katie can't join us, huh?" he says as soon as I sit down.

"Yeah, it would be great if she were here." I nod. "Like when we used to do brunches together in the Riverfront District on Sundays." The memory of this makes my dad smile. "But I know weekend mornings are the one time Michael can take the kids and she can volunteer at that smelly animal shelter she seems to love so much. Hey, did you lose weight?"

"Yeah, yeah, a little," he says, indifferently.

"Too bad you can't stay longer. I know you'd love seeing Sophie and Lola, they're getting so big! And did you hear that Sophie gave up meat? Kate swears she had nothing to do with it, but this would be the first six-year-old I've ever heard of discovering vegetarianism on her own."

"Actually," Dad replies, turning his attention to the muffin basket, "I stopped out there last night."

"You did? That's great. I didn't know you'd be able to find the time. I bet Lola made you watch the *Dora the Explorer* video, huh?"

The waiter interrupts to take our order, and I get the apple-cinnamon French toast so my father can order his virtuous vegetarian egg-white omelet and an orange juice.

"So how are you, chicken?" he asks once the waiter has left.

There's no reason to delay any longer. I've avoided telling him long enough. "I got laid off, Dad," I say looking up at him.

I can see a mixture of compassion and disappointment flash across his face. "Oh, honey . . ." he trails off. "When did it happen?"

"A little while ago. I haven't really told anyone."

He asks all the concerned dad questions—*Did they give you severance? What about health care? Are you okay financially? Do you need help?* I relay the details, and tell him I have no better explanation for "why me" than he does.

"I know you're going to be fine," he says. He is entering his default fathering method, the one in which *It's always darkest before the dawn!* and *Things will work out, they just will!* It's a routine fueled by well-meaning clichés, but never particularly probing questions. "You've gone through this before—and it's worked out. And hasn't every experience left you more prepared for the next? Remember that gay magazine you worked for?"

"You mean *Poz*?" I ask, tearing off a hunk of muffin and shoving it in my mouth.

"They fired you because they didn't like the way you looked!"

Getting fired from *Poz* was humiliating. Six weeks after my first day, the managing editor, Simon Hewitt, buzzed me at the front desk and asked me to stop by his office when I had a chance. That meant immediately. I took off my headset and programmed the phone to automatic voicemail pickup. I walked into Simon's office, and he asked me to close the door and have a seat. He said *Poz* was a magazine about a certain aesthetic and a way of living, and there didn't seem to be a *flow* between me and the magazine. He then said he preferred everyone working at the magazine to embrace its aesthetic, so unfortunately it wasn't going to work out for me at *Poz*. Translated, Simon was actually saying I was too fat, straight, and square to answer his telephone.

"But, Dad, *Byzantium* was *different*."

"Maybe you should take this time to think about going back to school? You've had a lot of different jobs since you've been out of college. Maybe this is the opportunity to step back and refocus. What do you think you would *really* like to be doing, Rach?"

I cut a large bite of the French toast that had just arrived, shovel on some of the browned apples, and advise my father to have his bite quickly as I deliver the dribbling pile to my mouth. My dad has always been a *whatever-makes-you-happy-honey* kind of father, in the most sincere way. After my mother died, he was as lost as we were, and when it came to raising two girls, if our hair was brushed and we seemed well fed and happy with our toys, then everyone was doing okay. Sometimes I wish he were more like Ben's parents, who have always had predetermined life-goal expectations for him and frequently remind him of them. And no matter what the situation, the Seidmans always have an answer. On days like today, I wish my father might offer one, too.

"So, Dad," I say, lifting my water glass, "you didn't tell me about the big project you're working on that brings you to New York."

"Well, I didn't actually come for anything work-related."

"You can tell me. I understand that *other* people still have jobs."

"Well, no, that's not exactly what I mean." He pauses and glances out the window. "Somehow I thought this was going to be easier to say."

I zone out as he begins a long wind-up to what I assume is a confession that he's started dating Miss Reese again. She is the home ec teacher at my junior high school. They've dated on and off for years, and he knows it bothers me. Specifically, *she* bothers me. She always used to come over to my cooking station in class and sneak a foil-wrapped package into my bag, telling me to take the goodies home to my "sweet dad." The fact that my father can find her appealing simply makes me want to toss my cookies. Aside from making an excellent apple crisp, the woman possesses no redeeming features and—

". . . malignancy in the lung," Dad says, nodding.

I look up at him. "What?" I'm pretty sure I just heard the words *malignancy* and *lung*. "What did you just say?"

"Dr. Baker wanted me looked at by the team at Sloan-Kettering, so . . ."

"You have *cancer*?"

"I have a lung tumor. But, I guess that's cancer to you and me, kid." He tries to laugh then stops. "Not really a good joke," he says.

"Dad, I . . ." I'm having trouble catching my breath. *What the hell just happened?* "When did you find out?"

"A little while ago," he replies, and I hear an odd echo of the conversation we'd had a few minutes earlier. But the tables have turned, and I have absolutely no idea what to say to him in his moment of need. "I hadn't been feeling well for a few weeks, but I just thought it was the flu there for a little while."

"Why didn't you tell me before, Dad? Didn't you think I'd want to know something like this?" My voice has become shrill.

"Sweetheart, I didn't want to worry you. Besides, I didn't really think there was anything to worry about—"

"So? So . . ." I swallow hard. "What changed?"

"Well, I started coughing up some blood, so I decided it would be a good idea to go talk to Dr. Baker about it. He wanted me to get a bronchoscopy and take a chest X ray. And that's when they discovered the tumor on my lung." He pauses and looks at me. I am just staring back at him, wide-eyed. "He recommended surgery to remove part of the lung, but encouraged me to get a second opinion first. He said he knows the head of oncology at Sloan-Kettering, and so when he mentioned the possibility of going to New York, I decided to do it. I figured I could find out what was going on here, then tell you and Katie. To be honest, Rach, I was really hoping I wouldn't need to be having this conversation with you."

"Oh, Dad."

I stare down into the remnants of the French toast I've just shredded with my fork. I don't know what to think. I don't know if this is something that can be treated, or something that's going to take my father from me tomorrow. "So what happens now?" I ask, not certain I want to know the answer.

"Well, fortunately, there is some good news," Dad says, nodding his head enthusiastically.

"What is it?"

"There's finally a decent reason for me to live in Minnesota." We both laugh briefly, but it can't be sustained.

"Okay, and what's that?"

"The Mayo Clinic," he says, "happens to be one of the finest cancer research facilities in the world, and it's right in our backyard. The doctor here told me it made sense to do the surgery and follow-up there. He said Mayo is a wonderful hospital and that I'd probably be more comfortable doing it there, close to home."

"Dad . . ." I trail off, choking up. He squeezes my hand as I close my eyes, and the tears leak out. The waiter comes by to refill our water glasses, but my father waves him away. I open my eyes to look at him and bite my lip.

"I'm sorry," he says, "did you want water?"

"No."

"Listen, honey, you know more than anything in the world I want to be able to tell you that I'm going to be fine."

"But you can't?"

"I really do think I'm going to get the best treatment that's out there. Both doctors were encouraged by the fact that they didn't see any spread of the tumor. So they're just going to re-move the part of the lung with the tumor and then whatever it takes to get better, I'm going to do. I can beat this." Dad smiles and tries to will me into belief. "I'll even eat your Aunt Barbara's soy-protein veggie burgers that she's been pushing on me for years."

"No, Dad, I want you to get better, not worse," I reply, taking a meager stab at humor, and he responds by giving me an appreciative pat on the knee.

"I know you do, chicken."

"Did you tell Kate?"

"Yeah, when I stopped by last night. She really wanted to be here this morning, but I told her not to come. In fact, I in-sisted. There was no reason to make her miss her morning at the animal clinic."

"Dad!" I say sharply, feeling familiar anger rise in me. "I think your *cancer* trumps some hemorrhoidal *ferret!*"

"Rachel, listen to me," he replies sternly. "This is not something that's going to kill me tonight, nor is there any-thing that Katie can do to make it go away. So I didn't see any good reason to ruin the one morning a week she gets to go out and do something she really enjoys. Got me?"

"I guess," I answer.

"Good," he replies, "and besides, I'm sure a ferret hemorrhoid is very uncomfortable for all concerned."

*   *   *

"Hello?" Kate says, picking up the phone.

"Why didn't you tell me? Why didn't you tell me he told you?"

After breakfast, I waited with Dad for his ride to the airport, trying hard to play along with his halfhearted chatting. When the car pulled up, I gave him a hug and then stared at him, too full of emotion and confusion to get out any words. "It will be okay, Rach, you'll see," he said, giving my hand a squeeze with both of his.

After the Town Car pulled away, I walked very slowly toward the corner, feeling as though everything had been momentarily suspended, like a videotape on pause. I saw a cab coming up Park Avenue and I hailed it, giving the driver the address to my apartment. I needed to talk to Kate.

"Rach, he asked me not to," Kate answers. "He said he wanted to tell you himself. He said he would have preferred to tell us both together, but you know how he is . . . he didn't want to make 'a big production' of it. I told him he was being absurd, that I should call you and you'd come right away, but he actually got angry and insisted we not 'ruin your evening with all this.' He also said he didn't want me to change my plans for this morning, either! He was so adamant about it, he was unlike himself."

"Kate, he's dying, isn't he?"

"He's not dying. He's got cancer," she replies quietly.

"I wish he'd told us sooner."

"Yes, but it sounds like things were caught in time and the surgery should take care of it. I think he was hoping it might just go away by itself, that he wouldn't have to tell us at all until he was in remission!" Her tone of voice is rising, and I recognize the anger as frustration, the same frustration with our father we've experienced our whole lives.

"My understanding is it was detected in a timely manner and that things are under control," Kate replies, speaking soothingly and methodically. I listen to her break down the same facts Dad talked about earlier. The massive void of panic that opened this morning begins to feel a little less all-consuming. She pauses, and there is just silence and understanding on the line between us for half a minute.

"They said Mom's cancer was treatable."

"I know," she says, almost in a whisper. "But I think everyone said that about Mom because they didn't know what else to say to us at that age. But her cancer was a totally different illness, Rachel. And they've made real progress in treatment therapies now. You have to believe that, because it's true."

I am silent again for another moment, letting Kate's calmness settle in. "I do want to believe that," I reply softly.

"Rach, what he needs right now is for us to be normal," says Kate. "That's the best thing we can do for him. The doctors are saying it's manageable, so what we can do is wait, and hope, and go about our lives like he'd want us to."

"But Kate," I say, another wave of emotion and frustration rising in my throat, "he's treating this like he treats every other problem!"

"This is just how Dad deals with things, Rach. We know that. If it helps him to believe that we're not worried, then we need to do our best to make it seem that way. It may be the only thing we can do to make him feel better."

"Are you sure he *really* knows?"

"Of course I am. I think we're all aware of what's going on, Dad especially. He's always trusted us to let him know when we've needed help, and I think we need to do the same for him."

"Yeah," I murmur.

"We've been through this before, Rach, I know. And it's not fair. Believe me, I feel it, too," she replies. "But we can do this for him—even if we'd rather do it another way—because we need to stick together and do whatever we can to make him feel better."

"You're right," I say.

We hang up a few minutes later, and I have to fight the urge to call her right back. Everything I'm feeling is too familiar and too horrible, and no one knows exactly how it feels more than Kate. I want to believe her when she says it's not like before, with Mom. I envy her composure and her conviction.

If she's convinced, then I need to be, too.

3

A few days later, I'm still "between temping gigs," which is about as unemployed as it comes. But I don't really care—getting fired feels like it was ages ago. I've been consumed with thoughts about Dad. Once he got back to Minnesota, I'd called and told him that I wanted to come home to be with him for the surgery, but he flatly refused. He said it with the same firmness—almost fierceness—he'd used at breakfast, when he'd insisted on not bothering Kate, as though first the tumor and now the surgery were an unfortunate nuisance that he refused to blow out of proportion. He'd left no room to insist, and then, as usual, cracked a joke, "You just want to come home so you can get behind the wheel of my minivan, don't you?" So I'm left with nothing to do. I need more of

Kate's coolness and her comfort. I don't even bother calling before hopping on the subway to go see her.

I make my way to the F-train stop, and twenty minutes later I get out at Carroll Street. Kate and Michael live in Carroll Gardens, a tree-lined brownstone neighborhood in Brooklyn. I walk down Sackett Street, a picturesque residential block just off the bustling main drag, Smith Street, and I spy the spill of my sister's life well before I arrive at her doorstep. The girls have colored the block with the oversize chalk sticks I bought them a few weeks ago. My three-year-old niece, Lola, is undoubtedly responsible for the rainbow made entirely of yellow. I recognize what looks like a turkey probably drawn by Sophie, who is in the first grade and learning about Pilgrims and Indians. Kate's done a pretty good caricature of George W. Bush in the hear no/see no/smell no evil monkey pose with a thought bubble that reads, "Keeping Sackett Street Safe from Evildoers." They've been adorning the sidewalk with similar works pretty much since the first day they moved in, but I don't get the impression their neighbors particularly mind. The other people who live on the block are a mixture of young boho couples who left Manhattan in search of more space and the lifers who've been in the neighborhood since coming over from their respective homelands.

I smile when I see the Big Wheel parked at the top of Kate's stoop. Not exactly the Kawasaki motorcycle she had bought and kept hidden when she was in college. She knew our father would have had been furious if he ever found out—for the six years she used it as her primary mode of transportation, she never once told him about it and swore me to secrecy. I kept the secret in exchange for her fantastic silver-and-garnet earrings. And the promise that I could count on her backup for that one summer in college when I came to New York to wait tables and lived with my boyfriend but told Dad I was living with her.

As soon as I get to the top of the stairs, their long-haired Irish wolfhound, Lucky Charms, starts barking at me ferociously through the window. Lola toddles up behind Lucky and presses her face against the glass. I bend down and do the same thing on my side, puffing out my cheeks. Lola starts shrieking with joy.

"Lola, Lola, honey, inside voices, inside voices," Kate yells from somewhere inside. A moment later Sophie comes to the window, sees me, and yells, too.

"Maaaahhhhm, it's Aunt Rachel!" I hear Kate quickly bound down the stairs toward the front door, which she flings open.

"Rachel!" she says, squeezing me. "C'mon in."

As I enter, Kate says, "Watch your feet! Tea party in progress—you don't want to knock over any of our special invited guests." In the middle of the vestibule Sophie has set up a little table with four chairs and seated a party of stuffed animals and dolls. I recognize her favorite, a one-eyed dog she calls Alfredo, sitting in the biggest seat. At each place setting Sophie has laid out sandwiches of Wonder Bread and peanut butter sectioned into triangles. Scattered on the floor around

the tea party sit countless other stuffed animals who are serving as restaurant atmosphere.

"So does this mean I'm not an *invited* guest?" I say, turning
to Sophie.

"You're always invited, Aunt Rachel," Sophie replies. "But
you're always too busy to come."

"Not anymore, my lovely," I say, scooping her up and
cradling her spindly little body in my arms. Kate approaches
and wraps her arms around both of us. She is taller and more
muscular than I am, and her long arms easily encircle us. We
share the same fair skin and dark, coffee-colored hair, but unlike mine, which goes past my shoulders, she keeps hers in a
shag, which she's always slipping behind her ears or pushing
away from her face. When Kate walks down the street with
her two creamy-skinned, dark-curled little clones, people
sometimes turn to stare at the striking threesome, or just at
Kate. "I called this morning to get an update." Kate strokes
the top of Lola's head, raises her eyebrows, and then looks
down. "We'll talk more about that later, but just quickly,
they've scheduled his surgery for this Thursday."

"Thursday? That's so soon! Don't they have to wait for an
operating room or something? Don't weeks usually go by?"

"They don't want to wait. If they do—" then Kate recon-
siders and instead says, "They just don't want to wait. C'mon,
we were just about to go the supermarket. If you're good, I'll
buy you some Double Stuf Oreos."

I help pack Lola into her jacket as Sophie slips into hers,
and Kate clips on the dog's leash. We set off en masse up the
street toward Metro Foods—Kate pushing Lola in a stroller,

Sophie pushing Alfredo in a doll-size stroller, and me getting pulled by Lucky Charms.

I tie Lucky Charms to the bike rack in front of the grocery store and follow the troupe inside. The cart fills quickly with three varieties of yogurts, gallon jugs of milk and juice, and a few boxes of sugar cereal Sophie manages to pull off the shelves when Kate turns her back. Lola sits in the small seat at the front of the cart eating blueberries out of the plastic container, and Sophie alternately walks alongside or beelines across the aisles, picking up and hugging boxes of any product that happens to bear a cartoon commercial tie-in on its label. Occasionally Lola points to a box or jar on a nearby shelf and, her little arm wagging as though she's found a treasure, cries out eagerly to Sophie, "That one, So-*pheee!*" They remind me of Kate and me. Whatever Kate was doing, whatever trouble she was getting into, I would observe breathlessly and then join in or try to copy. It was that way until our mother died. After, Kate would still get into trouble, but she wouldn't let me join in anymore. She became protective, even stern sometimes, although at the time I didn't understand, and she just seemed mean and moody to me. I look at Sophie and Lola and hope things will never have to change for them.

As Kate reaches for a carton of sour cream featuring a slender cow in a pink dress, Sophie runs up to her.

"Mommy!" she says excitedly, tugging on Kate's leather coat. "You know what?"

"What?" Kate asks, good-naturedly.

"That cow's a girl!"

"Umm-hmm."

"I'm a girl, too. I have a vagina."

My mouth drops open; Kate blanches slightly but isn't rattled.

"Yes, sweetie, that's right." She puts the sour cream in our cart. "You most certainly are a girl." My sister smiles at an older woman who's standing next to her, checking the expiration date on a carton of half-and-half.

"But my friend Benjamin, at school, he's a boy," Sophie continues, looking wise, "so he has a penis."

The older woman's head turns slightly as she keeps her eyes on the half-and-half, clearly listening intently now.

Kate tries to stay cool. "Uh-huh, that's right." She puts her hands on Sophie's shoulders, nonchalantly trying to steer her daughter out of the dairy section.

"Mommy, you're a girl, so you're supposed to have a vagina, too. Do you have one? Do you have a vagina?"

The old woman now looks directly at Kate.

"Yes, honey, I do," unflappable Kate says, sounding distinctly flapped.

"Well, Mommy," Sophie says triumphantly, "don't let anyone touch it! It is *personal private!*"

"Who wants to pick out some COOKIES!" I say, my eyebrows at my hairline.

Kate and I say nothing as we unload the groceries at the checkout counter, avoiding eye contact, fearful we might encourage Sophie to expound further on the human body for unsuspecting Metro Food customers. But as soon as we walk through the grocery's automatic doors, we look at each other.

I start laughing. "What in the *world* . . ." I whisper, while Sophie is busy chatting to the dog.

"Progressive schooling," Kate replies.

"And I thought she was learning about Pilgrims and Indians," I say, not knowing whether I should be impressed or horrified. As we walk back around the corner and down the street toward home, I am feeling better than I have in several days.

*   *   *

"Come on," Kate says, handing me the grocery bags as she folds up the stroller and kicks open the front door, "time to meet the menagerie." I follow her to the kitchen, and the circus follows me—Sophie, Lola, Lucky Charms, and two other dogs I've never seen before who suddenly materialize from the garden in the back of the brownstone.

"And these are?" I ask, leaning down to pet the fat black Lab whose chunky middle section metronomes slightly out of synch with his legs as he wags his tail.

"The neighbors' kids," Kate replies as she starts unpacking the bags, opening and closing cabinets as she puts away packages. "They're away for the week, and Sophie volunteered that they could stay here."

"Michael didn't object?"

"Object? He laughed. Said it looked like the girls were picking up all my bad habits. He thought it was adorable."

"It is kind of adorable," I say reaching for the Double Stufs and tearing open the package.

"Uh-huh, until you learn that Spanky, the Rhodesian

Ridgeback over there, is diabetic and depressed and requires insulin shots and doggy Zoloft three times a day. I swear to God, Rachel, sometimes I wonder how this became my life."

I sometimes wondered, too, remembering the borderline-punk older sister, who'd dropped out of college for a few semesters to be a roadie for a band.

"Good luck?" I say, winking at her.

"Fuck you," she replies, laughing.

Lola giggles and adds, "Fa-q."

I stay for the dinner of chicken fingers and plain pasta, read Lola the same good-night story three times, and then take my time getting back to my apartment. As I step onto the Manhattan-bound subway, I worry that as soon as I leave Brooklyn the provisional feeling of well-being will have worn off. Of course, as soon as you start worrying that the good feeling is going, it's already gone.

4

I'll never work again. I know it for certain. Other people, yes, they'll bounce back. They'll find employment. Not me. I am already tired, and I only woke up an hour ago. It feels like I'm paralyzed, like my body is giving up, knowing that nothing I'll be doing today will be remotely important. I've tried to distract myself as much as possible, to get my mind off Dad, off my unemployment, off anything that matters. I've done sightseeing around New York. I've cruised the aisles of Duane Reade looking for Club Card reduced-price offerings. I've loitered in so many Starbucks, I've been mistaken for a homeless person. I consider making myself some waffles, but then decide I don't deserve them. Waffles are a weekend treat, best enjoyed after a Hard Five.

I decide to lie in bed, stare up at the ceiling, and wallow.

But wallowing is old. I wallowed all of yesterday and the day before. I get up and tear off my bathrobe. I need to shake off the gloom. I walk over to my CD rack and grab REM's *Green* album. As soon as Michael Stipe's voice begins blaring through my speakers at level nine on the volume dial, I can feel my limbs again. First my arms regain animation, then my head starts bobbing loosely on my neck, my knees start bending, prompting my legs to start moving in a corkscrew of dance floor greatness. Then my roommate Christy and her boyfriend Carlos appear at my door.

"RACHEL!" Christy yells, catching me by the arm as I twirl, eyes closed.

"What?" I reply, stopping abruptly, as I catch sight of the two of them.

"Jor music woke us up," Carlos says, turning down the volume on my stereo.

"Sorry." I am actually closer to horrified than repentant.

"It's, like, eleven," she says, squinting at my alarm clock. "Why aren't you at work?"

"Pink slipped," I reply, realizing it's been over a month and I haven't yet told Christy. We haven't been on especially friendly terms since I asked her not to burn incense in the kitchen because it made my food taste like cheap cologne.

"Ouch," she says, and gives me an exaggerated frowny face.

"What is peenk slip?" asks Carlos.

"It means Rachel got fired, honey." Christy nods slowly at her boyfriend. "They call it getting pink slipped when your company doesn't need you anymore, and they give you all the reasons why they don't want you on a pink sheet of paper. Right, Rachel?" She turns back to me and nods some more.

"I didn't actually get a pink slip, *per se*," I mumble, "just a swift kick in the ass."

Carlos looks even more confused.

"I'm really sorry I woke you guys up," I say. "I'll keep the music down, I promise."

"Good," Carlos says tersely, under his breath.

"Excuse me, what?"

"Oh, Carlos is just a Mr. Grumpy Pants in the morning," Christy replies, shepherding him toward the door. Before she pulls it shut behind her Christy turns back to me. "So, like, do you think you're going to be hanging around the apartment much?"

"Why do you ask?" Why do I suddenly feel like a mother intruding on her teenager's slumber party?

"Just cause we were probably having some people over later," Christy says. "We've got our midterms next week, so a bunch of us are going to be practicing technique out in the living room." Christy and Carlos are studying to get their certificates in therapeutic massage. They met at "The Institute."

"Oh, what does that mean exactly?" I ask.

"You know, there are going to be a lot of bodies stretched out of the floor."

I clearly *am* going to be interrupting that slumber party. "I'll stay out of your way, I promise."

"Great, thanks!" she says, smiling, then closing the door.

*   *   *

"It was like a patchouli-scented orgy," I tell Ben the next day at the flea market, blinking hard in the Saturday morning sunlight. "I literally had to tiptoe my way through the bodies."

"Hmm," he says, picking up a Danish Modern martini pitcher and turning it upside down to look at the stamp on the bottom. "Wonder what the 'original-scented' orgy smells like?"

"Please, don't make me hit you with glass barware."

Ben puts the pitcher down and moves over to examine a selection of kitschy glasses. "You wouldn't think a classic martini set should be that difficult to find. What is the world coming to?"

"The question is not what is the world coming to, Benjy, it's what can we do to make it stop spinning."

"We make cocktails," he replies, "extra dry, just like the boys at St. Andrews have been doing since the dawn of golf." He puts down the shaker and practices the swing he's been trying to perfect since college.

"Anyway," he says, "you can't let these totally inconsiderate dipwads walk all over you like that. Tell them no. That apartment's your place, and their behavior is completely unacceptable. If you don't set limits they'll just keep abusing you."

"Look, I'm sure Norma Rae would be very proud of you right now, but I can handle the situation, okay?" I feel a twinge of anger flare, partly because I know Ben's right, and partly because I don't feel like being lectured by my best friend.

We move on to the next cluster of tables, and as Ben examines a silver cocktail shaker, his cell phone rings.

"Well hello!" he says enthusiastically, mouthing "Leigh." "Yeah, uh-huh, we're still at the flea market, but I think we're going to be leaving soon because just between you and me, all this stuff has been *used* before." Girlfriend laughter tinkles through the earpiece. "Oh, really?" Ben continues, "I'll ask her."

He keeps the phone at his ear but moves the mouthpiece away. "Leigh just got an invitation to go to a restaurant opening tonight. Wanna bail on the MediaSalon thing?" MediaSalon is a website dedicated to all sorts of media-related activities, and they frequently organize networking cocktail parties. Ben and I had planned to go together.

"I'll just go to the MediaSalon thing by myself." *Fantastic.*

"But it wouldn't be a problem to get you on the list," Ben says. "Leigh told me she could make you our plus one."

"No, really, I need to go to this MediaSalon party. I'll do some networking, get my life in order, that kind of thing."

"Free food and great company," Ben replies, weighing the option in one hand, "or bad wine and single in a sea of networking barflies," in the other.

"Ben!" I interrupt. "I want to go. Alone!"

5

As soon as I walk into the bar, Nuit Noir, I instantly remember why I never do these things solo. The bar is full, the MediaSalon party is operating at capacity, and I am alone, looking like a huge loser in a sea of networking barflies.

A woman in a red feather boa approaches me.

"Hi," she says, brandishing a clipboard and looking happy to see me. "And you are?"

"Rachel Chambers?"

"Okay, right. Good." She glances down at her list and slides her pen across my name. "There are a few people here I want you to meet."

"Really?"

"You're going to love these guys!" She grabs me by the wrist and pulls me toward two men who appear deep in conversation. One is prematurely gray in his early forties, and the other is in blocky black glasses and vibing Clark Kent. "This is Rebecca," she says, depositing me in front of them and leaving before I have the chance to correct her. We all turn to watch as the feather boa flutters behind her.

"That's Cynthia," the older one explains. "She's the greatest."

"Gotcha," I reply. "But I'm not Rebecca, I'm Rachel."

"Scott," Clark Kent says, extending his hand. "And this is Jim."

"So what do you guys do?" I ask. *Okay, this isn't so hard.*

"Freelance writer," Jim answers.

"Yeah, freelance writer," Scott says, nodding.

"Freelance writer," I throw in quickly and point to myself.

"Cool," Jim replies. "Who do you write for?" He smiles broadly and conveys a tinge of desperation that suggests he thinks I might be able to get him an assignment.

"I'm just starting out, looking to make some connections here," I reply, moving back slightly to reclaim some personal space.

"I come to these things all the time," Scott says.

"So you've found these parties helpful?"

"Not really," he replies, leaning in.

Jim nods. "Me neither."

"But, you know." Scott looks down at his shoes.

"Yeah." Jim takes a sip of his beer and the conversation stops.

"I'm going to go get a drink." I gesture vaguely to the back of the room. "I'll see you guys later."

I wedge myself into the crowd at the bar, thinking that perhaps this will all seem easier after a beer or two. "Hi, sorry, excuse me, can I just get in here please?"

"Whoo-boy, looks like we've got an alcohol-related emergency," says a short, stocky guy with a scruffy dark beard standing to my left. His two friends turn around and look at me. "Incoming wounded."

"Amstel Light," I practically bark at the bartender, struggling to extract my wallet from my bag. After paying for the drink and taking a swig, I tip my head and acknowledge the short guy. He smiles back at me, but because he's now listening to one of his friends talk, I don't interrupt further. Instead, I just eavesdrop.

"So I don't know. Over the last few months I must have written about . . . conservatively, maybe fifty pitch letters. And what do I have to show for it? Nothing. *And,* I'm going to have to move back in with my parents!"

"But, dude," Shorty says. "They live in a *huge* apartment on the Upper West Side."

"It's rent-controlled," Dude replies defensively. Shorty and the other fellow, a big guy wearing a rumpled button-down shirt, share a look. "Well how's it going for you?" Dude asks Big Guy with Rumpled Oxford.

"Freelance-wise?" Rumpled Oxford bats his hand at the air. "Brutal. I finally, finally get this commission to do an investigative piece and work on it for two months. Then the editor gets fired, and they drop the story. I get a little money for the kill fee, but basically I'm shit out of luck."

"Can you take it someplace else?" Shorty asks.

"I guess, but in the meantime I need to pay my rent."

I tilt my head in closer to hear what solution he's come up with. "And it's not like I'm about to move back with my parents in Minnesota." When I hear Rumpled Oxford do the native *Minna-so-dah* pronunciation, my head whips around. "Did you just say you were from Minnesota?" I ask.

"Go Wolverines."

"I'm from there, too. Originally. Today I'm a Hell's Kitchener. I'm Rachel."

"Ethan," Rumpled Oxford replies, extending his hand.

"Zach," Shorty adds, "and today I'm a Hell Raiser."

"I'm Ron, and I'm going to go to the bathroom," Dude says, putting down his drink and leaving us at the bar.

"Which makes him a real pisser," Zach adds.

"So where'd you grow up?" Ethan asks.

"Minneapolis."

"Me, too."

"But I've always thought of myself more as a St. Paulie girl."

"Me, too!" Ethan replies, clinking his bottle against mine. "Well, Rachel, it's been nice meeting you, but now with all this beer talk, I have to go to the little girls' room, too. Zach, watch my beer."

"Aye-aye." Zach salutes.

"And when I say *watch,* I mean with your eyes and not your mouth."

"Fiiine," Zach concedes as Ethan walks off.

"So," I say to Zach, "I'm sorry to admit this, but I was totally eavesdropping a minute ago, although I was trying to think of it as participating in the conversation nonverbally."

"And what fascinating detail was it about us that sparked your interest?" he asks, smoothing down his T-shirt and air-combing his hair like Fonzie.

"I'm new to the freelance biz, and I was just wondering—"

"Yes, everybody has another day job."

"Ah, overachievers," I say, and Zach laughs.

"Yeah, that's it. We're all worker bees at heart. And I can't believe I just used the term *worker bee*." He shakes his head. "Fucking Trees."

"That doesn't sound very pleasurable."

Zach laughs. "Trees is actually 'Trees-dot-org.' Ethan and I work there. They do environmental education stuff. A lot of freelancers work there, so if you ever want to find out more," he replies, reaching into his wallet for a business card, "e-mail me or something."

Ethan returns from the bathroom and chugs the rest of his beer. "I'll buy you dinner at Lil' Frankie's if we can get out of here in the next fifteen seconds," he says. "I think I've collected enough homemade laser-printed business cards to stuff a piñata." He taps his watch at Zach. "Fourteen, thirteen . . ."

"I never pass up a free meal," Zach says, tucking his wallet back into his back pocket. "But, uh, just to be clear . . . that wasn't a homemade laser-printed business card I just handed you." He smiles. "It was something for you to wrap your gum in later."

"*Of course,* that's what I assumed," I reply, returning the smile. "Nice meeting you." As they walk away, I look at Zach's card. It shows a big cartoon caricature of his scruffy head attached to a disproportionately little body. I laugh and decide that Shorty has the right idea. I look quickly left and right and make a dash for the door, successfully avoiding Cynthia's good intentions.

6

I push open the door to Merit Staffing and find a waiting room crowded with women, most of whom are much more professionally dressed than I am. They all look up when I enter, and a few smile. I see a box labeled "Résumés" and walk over to put mine on the pile.

"Un-uh, no," says one of the women rising out of her seat when I turn back to sit down. "You can't just put your résumé on top like that." She looks around to the other women, not merely to gain support, but to gauge the level of disbelief at my audacity.

"I'm sorry, what?"

"You have to put it at the bottom," instructs another one of the people waiting.

I take my résumé and place it underneath the six others in

the basket and glance around. "Do you have any idea how long it'll take to be seen?" I ask the less hostile woman to my right.

"Nope," she replies, and she turns back to examining her fingernails.

An hour later my name is called.

I am brought to the desk of Marjorie Goldsmith. A red pom-pom weevil with white feet dangles from the upper-left corner of her nameplate. Marjorie is in her mid-fifties and has a seen-it-all-and-am-not-impressed look. She wears a horizon-tally striped shirt that puckers across the chest, which in turn produces more horizontal stripes. Her desk is strewn with hundreds of résumés.

"Hi, I'm Rachel," I say, taking the don't-plan-on-getting-comfortable plastic seat next to her desk.

She looks at me over her reading glasses. "So you want to temp for us, Rachel?"

Want is a strong word, but I am willing to go with it. "Yes. Yes, I do."

"How many words per minute do you type?"

"Forty?" Sounds reasonable.

Marjorie purses her lips. "We won't take you on unless you can do at least fifty."

"Maybe fifty?" I smile.

"And you know Word, WordPerfect, Excel, PowerPoint, Photoshop, and HTML?"

I nod.

"We need professionals," she says.

"Of course. I'm very professional on the job."

"And I can see you've had a lot of them," Marjorie replies, scanning my résumé.

I try not to let this rattle me. "Yes, that's why I think I'd be excellent at temping. Short assignments are my forte."

The woman finally smiles.

We go over to the testing center, where three women are fiercely concentrating on their screens, deep into their exams. I am told to sit down at a computer terminal and then given an instruction manual. Marjorie tells me to come back to her desk when I'm finished. I open the instruction manual, which describes the test. It says that it will take approximately an hour and a quarter to complete. Another woman is brought into the room and told she'll just have to take the typing test. The woman nods, then, like a concert pianist, flexes her fingers and bends them backward. Her hands poised above home row, I watch her left index finger reach for the T. She then proceeds to break the sound barrier. The clatter of keys sounds like automatic weapon fire. By the time I start typing myself, she's already finished.

A little over an hour later, I walk back to Marjorie, who is flipping through several binders and has the phone wedged between her ear and shoulder.

"All finished?" she asks sweetly.

"I guess so."

Marjorie quickly glances at my typing test while continuing her phone call, repeating, "Uh-huh, uh-huh, yes, uh-huh, I know, uh-huh, got it." I score a lousy thirty-seven WPM. "Well you know, I actually have a girl standing in front of me right now who I believe will be perfectly adequate for your needs."

The description actually makes me smile.

"Let me make sure she's available." Marjorie takes the phone away from her ear and presses the hold button. "Now, Rachel, we have a wonderful opportunity at one of the finest investment banks in New York. And this job could be yours, but," she pauses for emphasis, "but, you have to understand that under *no* circumstances should you expect this to become a permanent position. The last thing these important bankers want is to be bothered with a girl at the front who doesn't know what she's there for, okay?"

I blink rapidly several times. "Okay?"

"Great," Marjorie says, turning her full attention back to the receiver. "It looks like she'll work out, Ellen. Okay, thanks, hon. Talk soon!" Marjorie hangs up and nods her head. "You're all set. Report to the HR department at Bear Stearns tomorrow morning at eight sharp, and they'll tell you where to go."

*　　*　　*

Mark Westerhoff, my new "boss," is exactly my age. His secretary has just gone on maternity leave. He occasionally comes out of his office to drop off work in my inbox, but seems to prefer doing this while I'm away from my desk. When there is no way of avoiding contact with me, he feels compelled to make idle chatter before handing me my assignment and bolting back to his office. During one of these chats he asks what I was doing before I started temping. I tell him I'd been a freelance writer—it seems like the easiest answer and close enough to the truth.

"But you need extra money while you're finishing up the novel, huh?" he asks. I can't tell if he's making fun of me or is actually interested.

"Something like that," I respond, staying vague.

"So are you pretty good with copyediting, too? I'm sure you've realized by now that I'm not the world's greatest at grammar."

"Are you kidding?" I say. "You're obviously much smarter than most of the people here." I have absolutely no basis for judgment on this, but it seems like something he would want to hear.

Mark starts walking back to his office, but after taking a few steps, he turns around. "Listen—I've got this thing that I have to get done and I basically just need someone to proofread it, to make sure I've got all my who's, whose, and whatnot in the right order, you know?"

"You're looking for someone to copyedit for you?"

"Yeah, do you think you could do that?"

"I'd be happy to." I smile.

"Cool," he raps his knuckles on the nearest desk, "I'll e-mail it to you. What's your address?"

"It's PinkSlip@hotmail.com," I answer. I'd set up the account as soon as I lost my address at Byzantium. Within a minute, his message appears in my inbox.

Subject: (none)
Message: As discussed attachment
Attachment: personalstatement

Personal statement? Is he asking me to proofread his ad for Match.com? Though unexpected and probably inappropriate, it could be kind of fun. Once I download the document it takes me a minute to realize Mark is asking me to edit his business school application. Scrolling down, I see that there are several different essays within the long document, each one starting off with the essay question in bold. I read the first topic and laugh out loud.

Many organizations have a credo or value statement that they follow. Please share with us your personal credo.

They're asking for the personal credo of a twenty-something banker? What kind of answer are they possibly expecting? *Play hard, work much harder, and never let the guy in the cubicle next to yours own a more recent model Blackberry.* I click down to the next essay question.

We believe that the best education for leadership in any sector of the world economy is two years of rigorous business fundamentals. This approach to learning will prepare you for any career you might pursue, be it in business, government, or a nonprofit arena. With this in mind, tell us why our MBA program is the right learning environment for you.

Don't they mean two years of rigorous schmoozing and balancing one's driving-range time with study groups? When Andy talked about going to business school, it was never about "learning." It was about reveling in two company-subsidized years of résumé building without the added responsibility of also being employed.

I scan the first few paragraphs of Mark's "credo" essay and then go back and reread it, carefully, to see if there isn't some nuance or a Greater Point that I'm missing.

As the captain of my college rugby team, I was the guy in charge. In moments of victory or in moments of defeat, when the buck stopped, it was in front of me. For better or for worse, I had to answer for the result. Team solidarity is so important when playing on a team that it was always my primary focus. In the now-infamous closing game of my senior year rugby season, things seemed to be going terribly wrong. We'd had a mostly victorious season, and this was the match that would define the fate of the team. The tension on the field was so thick you could cut it with a knife. But my credo has always been to never cave under pressure. When it looked like we were going to lose, I managed somehow to pull the team together. I took away from that experience a valuable lesson about myself and the importance of keeping things together.

The rugby stuff continues. He talks about another game from his sophomore year, about some "weak link in the chain," and then he concludes with the goal of teaching his " 'little brother' who lives in a project in the Bronx" how to play the game, because he doesn't see himself just as a leader, but as a role model, too.

Mark didn't strike me as the sharpest tack, but he didn't seem this dumb. His personal credo makes him sound like he has the values of a fifteen-year-old Abercrombie & Fitch model.

I start with a straight copyedit. But when I go back and read this proofed version, it's still stupid. There's nothing else terribly pressing that I need to do, so I decide to see what will happen to the essay if I rephrase a few of the topic sentences and reword some of the glaring clichés. I tweak the Little Brother in the Bronx story so it's less obvious that Mark did his two days of volunteering just to use the phrase "role model" on the b-school application. There's no way to get rid of the rugby metaphor entirely, but by the end of the afternoon when I'm done with the essay, Mark not only sounds like a dynamic team leader who thrives under pressure, but also a humanitarian committed to improving the lives of those around him. I e-mail the first copyedited version of the original essay back to Mark and also attach this second version of the essay with a note explaining what I've done.

Mark:
Attached are two versions of your personal statement. The first is a totally clean version of the essay you wrote—100% spell-checked and with grammar so perfect, Strunk & White would blush at your precision. The second version includes a few additions I think further clarify what a great candidate you are. Hope this is what you were looking for!
Rachel

I send the message and watch as Mark turns to the computer when he hears the new message arrive. He reads my note, looks around his computer at me, and nods. I glance at the clock and realize I have spent the entire day editing one essay. I became so involved in it, I didn't even stop for lunch and it occurs to me now that I still have hundreds of pages of documents to photocopy before I can leave.

I perch on the counter next to the copier, watching the high-speed machine flash. I had high hopes that I might be able to finish the task in a decently short amount of time so I could beat the rush to the elevator bank. But when the "Error—Tray 2" message starts flashing, I know I'm screwed—Tray 2 is notoriously temperamental. I crack open the gigantic copier and start hunting for the paper jam. My head is firmly planted in Area 3 when I hear my name called out from behind me. I turn and see Mark standing in the copy room doorway with a piece of paper in his hand.

"Rachel, can I talk to you for a second?"

"Sure," I say, closing the copier in an attempt to make it look less like I've broken the expensive machine. Mark slides the copy room door shut.

"So I read your essay," he says tentatively. "And I think it's pretty good."

"Thanks."

"I mean, you know, my version was really rough. It was just like my first draft, and I hadn't really had time to revise it yet. I mean I probably would have included all that stuff that you put in there, too."

"Of course." *Liar.*

"So I may just use this essay as is because I'm not sure I'm going to have the time to work on it anymore." Mark nods.

"Well, I'm glad I could help," I say. I point to the piles of bound documents.

"You think it's okay if I finish the rest of this tomorrow?"

"Oh, yeah, yeah sure," Mark replies, as he opens the door again and walks out. Even though I still have to ask Mark permission to leave, I know the balance of power has shifted a little this afternoon. I have done a job for him better than he did for himself, and made him look really good in the process. I believe that is what's called an ideal employee. I leave the paper jam for someone else to fix, gather the copies I've made, and walk back to my desk. I collect my things and unwittingly start to straighten up. It's almost as if I'm beginning to feel some pride in ownership again.

7

I see Ben sitting in the window table of his favorite Vietnamese place as I come run-walking up Columbus Avenue. He's flipping through a magazine and doesn't see me coming, so I press my butt up against the glass and wriggle. Ben pretends not to notice, but several other patrons begin pointing and staring.

"Despite the unlikely odds of actually enjoying a temp job, your butt cheeks seem to be telling me you've had a good day," he says as I enter the restaurant.

"And, despite the odds, I think I actually did!" I reply, with cheerleader pep that surprises even me. I sit down, shake off my suit jacket, and lunge for the menu. "And I'm *star*-ving. I forgot to eat lunch today."

Ben signals for the waiter and holds up two fingers. The

waiter nods and immediately brings two beers to the table. This is why Ben loves being a regular at his local Asian greasy spoon: VIP service.

"So you know how I told you about this guy I'm working for who has difficulty, you know, talking to the help?"

"Sure, the kid who does the dump-and-run trick when he has work to give you."

"Right. Well, today he says he's got this 'thing' that needs to be edited, and would I mind taking a look?"

"He asked you to take a look at his thing?"

I ignore Ben and continue. "It was his application to business school, and his essays were *awful*. They were so brainless they made me laugh. So I started to tinker with them, and once I got going, the time just flew." I take a sip of beer. "It was strangely satisfying."

"Oh?" Ben calls over the waiter and orders us two bowls of noodles. They appear on the table almost immediately.

"It was like I had some kind of perspective on how to package him. Sort of like being back at Byzantium, in a weird way."

"Sounds like Bear Stearns is getting more than their money's worth out of their newest Girl Friday." Ben says, slurping from his steaming bowl of noodles. My cell phone starts vibrating in my bag. I reach down and flip it open, but I don't recognize the number.

"Hello?"

"Hello, this is Linda from Merit Staffing. Am I speaking to Rachel Chambers?"

"Oh, hi Linda. You're working late tonight."

"Well, staffing never stops! I'm calling to let you know, Rachel, that Mr. Westerhoff from Bear Steams let us know he will no longer be needing your services."

"I'm sorry, what?"

"It appears whatever project you were working on there has been terminated. So your assignment at Bear Stearns is over."

"How can that be? His secretary is on maternity leave until—"

"Well, sometimes the collaboration with our staffers doesn't work out quite right. Mr. Westerhoff didn't elaborate as to the reasons for the termination."

"Um . . . okay."

"I'm sure we'll find you something again soon. But no need to report to the office tomorrow. Alright, hon?"

"Okay, thanks . . ."

I slowly close the phone and stare at it for a moment. I eventually put it away and look at Ben, who is holding his chopsticks in midair, waiting for me to speak. "That was Linda from Merit Staffing," I say. "She was calling to tell me Mark Westerhoff will no longer be needing my help." I am completely shocked. "I just spent all day helping this asshole, and he gets me *fired*? Could that possibly be what just happened?"

Ben doesn't look at all surprised. "You corrected him. Pointed out his flaws. To him, you're just a temp; how could you possibly do anything better than he can?"

I sit silently as Ben keeps talking, making infuriating sense.

I can tell he's winding down when he says, "He's a *guy*, Rachel. A successful guy who's rarely in the position of being told what to do, unless it's by another more successful guy." Then Ben leans forward over the table with a serious expression. "But, Rach?"

I look up from the soggy beer-bottle label I've been scraping off.

"Mark's reaction was absurd. You tried to do him a favor. There's no reason he shouldn't have been receptive. A lot of busy guys applying to business school would be grateful for anything that could make them more competitive."

"I was just doing a job that really, obviously needed to be done."

"Did you save the essays at least? I bet they're still in your e-mail archive."

"Yeah, they're probably in there somewhere," I reply, stabbing at the vegetables floating in my noodle soup.

"So what you're telling me is you already have the perfect 'before' and 'after' sample for the Rachel Chambers Essay Company. Your motto can be, "Bring us your rich, your functional illiterates, your rugby players yearning for an MBA . . . and we'll send you on your way with pure genius and correct grammar."

I laugh. "You make me sound like P. T. Barnum—revising essays as the greatest show on Earth."

"I don't know about the *greatest* show, but I bet it could be a pretty neat little business scheme. And there *is* a sucker born every minute," Ben says, nodding at me. He pulls out a few paper napkins from the metal dispenser on the table, unfolds them, then takes out a felt-tip pen from his bag. He starts writing on the napkin in block letters.

THE BUSINESS SCHOOL APPLICATION.
ONE SHOT TO IMPRESS.
YOU NEED KILLER ESSAYS.
WE'RE THE PROFESSIONALS.

"You're a professional, right?" he asks.
I nod. Ben continues writing.

PERSONALIZED COACHING IN THE ESSAY-WRITING PROCESS.
YOU GIVE US YOUR VITALS AND YOUR ATTITUDE,
WE GIVE YOU A PERSONALITY AND GET YOU IN.

I laugh out loud. I couldn't have written it better myself. Ben continues.

ONE-STOP SHOPPING FOR THE ULTIMATE APPLICATION.
CALL 1-800-HOT-STUFF FOR MORE INFORMATION.

I take the pen and replace 1-800-Hot-Stuff with my real name and phone number. "Let's definitely use my real digits. We can tape this up on the first lamppost we see and then I can score some of the most eligible freaks in the city," I say with mock glee.

"Fantastic. Let's go to Kinko's and design this baby, print it out, and plaster it all over Manhattan," Ben agrees.

"Better yet, I'll hand-deliver this napkin to Mark Wester-hoff's home. That'll show him!"

"I'm serious, Rach. This is how all great businesses got started, just two crazy kids with an idea and a copy card."

"Right, I definitely see myself as the next Bill Gates."

"Come on, what's there to lose? We'll make it fun. Go to the deli next door and pick up a six-pack, and I'll meet you at Kinko's in five minutes. There's one on Broadway, two blocks from here."

"Okay, I like fun. And what percentage of the profits will Ben Seidman Inc. demand for his investment?"

"No percentage, just one ultimatum."

"What?"

"Either we make these fliers and tape them up all over everywhere tonight, or I destroy this nasty soiled napkin now and forevermore."

I smile, thinking about the expression on Mark's face if everyone in his department at Bear Stearns actually did receive an ad from an essay-writing company that had my name and number at the bottom. The thought is very amusing.

"Okay . . . lager or pale ale, Seidman? You're on."

*　　*　　*

"Ben, that looks *great!* When did you learn how to use design software?"

"Uh, working at a design magazine?"

Large block letters at the top of the page spell out ON TAR-GET ESSAY, the name we came up with after looking through a big database of images in the design program and finding a graphic of a round archery target. Beneath the heading, Ben has created the image of an arrow nailing a rolled diploma to the center of the concentric rings of the target. Below the target, all the copy from the napkin appears in a large typewriter-style font. I delete the promise of giving a personality or getting anyone in, and replace it with a bullet-pointed list of a few other "services offered"—like "customized collaboration" and "intensive troubleshooting." Ben adds "highly refined bullshit meter," but I delete it. Ben makes a few more adjustments and then clicks print.

"Congratulations, Hot Stuff, you're in *bid*ness!"

We walk over to the copy machines and run off a hundred colored fliers. We splurge on Kinko's overpriced masking tape, tacks, and two staplers, fully prepared to plaster an ad on any surface—cork, glass, or metal. First we blanket the surrounding Upper West Side, then we catch a crosstown bus to the Upper East. When we finish, three hours and another six-pack later, we've covered a surface area of forty blocks by seven avenues.

8

"Hello?" I look at the clock: It's 5:59 A.M. *Why am I awake?*

"Hi, is this Rachel Chambers?"

"Yes . . ."

"This is Tisha at Merit Staffing. We have a job for you this morning. It's . . ." I can hear her flipping through papers. "It's an editorial and administrative job at an online educational company specializing in environmental and conservation issues," she reads aloud in a rapid monotone. "They need someone to start this morning at 9 o'clock for an indefinite duration. The offices are located at 127 W. 58th Street, that's between 6th and 7th Avenues. The dress code is casual, and you'll be reporting to Molly Carlisle, one of the directors. Remember to bring a copy of your résumé, so they can have an idea of what your skills are and why we referred you. Okay, Rachel? Good luck and have a great day."

I realize that she has given me all this information and I have written down none of it. "I'm sorry Tisha," I say, trying to flip off the covers and hold on to the phone. I grope for a pencil in the top drawer of the bedside table. "Once more?"

"127 W. 58th Street, between 6th and 7th, Molly Carlisle, bring your résumé. Oh, and the name of the company is Trees-dot-org."

*　　*　　*

I walk into the airy atrium of the company's building at 8:40 A.M. The lobby strikes me as surprisingly swanky for some kind of crunchy Internet outfit. I walk out of the elevators on the twenty-first floor expecting to see a reception desk, but there is just an empty foyer.

I wander into a vast, low-ceilinged space filled with large and mostly empty cubicles. Along the outer walls are half a dozen separate offices. Looking over the sea of cubicles and desks, all I see are a few heads facing screens, backs turned toward each other, workspaces blocked off by wooly gray dividers. I'm disappointed; Tisha had said that Trees.org was some kind of environmental educational company. I had imagined crepe-paper trees and poster-board clouds hanging from the ceiling, or maybe a rainforest diorama nestled into a wall.

I notice that there are nameplates hanging next to some of the office doors, so I start walking slowly down the row to my right looking for Molly Carlisle. At the far end of the office I finally spot her nameplate on the wall.

Her door is ajar, and I knock softly. "Hello?"

"Hello, yes, come in," says a woman's polite voice.

I stick my head around the door. "Hi, I'm Rachel Chambers. From Merit Staffing . . ."

"Great, have a seat. You're right on time."

I walk in and see that she's holding the phone receiver over one shoulder and pointing to a chair with her other hand. I realize she's in the middle of a phone conversation and mouth "Sorry," pointing to the door, to suggest I can come back. She smiles, shakes her head, gestures to the chair again, and holds up her pointer finger, mouthing, "One minute."

I sit down and focus on the view outside the small window behind her desk. The offices are just a few blocks below Central Park. From this high up, she has an almost unobstructed view of the treetops in the park, which look like a broad, textured blanket of golds and browns. I think it's the first time I've ever seen the park from this close and this high. The morning sun makes the fall leaf colors glow warmly.

"Of course, but not this week," she says into the phone. "We're shorthanded, but there is no question we'll be making that deadline." Her desktop computer emits the muted beep of a new e-mail. "Of course!" she says, and turns to look at the screen. "It's our priority, the website is our public face! In fact, listen, I have someone in my office now—the website person . . . Great . . . Will do. Bye now." She hangs up. "I am so sorry!" she says, still facing her computer screen and typing quickly as she speaks. She clicks on the mouse and then turns to face me, extending her right hand.

"I'm Molly Carlisle, the content director of Trees. As you

may know, we're an environmental action group," she recites, as though delivering a practiced speech. "We create online educational materials on environmental issues. We produce multimedia courses intended for students of all different types. College kids, activist homemakers—really anybody who's curious about the big environmental issues of today and wants to learn more."

I nod, trying to look interested. I probe internally, curious as to whether I can formulate any opinions about the big environmental issues of today. I cannot.

"Here, why don't I show you what one of our courses looks like. Just pull your chair up," she says, moving over to make room behind her desk. She inserts a CD into the computer's CD-ROM drive.

"This one is *Urban Waste Management*—that's what you'll be working on."

She rapidly clicks her way through a series of icons, describing briefly each of the course chapters as animated images, photographs, and short films materialize on the monitor. The course looks like a futuristic 3-D version of a ninth-grade science class filmstrip. As the images flash by rapidly, Molly explains how the course is structured, and I pick up a few terms like "reprocessing," "illegal dumping," and "toxic mineral content."

"Your job is essentially copyediting work. All those workbook exercises we just saw have already been created by our producers, but we need you to check for spelling and consistency, and generally make sure it all makes sense. One of the really urgent outstanding tasks is our glossary of terms." She turns to her computer again and calls up a spreadsheet of words and definitions typed in columns.

"Each of our courses comes with a hyperlinked glossary of terms. That means users can click on any term they don't know, and it will take them to a virtual dictionary that defines the term for them." She whiz-clicks until an animated pie chart floats across the screen over a background photograph of an enormous pile of garbage.

"Here, for example," she says pointing the cursor to one of the labeled segments of the pie chart, "let's say a user doesn't know what 'biodegradable' means. He or she can just click on the term"—Molly clicks—"and be taken straight to this animated definition." The screen flashes, and the word *biodegradable* appears in a large font on the left-hand "page" of an animated dictionary, and the definition appears on the right, with a series of numbered images illustrating the magnified decomposition process of a banana peel.

"All this—every single term and its definition—needs to be copyedited."

*   *   *

Except for one trip to the restroom, I spend the next four hours glued to my computer screen, silently proofreading tree-hugging terms. Toxic Persistent Pesticides, Growth Hormones, Fossil Fuels, Aquaculture, Alernative blabla, Bio hooha. I calculate that I average about twenty terms an hour, and there's an average of seven corrections per twenty terms.

All this adds up to a lot of staring and very little motion. By mid-morning I feel like I am operating in some sort of glazed fourth dimension.

When I go to the kitchen to get a soda, I notice that most of the surrounding cubicles remain empty. There are maybe a dozen people in the whole office. I wonder if Trees.org is just Molly and a bunch of temp workers like me, a little Wizard of Oz–style command center hiding behind the disguise of elegant marble elevator banks.

Along with the luxe atrium, the office also boasts a terrace, and it's even outfitted with wooden benches and some spindly potted plants. I take a can of Fanta from the fridge—check plus for the company's complimentary soda policy—and walk out into the late September sunshine to get some air. I'm starving, but I don't want to waste time to go get lunch. I stuffed a Keebler Snack Pack into my bag as I left my apartment this morning, and I bring that outside with me now, salivating at the prospect of the salty orange cheese. I sit down on one of the benches, and my mouth and ears are full of the crackling rumble of my own chewing when I hear the terrace door slam behind me.

"What's she *doing*?" I hear a male voice ask a few seconds later.

Another voice answers in a stage whisper, "Is she eating *processed* food?"

"*Processed* food? That's how the last girl got fired!"

They start laughing, and I turn around. There is a short guy with a dark-brown beard, glasses, and a Buddha belly who looks instantly familiar to me, but I can't place him.

"Hey, wait a minute. I know you," he says, wagging his finger at me. "Were you at that MediaSalon thing a while ago?"

"Oh yeah! You're . . . Zach! Right? You gave me your card."

"Yeah, that's right. And you're, um . . . Jen?" he asks, raising a dark bushy eyebrow and stroking his beard.

The other guy snorts. "Jen?! What, are you trying to play the odds with that one?" He was the guy who had dragged Zach out of the party.

"It's Rachel."

"Rachel," the big guy says, shaking his head at Zach, "you weren't even close with *Jen*." He turns back to me. "I think we met, too, and I'm Ethan. And don't worry, you'll see, it's not really so bad here."

"Not as long as you stay high, dry, and keep it organic," Zach adds, taking off his glasses and hooking them over the collar of his faded T-shirt.

"I didn't see you guys around earlier," I say, desperately hoping they hadn't been sitting on the other side of the cubicle the whole morning.

"Yes, well, that's normal. Molly lures you in and pep talks you, then begins the hypnotic process of sedation by excess information. By the time she walked you back to your cubicle you were probably well into the famous Trees trance."

"That's *exactly* what it was!"

Zach takes out a cigarette and extends the pack toward me.

"No thanks. I try to get all my carcinogens from my snack foods," I say. He laughs softly into his cupped hand as he lights his cigarette.

Ethan reaches over and takes one and points it at Zach. "He's the art director here, and that rare breed of Trees employee who is actually on staff. The rest of us are just fungible freelancers. Rachel, if I'm now remembering correctly, I know where you're from but I don't know what you do."

"Apparently, I'm the new director in charge of urban waste management." I reach for my empty soda can and cellophane garbage and stand up, not wanting to look like a slacker on my first day. "So if you have any urban waste management concerns," I say as I walk toward the terrace door, "don't hesitate to stop by my cubicle. I'm here to help."

By the end of the day, my brain feels inflamed, throbbing as though it's desperate to expand outside the confines of my skull. But as I emerge from the marbled atrium into the 6:30 dusk of bodies rushing toward the subway, I feel good. For now, at least, I've been welcomed back into the Great Society of the Gainfully Employed.

*   *   *

The problem with being a copy editor, I quickly realize, is that you're not supposed to add editorial comments like "Grow up, ya damn hippies." It's Friday morning, and I am staring at a particularly bizarre definition for the Trees.com glossary, when an instant message from Zach pops up on my screen.

Zippo: what type of Lunchables will we be serving on the Lido deck today?

Rach: why, you hungry? hungry enough to eat cheez with a "z"?

Zippo: maybe I'm just looking for a little mid-morning snack
    action
Rach: and looking to make a trade?
Zippo: what does pocket lint trade for these days?
Rach: same as always—navel lint
Zippo: tempting...but I got enough of my own. actually
    wanted to inform you of the rule at Trees that on your first
    Friday at work, you get taken out to lunch by the surliest
    (and most attractive) employee of the establishment
Rach: am I correct in assuming you hold said title?
Zippo: you am correct

For the rest of the morning I continue copyediting text
that's so radical it makes the Sierra Club look like an organi-
zation of sewage-spewing loggers. By lunchtime, I'm beginning to feel badly for the poor polluters under attack. Zach
stops by my desk at exactly 1 o'clock.

"Pencils down," he says. "Close your computer and pass it
to the front of the room."

I salute and grab my bag. "All set," I reply. "Get me to a
fast-food joint on the double."

"Local deli might be closer."

"But will the food glisten with oil and be heat-lamp hot?"

"Most assuredly." He nods. "It might even be bubbling in
oil."

"Then quit your yapping and get me to that deli, boy." I
look at Zach and he smiles as if he's not quite sure what to
make of me. I'm immediately embarrassed, and I can feel myself blush. I realize there's no reason he should know what to

make of me. Instant messaging has made us instant friends, and this is an abrupt reminder that trading quips on screen does not actually make us intimates.

"Sorry, I mean—"

"No, don't apologize. It's just my yap hasn't been shut quite like that in a long time," he says approvingly. "So get your rear in gear, and let's go."

There's a deli two doors down from our office building, and Zach and I load up our plastic containers with the salad bar's Chinese-looking fried food. We walk two blocks up to Central Park and find an empty bench.

"This is so nice," I say. "What a good idea to eat outside."

"Yeah," Zach replies, "I've found that if I don't get out of the office during the day, I go totally bonkers. Took me about a day and a half to figure that one out."

"So how long have you been at Trees?" I ask as I pop open the container and spear my fork into a gnarled chunk of General Chow's chicken.

Zach shakes his head. "Hard to believe, but I've been working there now for about twenty-one months—just one month shy of the Indian elephant's gestation period. All considered, I don't think I look too much worse for the wear." He strokes his gut and smiles.

"Well, I'm sure it's this ecologically aware vegan diet that's kept you so fit," I say, smiling also.

"No doubt," Zach replies, biting off a large hunk of barbecued sparerib. He is broad-shouldered and thick around the middle—and clearly at peace with his Fred Flintsone physique.

"So you've been the art director at Trees for almost two years, huh? Where were you before that?" Since my first day at Trees, I'd been wondering where the rest of the company's eclectic group of freelance randoms came from, and what they'd all done before working there.

"Cape May."

"*Cape May,* the Paul Simon musical?"

"Not even a little bit," Zach says, choking on his sparerib. "Cape May, the shore town in New Jersey."

"What the hell is in Cape May, New Jersey?"

"That turns out to be a very good question." Zach points to his cheek. "Go like this," he says, tapping lightly against the side of his face. "You've got a little decorative something there."

I feel my face getting hot more quickly than I can slide my hand over it, but eventually I find the offending food remnant and wipe it off. "Thanks."

"You've probably never had a beard, but sometimes I'll find a whole new meal in mine," he says, rubbing his hairy chin.

"That is beyond disgusting." I laugh.

"But that doesn't mean it's not delicious and nutritious," he replies with a grin. "So you asked about the attributes of Cape May, and I'll respond by telling you it's a town with charming townsfolk, cheap beer, and my girlfriend's older brother, who runs a B&B there. When I graduated from art school, he offered to exchange free room and board for our handyman and cleaning services. So we moved in, and it was a great deal— for me. Unfortunately for him, it was only after I spent most of those two years painting that he realized I wasn't exactly handy."

"You're a painter?"

"Yup, I've even got a tremendously useful fine arts degree from the Rhode Island School of Design to prove it. And you thought I only drew computer-animated landfills and illustrated angry droplets of acid rain."

"Do you still paint?"

"I do, but just a little. My girlfriend and I used to live in this tiny studio on the Lower East Side, and that's what I use as a work space now. But I focus primarily on drawing now. Actually, I have Cape May to thank for that."

"No paint-supply store at the beach?" I ask.

"I used to be really into abstract painting. I'd set up every day in this big empty room on the top floor of the inn that had a great view of the ocean and the clouds rolling in, and I'd create these moody canvases—you know, *Composition in Gray #1*," he says. "But when summer came, I'd look out the window and I'd be dying to be outside. So one day, on a lark, I set up a stand on the boardwalk and started doing caricatures for twenty bucks. My girlfriend would pose as my 'client' whenever business was slow at the beginning, and as soon as she sat down people would approach immediately and start watching me draw. The tourists loved it. I started selling four or five, and sometimes more, every day."

"And what about your girlfriend? Are you guys still together? Is she a painter, too?"

"Yeah, well, we're back together now, but we don't live together anymore. She works in an art gallery."

"So it all started because of the irresistible view of the

beach from your girlfriend's brother's house!" I reply, popping the last piece of overripe deli fruit salad in my mouth.

"And I realized I really loved drawing caricatures. They were quick, funny, and made people really happy. It was instant-gratification art. Not particularly arty by art school standards, but fun. I'd never really been into comic book stuff or graphic art before then, but after doing the caricatures that whole summer, I became totally hooked on drawing and illustration."

"I'd love to see some of your stuff."

"I'm afraid the Zach Stevenson Gallery isn't open to the general public—just to Gold Card–carrying art amateurs and to the pizza delivery guy."

"What if I brought pizza? And my MetroCard—it's blue *and* gold."

"Throw in some beverages, too, and I just might have to give you a tour."

9

I peer down to the street from the twenty-first floor balcony and feel dizzy.

"Rach," Kate says, her concern wafting through my cell phone, "you still there?"

"Yeah, sorry," I reply, moving back from the railing. "I just don't know what to say."

"I know."

I can almost hear Kate closing her eyes and nodding as she says this. I start pacing around the terrace as if trying to decide what to do next. Unfortunately, there's nothing I can do for my father from here. Although the doctors have reassured us that complications can happen after surgery, and that they can treat it, it doesn't make it sound less awful to me.

"I guess I should probably get back to work." I say. We both know it'll be impossible for me to get back to work. "Call me later?"

"Of course," Kate answers.

"Hey, Chambers," Zach calls, as I'm flipping my phone shut and he steps out onto the terrace. "You got any fire sticks to light my ciggie?"

I make a production of rooting through my purse, my back still turned so he doesn't see my face and the tears welling in my lower lids.

"I don't think so," I reply.

"I am going to look so uncool smoking an unlit cigarette."

"Yeah, I guess."

"Hang on now, you don't have to be so quick to agree. I mean there are certain people—" Zach stops speaking as he leans back against the railing and sees my face. "Hey, you okay?"

"Uh-huh," I say, with no conviction at all. "Well, not so fine really. I found out recently that my dad has cancer, and there was more bad news today," I blurt out.

"Shit, Rachel, I'm sorry," Zach says, sitting down next to me on the bench and looking away as my eyes continue tearing up. "That's so rough."

"My sister just called to tell me that after Dad's surgery he was given an intravenous line to deliver fluids, but they gave him too much and it caused some sort of mild heart failure."

"Oh, no." He pauses for a moment, staring at his hands. "Will he be okay?"

"This probably isn't the conversation you want to be having on your cigarette break," I reply, trying to let him off the hook.

"Come on," he says, softly, throwing the unlit cigarette over the railing, "where is your dad now?"

"At the Mayo Clinic in Minnesota."

"That's supposed to be one of the best hospitals, right?" he asks.

I nod. "I just wish there was something I could do for him," I say, "but I don't even know what it would be. Like suddenly I'm having these images of me enrolling in medical school and finding the cure. Or testifying in front of Congress to demand they give more money for research. It's so stupid."

"It's not stupid," Zach replies, shaking his head. "My mother's brother was diagnosed with lung cancer, and she felt the same way. I think one of the most difficult parts for her was feeling so helpless about the situation. It was out of her hands, beyond her control, and she would have done anything for him."

"Yeah," I say, "that's definitely part of it." What I don't say is that I'm scared. Scared for Dad. And scared for me.

"I don't mean this to sound flip or retarded, but I'm sure your dad is getting strength just knowing you're with him in spirit. God, I'm sorry, that sounded both flip *and* retarded." He leans back, looking at the buildings across the way, and focuses on staring straight ahead.

I wish I could tell Zach that what he said wasn't bad or wrong at all, and I'm the one who feels embarrassed to have forced him to find something consoling to say. Instead I say nothing. We both sit there for a moment not saying anything, just staring in the same direction across the skyline, but it's not uncomfortable. I stand up eventually and nod at Zach.

"Thanks," I say, "I really appreciate it. But I guess I should get back inside. I've been out here for a while." I want to be able to smile at him, too, but I can't muster it yet. He nods back and stands up.

As Zach holds the door open for me, my cell phone starts ringing. I stop and scoop the phone from my bag and see that it's an unidentified number. "Hello?"

"Ah, yes, hello," an accented male voice replies, "I would like to speak to the On Target Essay."

On Target Essay?

"Yes, hello?" the man repeats.

Flustered, I do the only thing I can think of: I stab at the "end" key on the phone, then snap it shut. A second later, while I'm still staring at the phone, bewildered—and Zach is staring at me, even more bewildered, still holding open the door—it rings again.

"Hello?" I say, nervously.

"Everything okay?" Zach whispers, letting the terrace door swing shut again. I shrug my shoulders at him for lack of a better response.

"Yes, hello. I'm looking for the On Target Essay," the foreign voice says.

"Oh, yes, I'm sorry. That's so odd, I think we were cut off somehow," I reply.

Zach laughs softly behind me.

"This is On Target Essay?"

"Yes, you've reached On Target Essay."

"And this is Rachel Chambers speaking?"

"Yes?"

Zach points to himself, then mouths, "Want me to go?" I shake my head no, and we both stand there for a moment, waiting to hear what nonsense will come out of my mouth next.

"Good," the man replies. "My name is Vladimir Cherov. I'm applying to business school, and I am looking for some professional help with my essays because though I believe my spoken English to be acceptable, my ability to write it is sub-acceptable." He pronounces each word slowly but with precision. And he's right, he clearly does speak English well, but it's equally clear that it's the English of a well-educated foreigner.

"And where are you from?" I ask.

"I am from Estonia," he declares and then pauses. "It is small country on the Baltic Sea."

I've heard of Estonia, of course, but I have only a vague idea of where it actually is. Vladimir continues with his introductions.

"I am living and working in New York," he says. "For a small investment bank. You are in New York as well, correct?"

"Yes," I reply lamely.

"Well, what can you tell me about your services?"

"Oh." *Oh, God.* "Well . . . we provide full-service application coaching and consulting. We start with an initial client interview to help us understand your goals clearly, as well as your strengths and weaknesses as a candidate. We then work with you to create detailed outlines for the required essays. And then we do a serious collaborative edit, making sure we've answered the questions strategically and depicted you as unique and attractive a candidate as possible," I reply, exhaling only after I finish the speech. Zach's head shakes back and forth—cartoon character quick—and he gives me a look of complete astonishment that all but shouts "What the fuck!?!"

"I see," Vladimir replies. "So you assist the client in writing the essay?"

"Well . . ." I hesitate, suddenly panicked about what answer he wants to hear.

"But you do not write the essay?" he interrupts.

"Absolutely not," I say, with a tinge of offense in my voice, wondering if this is going to be a deal-breaker. Where the sudden burst of morality is coming from, I have no idea, but it seems right to me.

"That is excellent," Vladimir continues.

Okay, chalk one up for a code of ethics, "I'm glad we're on the same page," I throw out, assuming I've passed this man's secret test and this will conclude the interview section of the phone call.

"Yes, and you possess samples of your work for my review?"

Samples of my work? No. "Yes, of course." Apparently, though I refuse to cheat, I'm quite capable of lying. "I'll be happy to send a few over to give you a better sense of my work." *I could send Mark Westerhoff's revised essay.* "You understand, of course, that I'll have to change the names to protect the innocent." I say this laughing, but Vladimir does not laugh with me. Perhaps this is a language barrier thing.

"That sounds reasonable to me," he says. "And now we must discuss your fee."

"Right, my fee."

"Your *fee*?" Zach cackles.

I wave my hand, frantically trying to shush him. "Well," I say, trying to stall as I start thinking of a logical way to calculate a fee. *Words per page? Words per hour? Combined number of meeting times, writing time, edit time, and the chunks of time I'd spend procrastinating?* "That would depend on what intensity of consulting you'll require."

"Yes, that is what I assumed. Okay then," he says, and sounds like he's nodding. I take this to mean he smells my bluff. "Later when we meet we can perhaps discuss the range of my needs and the plan of attack. I am trying to get my applications done by the next deadline, so there is a lot of work to complete as quickly as possible."

"Deadlines are my specialty," I say, not knowing precisely what I mean by this. I see Zach nod in firm approval. "So I suggest we meet for an introductory assessment meeting."

"And how long shall this introductory meeting last?"

I have no idea what will sound reasonable. "An hour and fifteen minutes?" I reply. "This will give me the chance to get a sense of you as a person, as a professional, and as an applicant. It will allow you to ask me any further questions you may have concerning the process. I think we should plan to meet some time in the middle of next week—"

"No, I think sooner is better," he adds quickly. "And where shall I go?"

With that level of enthusiasm, we've just ruled out intimate or dimly lit spaces.

"Starbucks. Why don't we say we'll have our initial meeting at the Starbucks on 57th Street between 6th and 7th Avenues?"

"That's fine. How is tomorrow night for you?" he asks.

"Let me check my schedule." One-one hundred, two-one hundred, three-one hundred. "Yes, tomorrow night will work for me."

"Until then," Vladimir says.

"Great!" I say, instantaneously reprimanding myself for sounding so unprofessionally excited. "Tomorrow." I hang up the phone and cover my face with my hands.

"Okaaaaay," Zach says, with a full-face smirk. "Maybe you'd like to explain what sort of fee-paying 'client interview' you're setting up. I've never heard of escorts meeting their dates at Starbucks, but why not?"

I smile—finally—and pull Zack back over to the bench. I tell him the whole story about the caper with Ben and how On Target Essay was "launched" with tape and tacks and a couple six-packs of Bud. I give him a little bit of the backstory concerning my tremendous experience in the world of business school applications—and how I got fired for it—and when I finish babbling, Zach starts clapping.

"So this guy saw one of your fliers and thought you were the real thing?"

"I guess . . ." I shake my head.

"That's brilliant! I love that," he says jumping to his feet. "And just think, when I heard you discussing your fee, I assumed it would be hourly and not include kissing on the mouth."

"Zach, holy shit. What am I going to do? This guy thinks I know what I'm doing—unless he's just a psychopath with a penchant for low-rent advertisers."

"I'll bet he's the real deal. He saw your ad; he wants your service."

"I can't do this!"

"Of course you can."

"No. I can't," I reply with emphasis, "and I'm not just being modest here."

Zach claps his hands around my cheeks. "Rachel," he says, shaking my head back and forth. "Not only *can* you do it, you should do it. Just listening to you tell this story once, I'm excited for you. It's a fun idea that turned you on and made you take action—I dunno, but to me that's a good sign."

"But it was a *joke,*" I protest, looking at Zach, my cheeks still scrunched between his hands.

He smiles back at me. "Aw, that's crap. A joke doesn't come up with a brand name and a logo and then poster itself all over Manhattan. You've got something here! In your gut, you know it."

"But Zach," I remove my face from his grasp, "I don't know if my gut's ready for a client."

"Well, Rachel, your gut doesn't have much of a choice, because you've already got a client. And as it happens, your gut comes wrapped in a savvy package, with a good head on its shoulders. Which, if nothing else, knows how to improvise some *very* credible wheeling and dealing. I just saw it in action."

"Okay, but—"

"Honestly, I think you owe it to yourself to just give it a go. Once. Test your gut." He pauses. "Also, this is your big chance."

"My big chance?"

"To live the words of the founding fathers of this great nation."

"E Pluribus Unum?"

Zach shakes his head, "Little known fact: When those great men gathered to sign the Declaration of Independence at the Second Continental Congress their official motto was, 'Aw hell, why not?'"

10

The next day I head into work wearing a fitted cashmere sweater over a full skirt, dark black stockings, and faux-python heels (eBay acquisition: $75). I hope the look reads charming, cerebral working girl. I hope the look reads poised professional, rather than terrified fraud, which is much closer to the way I'm actually feeling.

I'm horrified that I've let things go this far. *What was I thinking?*

As I'm taking off my coat and hanging it in the closet by the elevators, Zach and Ethan walk by on their way for a smoke on the terrace.

"Well, hellooo stilettos!" Ethan exclaims and nods approvingly at Zach, who nods back. They both stop, and I do a full turn in place and then present myself for inspection, looking down at my shoes and smoothing my skirt.

"What do we think? Does it look like I'm trying too hard? Should I have worn something a little lower key? Do you think he'll think—"

Zach holds up his hands in a time-out sign. "May I?"

"I just feel like I—" I giggle, then stop, acknowledging the time-out sign.

"I was just going to suggest that I, personally, think you look terrific. I might even say polished. And I think it's fair to say"—he turns toward Ethan and places a hand on his shoulder—"that my colleague here feels the same way."

Ethan nods some more. "Terrific *and* polished. And I know I'd hire you if you were, say, coming to my office for an interview after sneaking out of here at lunchtime." Ethan doesn't know the real reason I'm dressed up, but I'll take all forms of affirmation today.

"Honest, really," Zach adds. "A very convincing first-impression look."

"Thanks guys, I hope you're right . . ." I add, trailing off, reaching for my bag on the ground and turning in the direction of my desk.

"I *am* right," Zach replies, following me, "but . . ."

I turn. "But what?"

"Well, there is one thing I think you're missing."

"Missing? What am I missing?" I raise my hands, palms up, and anxiously look myself up and down. "Tell me!"

"I'm talking about TEDs. You need some TEDs, teacher."

I'm not following. "Teds?"

"Tactical Eyewear Devices."

"Huh?"

Zach gives an exaggerated roll of his eyes, "You need *glasses!*"

"I have 20/20 eyesight, Zach, why would I need glasses?"

"Allow me to rephrase: You need glasses *frames,* with clear lenses. They're instant credibility," Zach says. "You know, some big-deal tortoise-shell number, something that screams Smart Girl and No Nonsense. The whole sexy librarian thing. Men really respond to it. He'll eat it up with a spoon."

"Oh!" I laugh. "Sure, of course. In place of actual skill, I'll have mad style. He'll take one look at me, see some killer glasses and pointy shoes, and know without a doubt that I can be trusted to manage the outcome of his professional future."

"You got it," Zach replies. "People totally get off on that air of authority. And I know just the place where you can get set up. There's this street in Chinatown with a bunch of glasses-frame wholesalers, where you can get good knock-offs, clear lenses and all, for cheap. We can swing by during lunch, if you want."

I think about it for a few seconds and it's exactly what I need. A good-luck talisman. Something to keep my mind off tonight. "All the way downtown . . . are you sure you have time?"

"Yeah, sure. We'll hop in a cab, get you all set up, and be back before Molly's even eaten her tofu-on-organic-rye."

I look at Zach and smile. He smiles back then turns in the direction of the terrace.

"Go on, git," he says over his shoulder. "And don't try distracting me until lunchtime because I have very serious work to do animating toxic clouds of incinerator dust. Toxic dust." Zach shakes his head as he steps outside. "I think I was briefly addicted to it in college."

*   *   *

At 12:30, we hop in a cab to Chinatown.

Zach leads me through a series of left and right turns, down streets lined with shops selling everything from Chinese produce and seafood, to ceiling-high piles of porcelain soup bowls, huge baskets of unrecognizable dried fruits, and all sorts of packaged soaps written in Chinese. It's a twisting maze of streets, but Zach seems to know exactly where he's going. We stop in front of a store next to a take-out food shop with glistening orange roast ducks hanging on hooks in the window. We walk inside, and the entire shop is lined, floor to ceiling, with cases and cases of glasses frames.

"Wow!" I laugh, spinning around, staring. "If I felt the same way about glasses as I do about pointy shoes, I would be catatonic with joy right now. This is amazing!"

"It's true." Zach nods, shrugging lightly. "Can you imagine all the little people with little screwdrivers sitting in a little room attaching the legs on these things?" He nods a greeting at the shopkeeper, who's sitting on a stool behind the counter and then turns back to me. "So what's your aesthetic preference? Eurotrash poser? Ivy League douchebag? Design student wannabe?"

"I'm partial to the rectangular, Helmut Lang minimalist severe look," I say.

"Helmut Lang! Right here!" The shopkeeper jumps up from his stool and points to a glass case in front of him. He takes out the shelf and places it on top of the case, and I walk over for closer inspection. Most of the frames are made of delicate black plastic or silver wire in geometric shapes. I try on a pair of black frames that stretch across my face in two narrow rectangular bands and turn to face Zach. "What do you think?"

"I think dark, smoky nightclub in East Berlin with industrial music in the background, sort of intense-but-groovy grad student. It makes me want to call you Helga. The Estonian might not dig it. I understand the Baltic countries had a rough time with Stalin."

"Fair enough," I say, smiling. "Let's see, which ones say loud, proud capitalist pig?" I try on another pair of the knock-off Helmut Langs, this time in a practically invisible, oval-shaped titanium frame. I look at myself in the mirror; it looks like I'm wearing two monocles suspended in front of my eyes by some mysterious force. Zach hands me a frame that he's taken out of one of the displays on the wall.

"Try these," he says, handing me a pair of big tomato-colored plastic frames with the name of a designer I've never heard of inscribed on the stem. "They look sort of funky serious, right?" I slip them on and look at him. He snorts, and then I turn to the mirror. The glasses are gigantic and incredibly red, and they make me look a little girl playing dress-up. "I love them!" I cry, and turn to look at Zach. His expression freezes, and he is clearly uncertain whether I'm being serious or not. "Halloween is right around the corner, and I've *always* wanted to look like a stupid near-sighted clown," I squeal.

At first the shopkeeper keeps showing us frames, taking out shelves and directing us to other glasses that look like the ones I'm trying on, but after a while I think he gets confused keeping up with which ones we like and which ones we're pretending to like. He sits back down on his stool and picks up his newspaper, letting the pile of rejects on the counter grow. Zach is trying on frames now, too, as a taste test before I try them, he says. We establish a rhythm where I try on a pair and turn to him, he gives a reading—school marm, downtown architect, eccentric single mom, Wall Street power player—and then we come up with a verdict: reject or reevaluate. The shop guy is indifferent to our guffaws and Zach's occasional mime act when he tries to do a charades version of what I look like in a pair of frames. When we finally narrow it down to two frames, I turn triumphantly to the shopkeeper to ask him if either frame comes in a different color.

"It dee-pend," he says. "Yoh buy or not buy? Yoh and boyfriend here long time. Yoh buy or not buy?"

I glance sidelong at Zach, a sheepish smile on my face, but he has suddenly taken to studying a pair of glasses in the opposite corner of the store and his back is turned to me. "I would definitely like to buy. In fact, I'll take these, please," I reply politely, handing him a pair of dark tortoise-shell frames in a slightly cat-eyed shape. Zach's reading on them had been

"Sassy but serious cool girl." I think they gave me the look of a chic 1950s court stenographer, a working-girl type who could still go home and whip up deviled eggs for her friend's potluck.

As Zach and I walk out of the store and back in the direction of Broadway, I slip on my brand-new glasses and make a point of examining my reflection in every store window we pass. "You just might have given me good advice," I say to Zach, smiling, still looking at myself in the passing storefronts. "I think I am getting serious but sassy vibes. I hope it works for the Estonian."

*   *   *

It seems to take forever, but finally the clock on my computer screen changes from 6:59 P.M. to 7:00 P.M. I reapply my lipstick, shove a legal pad and some ballpoint pens from the supply closet into my bag, slip on my coat, and head out to meet my first On Target client. Starbucks is only a block and a half away, so I'll get there with ample lead time to scope out a discreet corner table.

As the elevator descends, I review the scenario: When Vladimir walks in, I'll recognize him and raise my hand in a subtle wave. He'll walk over, and I'll stand up and introduce myself with a firm handshake. Then I'll point to the chair opposite me and ask him to sit down. I'll offer to buy him a cup of coffee, give him a quick summary of the purpose of this Orientation Meeting, and then I'll suggest we get right to work. I'll take quick efficient notes on my legal pad as he reels off his résumé. I'll probe for some family background and some personal interests, whatever little nuggets of uniqueness he has, and then ask him if he thinks there's anything else I should know. Easy.

A few doorways before the Starbucks entrance, I reach into my purse and pull out the burgundy pleather case, open it, and slip on my new glasses. I silently thank Zach for his genius idea. I pull open the door to Starbucks and look around—the place is full, and most of the tables are occupied. Who drinks coffee at 7:30 at night in a midtown Starbucks?

"Rachel Chambers?"

I turn, and standing behind me is a man considerably taller than I am, with a wide build draped in a long, camel-colored coat. His eyes are large and blue, and his eyebrows are raised in a question. "Are you Rachel Chambers?" He asks, with a slight accent and extra-clear enunciation.

"Yes, I am. You must be Vladimir?"

"Yes, Vladimir Cherov," he says, extending his hand. "I am here quite early. I had a meeting nearby, so I came directly," he explains. "Nice to meet you, Rachel."

This isn't at all how I am supposed to meet him. I shake his hand, desperately trying to figure out what I can salvage from my original plan.

He gestures to a table in the corner with a black leather briefcase open on top of it. "May I get you a coffee or tea, or something else to drink or to eat?"

He has preempted every single one of my planned moves so far. "Oh no, no, thank you," I stammer, smiling, "I'll get a tea, but please have a seat. Can I get *you* something?"

"No, I insist," Vladimir says, stepping up to the counter. "I would like a tea, please, and also a large coffee, the flavor of the house. What kind of tea would you like?" he asks, turning his head toward me.

"Earl Grey," I reply, feeling exceedingly uncomfortable. He hands me a cup of tea, and then hands the cashier a fifty-dollar bill.

"No, really, Vladimir, I—"

"Rachel, it is pleasure for me. Would you like to sit?" He gestures toward the table in the corner.

"Well, thank you then."

He stops by the condiment bar to put milk in his coffee, and I walk ahead to the table, take off my coat, sit down, and get out my legal pad and pen. The only part of the plan left is the get-right-to-work part, so I am sipping my tea with one hand and holding my pen poised in the other as he approaches the table.

"Is your office near here, Rachel?" he asks, as he pulls out his chair.

"It's on 58th Street," I answer, pushing up my tortoise frames.

"And what is your job?" he asks, taking a sip of his coffee. "It says on the advertisement that you are writer and editor by profession, no?"

I am marveling internally, aghast at how completely my plan has been wrecked. I had not factored in the possibility of his seeing me before I saw him, his insisting on paying for coffee, let alone his asking *me* any questions, and in general raining on what was meant to be *my* parade of Authority and

Professionalism. I am slightly pissed off that he's stolen my thunder.

"I'm mostly editing right now," I say crisply, intent on regaining lost ground. "So, Vladimir," I continue smoothly, "let me explain a little bit—"

"Call me Vlad, please."

"Vlad, let me explain how we'll use this hour and fifteen minutes. I'll be asking you questions in order to put together a thorough profile of your accomplishments and interests. All this is information we'll then use, together, to create outlines for your essays. It might feel like an interview, but try to relax and be as honest as possible." Then I say grandly, "Remember, it's not me you're trying to impress, it's the people who are going to be reading your applications." I pause to let this sink in, then finish up with, "So it will be helpful for me to get as complete an understanding of you as I can—warts and all."

"Warts? What are warts?"

"I'm sorry, there's no reason you would know that." I try not to smile as I explain, " 'Warts and all' is an expression that means telling the whole truth, the good and the bad all together."

"Yes, of course." Vlad nods. "That is the only truth."

Excellent—we haven't been talking five minutes, and our man has already spat out a personal credo.

"So, Vlad," I plunge, "what brought you to the United States? You obviously have a very unusual background, and this could be a strong selling point for you."

"Yes, you think so? I have been here now many years. It seems such a long time ago when I first came."

"Well, let's start with that. Tell me about where you grew up."

"I come from a small town called Kunda, in the northeast part of Estonia, yes? Kunda is famous for its cement plant."

I smile and nod, hoping to convey familiarity with Kunda. In truth, I wouldn't be able to tell Estonia from Eritrea on a map.

"Nearly the whole town works for the plant," he continues. "But the reason it is famous is because it was one of the worst polluters in the former Soviet Union—and this is saying a great deal." Vlad chuckles. "The plant's emission of cement dust was so high, it made the entire town look completely gray. We often joked that our tourism slogan should be: 'Kunda, it's a nice place to visit, but I wouldn't want to breathe there.'"

Now *this* is money. *Small-town boy grows up in miserable company town. Learns in deeply personal way that running a company isn't just managing a business, it's managing the welfare of all the lives dependent on that business.* "But things have changed there now?"

"Oh, yes." Vlad nods. "Everything changed with the end of Soviet Union. My father was one of the managers under Soviets, but after we gained independence, there was no state left to run the plant, just the people of the town. So my father, because he has been there for many years, and he is top manager there, he decides he has to take charge and run the plant."

Crap. The boss's kid. Much less sexy than the son of a poor worker disillusioned by the monumental failure of a historical ideal. But there's still potential, I think: *Unlike most children of privilege, having watched his own father struggle with newfound authority, he grows up understanding firsthand the heavy responsibility incumbent upon the decision makers.*

"The factory was killing the town, but closing the factory would then have killed Kunda's economy. My father realized we must make changes to the plant, modernize it. He would come home exhausted every day, but he had expression, he would say this often, very serious. 'You do what you can, and you do what you cannot, to keep the company running.'"

I am scribbling furiously, quivering inside with excitement. Vlad's father's expression is pure unalloyed gold. I can make it into *anything!* Vlad's field-tested principle of leadership. The deep source of Vlad's burning personal drive. The real-world roots of Vlad's unwavering work ethic. A few more of these and I can dismiss Vlad and go home and write him straight into business school.

As Vlad is filling me in on some of the details of his job, my stomach starts rumbling loudly. I look down at my watch curious to see what time it is.

"I am sorry," Vlad says, interrupting himself. "I have taken too long. I feel as I have spoken too much—"

"No, no!" I say. "Not at all. We're right on time. I think you've given us a lot of elements to work with."

"Good. I am glad. Perhaps we can talk payment. What are your rates?"

"I'll get back to you with an e-mail about that," I say quickly. I still have no idea what my rates are. "Meanwhile, the next step is outlining. Why don't we say I'll get back to you on . . . Friday with some preliminary ideas for essay topics? After that, if you think On Target's work will be helpful, we can proceed from there."

"That sounds very excellent," Vlad says, smiling, and reaching for his coat. "Can I walk you to the subway, yes? Midtown is so empty at night."

"Thank you, no. I'm going to stay and make a few notes while this is all still fresh. But it was so nice meeting you, Vlad. Your story is fascinating."

"Yes, I imagine you've had not many clients like me before."

"No I haven't," I reply extra-enthusiastically. "Which makes it all the more interesting. And better for the application, too!"

"Well, good-bye, Rachel," Vlad says, extending his hand again.

As soon as the glass door swings shut behind him, I feel giddy and relieved. I grin to myself. On Target Essay has weathered her virgin trip without crashing, burning, or getting busted.

11

Finally, some good news to tell Ben. I can't wait for dinner with him and Leigh tonight. He will love the Vladimir story. First, he will find it completely hilarious that we have a client at all. And I know he'll adore hearing about Vlad—especially if I get his accent right.

As I walk down West Broadway toward the restaurant, I hear my name called from behind me.

"Rachel?"

I turn and see it's Leigh. She's striding toward me very quickly for a small woman with so much baggage. On one arm she's carrying a bulging Marc Jacobs Stella tote, and with the other arm she holds a yoga mat and her suit jacket. I watch her as she approaches, smiling and silently betting all my future earnings that the gorgeous razor-sharp black suit she's wearing is this season's Gucci or Chloé. "I thought that might be you," she says when she catches up to me.

"I'm not sure I want to know what distinguished me from that angle." I laugh.

Leigh cocks her head, smiles politely, and says nothing, ignoring the ass joke I lobbed right to her. She has been my best friend's girlfriend for over a year, but I haven't actually spent much time with her. It always feels a little awkward when we do, like each of is trying hard to create the appearance of being comfortable.

"That's a lovely color lipstick on you, Rachel," she says.

"Thank you, yeah, I got this one at Sephora. It's called 'Ruby 411,' which is a slightly deeper version of their 'Vermillion 212,' which I also own, and it has a tad more shimmer than the 'Scarlet 917.' Which I *also* own. But don't get me started on their 'Crimson 646,'" I reply.

"Seriously?" Leigh responds. "What's wrong with the Crimson 646?"

"No, I was kinda kidding."

"Oh, right." Leigh smiles. "No, that *was* funny."

We arrive at the restaurant's entrance, and Leigh grabs The Odeon's heavy glass door with her left hand. As I reach for the handle to help her pull it, I see a large gleaming rock attached to her ring finger.

"Ho-my-God!" I say, my mouth dropping open.

"Oh, no! Oh, shoot!" she says, biting her bottom lip. "This wasn't how you were supposed to find out. He wanted to tell you himself. He had it all planned."

He had it all planned? The sentence replays in my brain. I know I need to respond. Stunned silence is definitely the wrong reaction.

"Could you forget you saw this?" Leigh whisks the manicured, diamond-adorned hand into her pants pocket.

"Congratulations," I say, at last. Then questions start rolling out of my mouth. "When? How?" *Why?*

"I told her she had to marry me or doom me to a life of rejecthood," Ben says, walking up behind us, kissing his fiancée hello. He turns to me and says, "I am now ready to receive your congratulations, your awe, and your disbelief that I managed to convince this beautiful creature to be my bride."

"If I knew you were going to start calling me a creature," Leigh says, patting Ben on the cheek, "I might have thought the wiser of it."

Oh, God. They're a cute couple. "First round's on me!" I exclaim, desperate for a drink. "Let's toast!"

They give me the details over dinner. Ben takes pains to assure me that no rings were hidden in pieces of food or glasses of champagne. "That would have been just too too," Leigh remarks, shaking her head, then brushing back her blonded hair. "If I have to read yet another one of those cheesy proposal stories in the *Times* wedding announcements, you know?"

"Instead," Ben says, "while sipping mimosas over brunch at the Boathouse in Central Park and finishing the crossword together—"

"*Ben*," Leigh scolds, stroking his hand, and then erupting in an irrepressible giggle. "Just tell her!"

"So we actually were having brunch and we both ordered

mimosas, but beforehand I'd arranged for the waiter to bring a bottle of champagne instead. That's when I bent down and asked her to give me the greatest gift in the world by becoming my wife."

I'm sure I would have found the story incredibly charming if I didn't feel so nauseous. There is a lot of toasting and thigh stroking throughout dinner. Ben asks, in passing, how things are going with me, but I decide against telling them the Vladimir client news. It doesn't seem like the right time. "Things are fine," I say, nodding quickly and turning up the corners of my mouth. Ben nods back as he reaches over and grabs a french fry from Leigh's plate of *steak frites*.

We are splitting dessert when Leigh turns and puts her hand on my knee.

"Rachel," she asks, "what are you doing Saturday night?"

"Nothing, I guess, why?"

"Casey, my old college roommate, is throwing an engagement shower for me—why don't you come?" She smiles widely and I smile back, doing my best to show teeth. I look at Ben, who is well aware that this type of activity is as appealing to me as gum surgery. But Ben is gazing at Leigh, and I can't catch his eye.

"What can I bring, Leigh?" I try not to let the modulation in my voice reveal what an effort I'm making to sound upbeat.

"Just bring your best Ben stories," she says. "You're going to be the only representative from the groom's side."

"How come I don't get to come?" Ben asks.

Leigh looks skyward, then rolls her eyes. "If you think I'm stupid enough to let my fiancé loose in a room full of desperate Manhattan single women!" Leigh turns to me with an "Am I right, or am I right?" expression. Our eyes meet, and her expression changes as she realizes I'm very much a part of that demographic. She looks frozen between a smile and a grimace.

"I totally agree with you," I say, ending her distress. "Ben'd be lucky to get out of there alive. Or with his pants on."

"You know," Ben says, "this party is beginning to sound pretty good to me."

As a celebratory gesture, I try to pay for dinner, but Leigh won't let me. She says she owes me far too much already for all the time I have spent training Ben. I thank her, hoping she realizes exactly what a gift she's received. I kiss both Ben and Leigh when we reach the restaurant door. I tell them I'm going to walk for a while to clear my head after all the wine. Leigh doesn't think it's safe for me to be wandering around at night, but Ben slips his arm through hers. "Rachel will be fine," he says, as they walk in the opposite direction.

12

"Hi Rach." It's Kate.

"Hey," I answer, not bothering to conceal the obvious mopiness in my voice.

"I'm going to be in your neck of the woods later this afternoon to buy a tutu for Sophie at the Capezio store on 57th Street. Can you get away for an early dinner? A big juicy burger on your big sister's dime?"

"I don't know . . ."

"You've got to eat," she replies.

I say nothing for a moment, debating whether to tell her why I've lost my appetite, the memory of last night's meal at Odeon still overwhelmingly present. I decide not to and Kate tells me she'll pick me up in the lobby at the end of the day.

"And if we don't feel like going out, we can just grab some

take-out and go back to your place. Okay? Good. See you around six," she says.

I get up to go to the bathroom, but as I walk past the terrace I see Zach standing outside smoking, and I decide to go out and say hello.

"I don't want to nag," I say, as the door slams shut behind me. I walk over to the edge of the terrace where Zach's standing and prop myself up against the railing.

"Good impulse. Go with that," he smiles then takes a long drag.

"But if you're really serious about being a good artist, you're going to have to give up smoking."

Zach cocks his head to the side and his lips curl down. "Really? And why is that?"

"Because having to get an iron lung is so cliché. One could even say it's been done to death, you know, if one wanted to get cute about it."

He considers this for a moment, then rejects it with a shake of his shaggy head. "Sure, but imagine how much fun it must be to get through airport security packing one of those. 'Seriously, sir, it's my iron lung!' Or how about whipping it out on the golf course. 'Oh, Trip, I wouldn't use a nine-iron, I'd use an iron-lung.' How about—"

"Okay, shut up, I'll stop," I say, holding my hands up in surrender.

Zach flicks his cigarette butt to the ground and stamps it out. "I know it's stupid to smoke," he replies, "and I've been meaning to quit." He pauses, and an evil grin spreads across his face. "Soooo, Rachel," he says slowly, "I have a deal to strike with you. I'll give up the demon nicotine if you give up those cheesy snack packs and anything else with more than fifteen ingredients on the label."

I look at him with wide eyes and then blink once and shake my head slowly absorbing his words. "You must be joking," I declare in a low, grave voice.

"Addiction is hard," he nods, "but together we can beat it."

"No way, man. Definitely not today, and possibly not ever."

"There is no time like the present. Every day you lie in wait is another day you lie to yourself. Putting off until tomorrow what you can do to—"

"Yep, I see where you're going with that. But right now I don't have a whole lot to work with in the small pleasures department, and spreadable cheese happens to be one of the very few things in my life that's always reliable and provides 100 percent dependable satisfaction. So I'll be damned if I'm going that let that go, too."

"That sounds much more serious than addiction."

"Well, the past few months *have* been a little heavy on unpleasant surprises. You already know about my dad . . . and a few weeks before that, my boyfriend of two years checked out, and then, last night my best friend announces that he's engaged. To this perfectly perfect girl he completely and grossly worships."

"That sounds like a lot to deal with all at once," Zach replies quietly, with a neutral expression. A laundry list of woes probably wasn't the answer he expected. I'm wishing I hadn't unloaded, and I can feel the heat rising in my cheeks.

"What was the deal with the boyfriend?" Zach asks.

"His name was—is—Andy. He works on Wall Street," I reply, doubting that he really wants to know more.

Zach says nothing for a moment and then a curious smile begins to form on his face. "Those Wall Street guys apply to business school, right?" he asks.

"Yeah, sure. I bet Andy's applying right now."

"So, you must have met a whole bunch of them in those two years, right? Why don't you pitch your essay business to them? Get them all onboard, and the next time this guy Andy turns around, all his buddies will be paying to have an audience with you."

I laugh, grateful to Zach for shifting the mood away from maudlin. "For a nice guy, you're pretty good with revenge schemes," I say.

Zach bows slightly. "Much like you with the Estonian businessmen clients, we aim to please. Nonetheless, we also aim to perfect. So despite your current circumstances I still think we should agree to a smokes-for-snacks exchange."

"It's a deal, you bastard."

"And speaking of Estonians—how'd the first meeting go?"

"I think it went really well!" I answer instantly, like an actress who's finally heard her cue.

"So what's the guy *like*?"

"He was this big tall blond guy in a suit, three buttons, expensive tie. He pronounced my name, 'Ray-chelle Chaymbers,'" I say slowly, rolling my R's, trying to imitate Vlad's careful overenunciation. Zach smiles. "He was so *proper,* sitting up straight behind this black leather briefcase and firing questions at me."

"Very KGB!"

"Except I don't think the KGB wore custom-made shirts and used hair product. He had some serious Euro style going on—"

"Not unlike my own perhaps?" Zach interrupts, opening up his worn suede jacket to reveal another one of the vintage-looking T-shirts he seems to wear every day. "Maybe I could interest our man in buying one?" He says, pointing to the faded picture on his belly.

"I'm thinking our man probably doesn't shop in used clothing stores."

"Well, then I promise to sell him a brand-new one," Zach replies.

"So you deal in TEDs *and* T-shirts?" I ask, smirking.

"Actually, yes. I design and sell T-shirts. Including the attractive if much-worn sample I'm wearing right now."

"You *do*?"

"Yeah, kind of a side thing. So you never know who'll pop up wearing one. In fact, maybe Vladimir already has one. Maybe he was wearing it *under* the custom-made shirt."

"Sure," I reply, amused by the image of Vlad as poster boy for Zach's T-shirt empire.

"But you were saying: stiff KGB spy guy with Eurotrash tendencies."

"Right, and Vladimir does have this total Communist story, but now he's bringing home a serious banker's salary. And eventually he wants to 'geef sometheeng beck to *Kunda*,' his polluted cement-factory town." I say the town's name in a growl, with a thick accent.

Zach cringes dutifully in response. "So Comrade Cinderella turns into a pressed-shirt banker. Then gets into prestigious American business school—with aide of visionary American entrepreneur—and most likely becomes CEO of the world."

"Something like that, I hope."

"Well I hope you're planning to bilk this bespoke dude. You should be charging what you're worth then doubling it. He'll wind up respecting you all the more for it."

* * *

At the end of the day, Zach and I head out of the office together. The elevator doors open in the lobby, and I see Kate leaning against the security desk. I point at her and she points back at me.

"Zach," I say walking over to her, "meet my sister, Kate."

"Hi," he replies, "I'd shake your hand, but—" He motions to Kate's hands, which are both holding Capezio shopping bags.

"Nice to meet you," she says, "and despite what you're seeing now, I'm not really a refugee from the Nutcracker Suite. I'm just an overindulgent mother."

"Well, I would have guessed prima ballerina," he replies.

"You hear that, Rach? Your friend thinks I look like a dancer."

"You won't like him when I tell you what he made me do today," I say, tilting my head toward Zach. "He made me give up spreadable cheesefoods."

Kate laughs. "Are you really going off the junk?"

"That's what I promised."

Kate nods, looking impressed, "Good work, young man."

"Thank you. Well, I should probably run," he says, "My own sister's coming into town, and I have to do a little emergency cleaning in my apartment before she gets in."

"I didn't know you had a sister," I say.

"Two." Zach nods. "But they both live in California. The younger one is threatening to move here if she gets this job she's up for, though. Part of me thinks it'd be fun to have her here, and then the other part of me—the part that used to live with her—is thinking the town ain't big enough for both of us. Nice meeting you, Kate," he says, smiling, and waving as he walks off.

Kate waits until he's out of earshot. "Aw, he's cute . . . they all like him up there?"

I shake my head no, taking a package from her and heading to the doors.

"He seems like a nice guy, too."

"He really is a nice guy," I say, nodding. "He makes work a lot more fun than it would be otherwise."

"Do you guys spend a lot of time together?"

"Well, no, we just work together. But," I add after a pause, "actually, yes, I guess we do, at work. He's sort of the guy who welcomes the new people."

"You're lucky the welcome wagon is so sweet. Does he have a girlfriend?"

I stop in the middle of the sidewalk and turn to look at Kate, my eyes narrowing and brows furrowing, as though I haven't heard her correctly. "Actually, yes, he does have a girlfriend, Kate. But if you're suggesting what I think you're suggesting, even if Zach didn't have a girlfriend, he is completely and wholly not my type."

"How is charming and funny not your type?"

"Kate," I start walking again and she follows, "You saw him. Zach is a really good guy, but he's way too . . . *messy*. He's the classic, hand-to-mouth hipster type, who probably lives in some dangerous neighborhood with a zillion roommates, you know? Zach is great, but he's so not for me. He just doesn't seem like a grown up to me. *And* he's short. *And* he has a girlfriend. Who's probably equally disheveled."

"Well, relationships don't last forever."

I look over, exasperated and preparing to glare menacingly at her, but I see she's smirking, delighted that she's succeeded in provoking me.

*   *   *

"So how was the trip? How was he?" I ask, as we open the plastic containers of Indian food spread out on my kitchen table. Kate had flown back the day before from a brief trip to Minneapolis. I had already asked those same questions last night when she'd called on her way home from the airport, but I suppose I am expecting different answers now. I don't think her shopping excursion today in my neighborhood is a total coincidence.

"Well," Kate says slowly, "he doesn't look great. He's lost a lot of weight." I nod and spoon out some chicken curry and rice onto her plate. "I thought I would be more, I don't know, prepared or something. I mean we *know* what the effects of the treatments are. We've seen them before." I nod again slowly, looking her in the eyes. "But he just looks awful. I guess I'd forgotten, or didn't really think it'd be that bad. He couldn't even keep up his front, couldn't even make a joke about it, so I found myself trying to make the jokes you'd be cracking . . ." She reaches for my hand and squeezes it, and I force a half-smile. "We went over his will," she says, "he wanted to make sure I understood everything." She pauses and looks down at her plate, pushing her food around with her fork.

"Oh, my God."

"Look, we'll pull through this together. That's what I told Dad, too."

I nod silently in response. I've been grasping one of the hot containers of food in my hands, as though trying to warm myself.

"We *will* pull through this, Rach," Kate repeats. She reaches for the container I'm holding. "I just want one spoonful of this potato stuff—I promise to give it right back."

Neither of us speaks for a long moment, and I concentrate on the sounds of our forks and knives clinking on the ceramic plates.

"Now tell me about this essay writing stuff," Kate says in a refreshed tone, blowing on a spoonful of hot daal. "Didn't you have a meeting while I was gone? And how is it that Ben talked you into this again?"

"Funny you should mention Ben," I say. "Actually he doesn't even know the latest."

"How come?" Kate asks.

"Well, Ben and Leigh and I got together for dinner last night. And I had been waiting all day to tell him about our very first client meeting, but before Ben even shows up, I find out from Leigh that—"

"They got engaged?"

I quit chewing and look at Kate, who's spooning lentils into her mouth. "Yeah, that's right. How did you know?"

"It's not so unexpected, is it? Maybe a little sooner than you might have thought . . ."

"Yes, they got engaged, Kate!" I say with emphasis, the pitch of my voice rising, as though stating something that clearly challenges credibility, trying to incite some astonishment. "And I was completely and totally surprised—*I* had no idea Ben had even been planning to propose."

"Yeah, he really should have told you."

"Thank you!" I reply. "Anyway, then the whole dinner became 'The Engagement Dinner.' I had this news I was so excited to share, but it wouldn't even have registered on Ben's radar, so I didn't bother telling him anything at all."

"Rach, an engagement is huge news."

"Of course it's big news. But just out of the blue like that, when I thought we were sitting down for a regular end-of-the-week dinner? Suddenly, the dinner gets hijacked—"

"C'mon, you're not upset because On Target Essay got upstaged. You're upset because Ben got engaged. You've been best friends, and . . . and I know you're not wild about Leigh. But it doesn't really matter who the girl is. It's like suddenly he announces that the thing previously known as your friendship is changing, it's different now . . . it's a little bit over."

"Kate, that's melodramatic. So Ben got engaged. I'm okay with that. I just didn't see it coming *last night* when I wanted to do a little victory dance."

Kate nods slightly. "So tell me about the meeting and what happens next with On Target Essay."

I feel like the previous conversation isn't concluded, but I also feel myself getting wound up, which I don't want to do with Kate tonight, so I let it drop. "Well, it sounds like this client needs *lots* of work done. So later tonight I'm going to start writing a few suggested essay topics and drafting an outline for one of his application essays. Then we're meeting again, probably early next week, to see how he likes it all."

"That's amazing, Rach." Kate smiles. "And don't be mad, but I also think it's totally hilarious."

"I know! And Zach came up with this other really funny idea today. He suggested contacting all Andy's friends at Morgan Stanley because a lot of those guys are applying to business school now."

"*That's* a great idea," Kate replies immediately, raising her eyebrows and nodding approvingly. "Who knew you could grow a business with vengeance?"

"Thank you. As you know, I've always been partial to expansion plans," I say, opening the pint of now-softened ice cream we bought for dessert and sticking in two spoons. Kate empties what's left of the bottle of wine into our two glasses, then raises hers. "A toast to expansion: your business, Dad's health, my breasts."

13

I am sitting on my bed, computer open on my lap, fingers poised above the keyboard. The rest of the mocha chip ice cream Kate and I didn't finish earlier is melting on the night table next to me as I contemplate the screen. Finally, I click on the new message icon and start typing:

To:
Cc:
Bcc:
Subject: Your Business School Application

The Business School Application. One shot to impress. You need killer essays; we're the professionals.

We offer personalized coaching in the essay-writing process:
- One-on-one outlining
- Customized collaboration
- Intensive troubleshooting
- Constant feedback

And most importantly, we never miss a deadline. Because you have no time to waste when your future is on the line. One-stop shopping for the ultimate application.

Contact On TargetEssay@hotmail.com or call Rachel Chambers at 212-975-9595.

It's essentially the same information Ben and I wrote on the original fliers. But there is one major difference: This isn't a shot in the dark. In the "To" box of the e-mail, I paste all the Morgan Stanley e-mail addresses I have in my contacts list from when I was dating Andy. Then I open another window and go to the Morgan Stanley web page. Using the password Andy told me to remember in case he forgot, I log into the company's employee directory. There I find the profile—with tasteful photo—of all the employees of each of the giant bank's departments. I go to Private Equity and scroll down this virtual face-book. I feel like I'm catalog shopping the finance set.

I copy and paste the e-mail addresses of thirty-one additional targets, then I click Send and quickly shut my eyes, waiting for the computer to process the command and for it to be too late to take it back. When I open my eyes, a "Mail

Sent" message has popped up on the screen, listing all the names of all the potential applicants.

I feel like I just pulled off a bank heist.

*   *   *

The next morning is like Christmas Day in my e-mail inbox.

When I arrive at work and log into my computer, the e-mail summary box on the side of the screen boasts 44 new messages. Sitting at my desk with my coat still on, I check the clock. Molly won't get in until 10:15, so I have about forty-seven minutes to fully vet my personal e-mail before she whisks by. I throw off my jacket then click the New Mail icon. I scan rapidly down the list of new e-mails. A dozen or so are any morning's usual array of junk, sample sale updates, friends, and penis extension offers. All the rest have subject headings reading "RE: Your Business School Application."

Just minutes before Molly walks by my desk, I've made my way through all the Morgan Stanley responses. Many of them are just greetings, friends of Andy's responding to say hello, that it's nice to hear from me, that this sounds like a really cool idea. Much more interesting are replies from the six people who have written that they want to find out more about On Target Essay. I feel a special thrill as I read and then re-read their replies. I respond carefully to each of the interested e-mails, including one from a woman asking me if she could forward my information to her best friend at J. P. Morgan. I resist the urge to tell her to mass e-mail the entire asset management and investment banking departments there.

I answer all their questions about On Target's rates (thoroughly reasonable), how quickly "we" can work with deadlines (it's whenever you want, baby), if "we" have any references (I refrain from telling them to contact Mr. Ben Dover). One woman asks only about the cost of a "full-service package" and requests an appointment, "for as soon as possible. In fact, could you accommodate me the day after tomorrow at 6:45 P.M. in my office located at 345 Park Ave. on the 11th floor? Assuming that will be suitable, please just give me a call once you've arrived at the security desk downstairs, and could you give me a contact number should something come up on my end at the last minute? I look forward to getting to work tomorrow. Best, Jessica Tucker."

Certainly, Jessica, we'd be happy to accommodate!

Over the next few days I continue corresponding with each of these potential clients, creating "company procedure" and "revision method" as the need arises, hoping I'll remember and be able to repeat it in the next e-mail. It's only been a few weeks since I laid eyes on a business school application essay for the first time in my life—Mark Westerhoff's ungrammatical piece of crap—but as I compose professional-sounding responses reassuring interested applicants about "our expertise" and "our established experience" and explaining "our general methodology in applicant packaging," it begins to feel like centuries ago. I begin compiling a chart of responses to the frequently asked questions so I don't have to keep retyping the same sales pitch, and mostly so I don't forget whatever executive decision I just made five minutes ago.

I download applications to the top-ten business schools and

read them over, trying to get a sense of the types of essay each school requires. Some schools ask for 250-word responses to a dozen questions (*Creatively describe yourself to your MBA classmates*), but others request two or three personal statements of 2,000 words (*Tell us why the Yale MBA program is the right learning environment for you*). I have to get back to Vlad tomorrow about "my rates," but I still have no idea how to charge for all this work. A fee per word, say, 33 cents? Too measly. Per application, say, $1,500? Too off-putting. A person-based fee? Because what if the applicant is a real asshole and karmically doesn't deserve to get in anywhere? Ultimately I decide to fix my rates according to essay length: It seems like the most objective measure, but also leaves room for some real cash intake, because length adds up fast, and full applications could potentially yield a few thousand dollars. And for the wily consumer who actually does the math, I decide to offer discounts for multi-application packages.

On the one hand, it seems perfectly reasonable.

On the other, it seems like arbitrary bullshit, but it's occurring to me now that that's what determines the cost of things, anyway: $15,000 for an Hermès bag . . . $1.50 for generic toilet paper . . . $1,500 for an acceptance from Wharton compliments of On Target Essay. As the founding fathers might say, "Aw hell, why not?"

14

I ring the doorbell to the twelfth-floor East Side apartment of Leigh's maid of honor. I can hear the muffled sounds of chatter; then the door opens and a pretty blonde with an inquisitive smile says, "Hello?" I'm about to introduce myself, but suddenly her expression changes and her hand flies up to her mouth. "Oh! You must be Rachel! *Ben's* friend! I'm Casey!"

I nod yes and smile as Casey extends her hand.

"Right!" Casey says as though to confirm things and then laughs easily. "Come on in!" she adds, stepping back and gesturing for me to follow her. She's wearing tight white jeans that sculpt her bottom, a sleeveless silk top with a green-on-white fern print that ties in a loose bow around her neck, and high-heeled strappy sandals: not exactly an outdoor outfit, given the evening's seasonal forty-two-degree low, but it does make her butt look hard and fab. I walk down the hall behind her, my hands tucked into the pockets of my long, weather-appropriate wool coat. "Just dump your stuff in here," she says, stopping in front of a closed door and placing her hand on the knob, "and then come on out and join us." She smiles again. I wonder if she and Leigh have the same dentist to bleach their teeth so brilliantly white—the guy I read about in last month's W magazine. "We're all just chatting in the living room."

"Thanks, I'll be right out," I reply with a tight smile, hoping she didn't glimpse my less-than-pearly whites. I walk into the bedroom and take my coat off slowly, not prepared for whatever onslaught will surely follow. I haven't met any of Leigh's friends, so I'm not sure what to expect. Assuming they're like Leigh, they'll be well-to-do, pretty girls, politely friendly to a fault. Most of them have probably narrowed down when their boyfriends will be proposing, and a few may already be thinking ahead to the mortgage on a four-bedroom house in Greenwich. Underneath my coat, I'm not looking much less wintry, with a chunky turtleneck sweater and black pants over brown leather boots, an outfit I'd thought—until Casey answered the door about thirty seconds ago—sent a casual-but-stylish weekend vibe, perfect for a chilly fall night of drinks at home with the girls. These girls evidently dress differently for that kind of night. I pause in front of the mirror over Casey's bureau and reapply some lip gloss, thinking, *I'll inhale a drink and then I'll go.*

Casey's apartment is a spacious two-bedroom, with an open kitchen separated from the living room by a long counter lined with high-backed bar stools. On the other side of the big living room, a sliding glass door opens onto a balcony. There are flowers all over—bunches of calla lilies mingled with brilliant fuchsia hydrangeas—gathered in heavy-looking white vases on the coffee and end tables, and white tea lights and orchids float in glass bowls of water. In each of the far corners of the room, huge, hip-high vases hold half a dozen giant palm fronds.

Scanning the room quickly, a smile ready on my face in case I spot Leigh, I see about a dozen women draped over the chintz furniture drinking pink and orangesicle–colored drinks from martini glasses. If I'm not mistaken, I think I see petals floating in them. I grasp that there's a theme, which is obviously tropical, or Tahitian, or Bora Boran. An engagement party with a theme. Who knew?

I feel someone grab my arm. "Rachel, hello!" says Leigh, giving my arm a two-hand squeeze, "I'm so glad you could make it. How are you? Isn't this *beautiful*?" she asks, her voice rising softly as though she can still hardly believe it, beaming and gesturing at the room around her. "Casey did a *gorgeous* job, didn't she? It feels like Saint Bart's in here . . . those palm fronds, the nibbles, the drinks—which you don't have!" she interrupts herself accusingly, then turns me in the direction of the kitchen. I hadn't noticed that the woman standing behind the kitchen counter is not a guest, but a waiter wearing a tuxedo shirt and a white apron.

"What would you like?" Leigh asks when we've stopped in front of the counter covered with platters of elaborate-looking finger-sized appetizers. "A rose martini, an orange fizz, or the tango punch—it's this delicious tangerine and rum thing Casey's caterer invented."

I raise my eyebrows at Leigh in anticipation. The bartender hands me a martini glass filled with a pale orange liquid and garnished with a dusting of small white flower petals. It looks like the pattern of a Lilly Pulitzer dress. When I look up from my first sip, the bride has wandered back into the gathering in the living room, but the bartender is smiling politely and gesturing at the spread in between us.

"Just to let you know about the choice of appetizers, there are skewers of grilled mahi mahi with a sweet and sour dipping sauce, vegetarian island rolls," she says pleasantly, indicating each of the platters in turn, "and mini crab cake burgers with chipotle mayonnaise."

"Lovely, thank you," I reply, looking to see if anybody else is eating. Several of the women are holding orange and fuschia paper napkins and balancing plates of food on their laps, but I decide I need to drink more before I eat. I need to drink a lot before I eat. I slowly approach the cluster of girls and couches and sit down in an empty chair next to a petite girl who is doing her best to take meticulous bites from an unwieldy island roll.

"Have you looked anywhere but Vera, yet?" she asks Leigh, who is sitting on a couch across the coffee table from her. The petite girl's left hand displays some serious platinum hardware—a hulking solitaire above a sparkling anniversary band, although she doesn't look old enough to have been married a year already. Let alone however many years it takes to earn a reward like that.

"Except for Barneys and Saks, not yet," Leigh replies, "and I loved Vera's stuff—how can you not, right?—but wouldn't it be fun to do something a little less done? Like Badgley Mischka or Reem Acra?"

"Well," says Hardware Girl, "I went with my friend Dana—you know Dana Friedman, right? She used to work at Rubenstein PR?—to her last fitting at Carolina Herrera, yesterday. Leigh, her dress was a-maaaa-zing."

"*Really?* You know, I feel like Carolina's ready-to-wear stuff is sort of old, but her gowns are gorgeous . . . but I don't know!" she exclaims, balling her hands into fists and screwing her eyes tight. "There is just *so* much to think about!"

Everyone lets out a chorus of sympathetic laughter. I join in. Hardware Girl seems to notice me when I do, and she turns.

"Hi, I'm Jackie," she says extending her other hand, "I'm a friend of Leigh's through my husband. He works with her fiancé."

"I'm Rachel. I'm also a friend of Ben's—of the fiancé," I reply, shaking her hand.

"Oh that's you! Leigh mentioned that a friend of Ben's would be coming. How funny that we've never met before! My husband's one of the directors at DL Group. The parent company of *DesignLab?* Jason Zelnick? We totally *love* Ben."

I totally love Ben, too, Jackie. But I don't find it funny that we've not met before. "Yeah, he's great, he—"

"Oh my God, Jackie!" Casey calls out from across the room with extreme urgency. "Weren't you the one telling me the story about that girl whose husband got cut from the *New York Times*?"

"Oh, yeah," Jackie replies, shaking her head with dismay. "My friend Marina was marrying this adorable guy Seth. He is totally pedigreed, and Marina's dad is a big developer—so they were total shoo-ins for the wedding announcements. They send in a beautiful picture of them together, but that Sunday, they open the paper and it's a gigantic close-up of *just* her! It looked like she'd sent in a portrait of herself alone. It was *mort*ifying."

"Seriously," agrees Leigh. "How can you make sure they don't *do* that?"

"You can't," Jackie answers, shrugging, "you just have to hope for the best. I think you and Ben are also total shoo-ins. Media job guy, marketing girl, Manhattan wedding—you guys are totally in."

"You *have* to talk to Leslie about her florist. She had all white and peach tones, so old-school elegant."

"My mother is talking about bringing in a florist from Charlotte, the woman who did her best friend's daughter's wedding. I saw the pictures in *Southern Living*, and it was really stunning."

I feel like a foreigner in a circle of natives, all chattering in a language I don't understand. I quit trying to follow the volley of comments and concentrate instead on my tangerine drink. I'm jerked back to attention when someone says my name. I look up and see all eyes are on me.

"Sorry?"

Casey is asking me a question. "How about you, Rachel, are you seeing anyone?"

"Uh . . . no, not really. Nobody, no."

"Dating in New York *is* hard," Leigh offers from her position in the middle of the couch. "Rachel was dating a guy from Morgan Stanley for a long time, but things ended just recently, right, Rachel?" she adds, sounding like she's trying to make up for my otherwise shameful shortcoming. There's a brief lull in the conversation. I suppose I am meant to have some views on the matter, but I don't know what to say.

"So, Rachel," a girl I think named Stephanie says, "tell us about Ben. What was he *like* in college?"

"Well." I pause and shift my gaze toward Leigh. I have foolish Ben stories, as well as endearing and embarrassing Ben stories, and even a few gross Ben stories. I presume Leigh knows most of them, because quite a while ago Ben had tacitly established the Full Disclosure to Girlfriend rule: that important relationship landmark in which the man no longer feels comfortable withholding secrets from his girlfriend. I'm not sure, though, how thoroughly Ben has actually adhered to the Full Disclosure rule, and if he has, if Leigh feels comfortable with my sharing unedited versions of some of those stories.

But when I look over, Leigh is nodding vigorously, trying to bite off a delicate chunk of mahi mahi from a skewer. "Tell us some stories! I'm sure I've only heard the rated-G versions," she laughs, covering her mouth. "Like what was that one about that night with those guys from the gay bar?"

I smile, knowing exactly which story she's talking about. "Now, *that* was a ridiculous night," I start, thinking of how many other ridiculous nights there had been. "So senior year of college, Ben gets really serious academically and he decides he's going to write a senior thesis. Of course he's totally on top of the research and the writing. It's not even close to the due date, but he has it all planned so he'll finish with a two-week margin. But obviously this is *way* too anal, so a group of us decide to put a few kinks in his plan. We grab him on his way back from the library one night, drag him into my car, and drive him to this gay bar in Minneapolis. On the way, we tell him we're holding his books and notes hostage and won't give them back until he manages to pick up a nice boy and brings him back to meet us.

"Ben is *insanely* furious. He doesn't say a word the whole way there, and I'm sure the second he gets out of the car, he'll go straight back to campus, right to campus police, and turn us all in for assault and kidnapping. But," I say, pausing to gauge the effect on my audience, "a couple hours later, the doorbell rings at the house we all share. I answer the door and it's Ben, with not one—but *three* guys, each more flamboyant than the other. Ben's shirt is unbuttoned to his navel, he's wearing eyeliner and carrying a bottle of jug wine."

Jaws are dropping around me, and it reminds me of just how utterly unself-conscious Ben is. "He's jutting his hip out and gestures one by one to each of the guys. 'This is Otto 'n' Dirk 'n' Derek, and I told the boys we totally had to come back to my house and play spin the bottle with my hags. So, come on everybody! Time for us all to play *together* now!'

"Long story short . . . Ben eventually has us all sitting around drinking cheap wine, spinning an empty Snapple bottle and making out with these random guys he picked up. He doesn't let down his front for a second, and the joke ends up being on us—especially the next morning when we wake up completely hungover and find Otto, Dirk, and Derek curled up on the couches downstairs. And no sign of Ben except a note on the breakfast table with a drawing of a hand extending its middle finger."

I skip the part about the bong, the ecstasy, and that it was actually strip spin the bottle. I'd thought about that night a lot over the years, about how, when Ben spun the bottle, and it had finally landed on me, I had butterflies. I had completely forgotten we were in the middle of a circle of stoned people, and when our time was up, we were still kissing. At four in the morning, when everyone had finally gone to bed or collapsed on the floor, Ben and I lay down on his bed, exhausted and laughing. He'd pulled me close and held me, and we fell asleep together. I wonder again now, as I look at Leigh laughing at what she thinks is the uncut version of a Ben story, what would have happened if things had ended differently that night. Even though we stumbled home late together plenty more times before we graduated and after, we never discussed the way that night ended.

I am the direct access to Ben's past, and the girls take full advantage, falling silent after the laughter or the loud group "Awww!" at the end of each story. It appears Jackie and Jason Zelnick aren't the only ones who *"love"* Ben. How is it that these women can be so foreign to me and so familiar with him? Leigh seems to be loving it, hearing all these adventures starring her future husband, sometimes comic, sometimes absurd, but always the hero. I had told these stories a million times before, when Ben and I would try to one-up each other with *you-did-it-and-I-was-a-witness* stories, but this time they seem to mean something different to me. It's like suddenly, now that Ben has made this irreversible commitment, I've never found him more sweet, and more brave, and more hilarious.

It's like I'd never realized just how much history we did share.

The stories are funny, but I'm not laughing, even if I am smiling on cue.

With every story I tell, I'm giving up a piece of Ben and handing it over to Leigh and to her world. And with each additional piece handed over, I wonder if I haven't made the worst mistake of my life.

What if we had gotten together that night and then stayed together?

What if I should have been the one to marry Ben?

15

"Question for you," Zach says, jutting his chin over the edge of my cubicle panel.

"The answer is no," I reply, without looking away from my screen, "tinfoil in a microwave is never a good idea."

"Check. Now say I was looking for your opinion on Jim Deal."

"Um . . . who?"

"The painter?"

"Ah," I pretend to think for a moment. "Don't know him."

"Exactly the answer I was hoping for," Zach replies. "So you want to go to his gallery opening with me tonight?"

"Why would you want me to come to his opening if I don't know who he is?"

Zach strokes the bottom of his beard and looks philosophical. Or, more precisely, like Jerry Garcia mid-trip. "Because you'll have a totally unbiased view of his work and you'll be able to tell me—in all honesty—how you feel about his crap. I mean his 'art.' Would you be up for it?"

"Is Jim Deal really a pseudonym for Zach Stevenson?" I ask.

"Nope, I swear. But the artist and I are friends. Sort of. We used to work together in California. This is a pretty big show for him tonight, and I'd like to check it out, enjoy the free wine, and show my support. And, of course, snicker in the corner if it sucks. We weren't really the 'closest' of friends."

"Free wine and snickers? Sounds like my ideal dinner. Sure, thanks, I'd love to come."

"Great. I'll e-mail you the details," he says smiling, then raps on my desk and walks away.

*   *   *

On the subway heading downtown, I look at my office outfit and wish I'd had time to change clothes. Normally I'd go to a gallery opening in something more artful—something that wouldn't look like I tried too hard, but that could be described as stylish and maybe even fierce—but I'd had to meet with Jessica from J.P. Morgan for the second time immediately after work. Sadly, my look is cubicle-cutter bland. Zach's not exactly the type to care about dressing for the occasion, though, so I doubt it really matters.

When I find him milling outside the Laine gallery, he is in fact still wearing the same layered T-shirts, cargo pants, and scruffy hooded sweatshirt he was wearing at work. He's also laboriously working over a piece of chewing gum. "Look what you've turned me into!" he says with exasperation. "I'm chewing to save my life, and this is no way to live—I'm disgusting. Besides, look! All the cool kids smoke at art openings. It's like a rule."

"Would that be the rule of conformity?" I say, arching my eyebrows.

Zach smiles, then spits out the gum. "Come on, let's go inside."

We walk into the gallery, which is overflowing with eclectic hipster clothing and asymmetrical hairstyles. Most of the people look like they have jobs where they never work in an office but still live in high-end real estate. As we wander the gallery, sipping white wine from plastic cups and squinting at large abstract canvases, I ask, "Remind me again how you know this artist?"

"We used to share studio space," Zach says succinctly. His eyes dart across the room, and he nods at someone before turning back to me. "Sorry if I seem out of it. This is all a little weird for me."

I realize I've never seen Zach be anything but laid-back. "This show is really that big a deal then?"

"Yeah," he replies, "Jim's had a good buzz going for a while, but this show is definitely the billboard for his arrival." He examines the card hanging on the wall below one painting, then lets out a soft whistle.

"Sticker shock? How much?" I ask.

"Nah, they don't put prices on the tags. I'm just impressed by the profundity of the title. Kind of says it all, don't you think?" He gives a dismissive laugh.

I look at the painting, which consists of a canvas divided between two similar shades of blue, then I look at the title card. *Tru Blu*. I actually like it, though I hesitate to admit this to Zach.

"Isn't it great!" a woman's voice exclaims from behind us.

I turn around and see a dewy complexion and high, artfully rouged cheekbones on a petite young woman wearing a blousy silk top and a tight black pencil skirt. A loose mass of curly brown hair is piled up and pinned behind her head. She's stunning, and she looks like exactly the kind of woman who would purchase this painting to hang in the bathroom of her Soho loft.

"Eva, hey there," Zach says.

"Hey, yourself," she replies, moving in to kiss him on the cheek.

"Eva, this is Rachel," Zach says, turning to me. "Eva works at Laine."

"Nice to meet you," I extend my hand to shake, and she gives me four delicate fingers in exchange. I am the Incredible Hulk standing next to this woman.

"And how do you and Zach know each other?" she asks.

"We work together at Trees," Zach answers.

"Oh, is that what we do there?" I say. "I thought I was showing up for the free soda."

"And don't forget the instant-messaging privileges," Zach adds.

"He is so funny, isn't he?" Eva replies, leaning in. "And so talented, too. I've been telling Roberta Laine she should look at his stuff. Graphic art is coming into its own—comics are completely *now,* and I know *the* artist."

Zach has been looking down uncomfortably at his feet, which are lined up as though he were standing at attention. Eva moves closer to Zach, angling him toward her. "I know that if she took a look, she'd absolutely flip out. I'm so sure of it."

Zach looks up quickly and turns to me. "She has to say that. She's my girlfriend."

Girlfriend?

"Rachel, have you seen Zach's work?" Eva asks, smiling effusively.

"Just what he does at Trees. Which is great!" I add quickly.

"That's what he does for a paycheck. You've got to see the characters he draws."

"What type of characters?"

"Ev, c'mon, that's enough," Zach replies.

"Hey, this is what I do for a living—I tell people about emerging artists—so just shut up and let me do my job," Eva says with a smile. "Zach's created this whole universe of characters that look like they walked straight out of a comic book—except they're doing everyday things. Things you'd never consider making art about." She readjusts the strap of her silky tank, which has just slipped off her delicate shoulder bone. "His drawings are the irony of seeing life as a comic book adventure. You *have* to make him show you!"

We notice simultaneously that a distinctively dressed older man at the other end of the gallery is beckoning to Eva. "I've got to take care of something," she says. "But I'll be back."

As she moves away, Zach grimaces. "I can't stand it when she does that."

"Are you kidding?" I reply, watching her walk away. "If my gorgeous girlfriend wanted to brag about me—"

"Now that's something I would enjoy listening to," he laughs, and moves in front of another painting.

I finish my cup of wine, toss it into the steel garbage can, and peer back toward Eva. I'm not the only one looking at her, either. Zach's girlfriend is one of those striking women who both men and women alike turn around to check out.

"How about you, Rachel?" Zach asks. "Have you started dating anyone new yet?"

I turn back from gawking at Eva. "Well," I reply, tempted to lie, "I *am* about to have a date."

"Oh, good." Zach nods. "So you're back in the game?"

I look at Zach, smiling at me encouragingly, then abandon my pose. "Sort of. It's a date, but it's what I suspect will be a spectacularly awful blind date."

"A blind date, ugh. They're the worst." Zach grunts. "At the end of it, you curse yourself for agreeing to it, get pissed at the person who made you do it, then wonder how badly you possibly could have needed companionship to have thought it sounded like a good idea."

"And don't forget the part at the end when your friends tell you the problem is you. *'You're too picky.'* Anyway, my friend Ben's brother went to college with this guy or something."

"Friend of a friend once removed," Zach notes. "Dangerous."

"Ben doesn't even know him."

"But he's sure you'll get along famously, right?" Zach smiles.

"Exactly. His name is Steve, he's studying to be a psychologist or something. So I believe the thinking goes like this: He's fascinated by nut-jobs and you talk about yourself obsessively—you guys will love each other."

"Or," Zach adds, "just as likely, he'll be completely insane himself."

"And I'll bend over backward to be pleasant even if he is."

"*Especially* if he is!"

"You're right. He'll come to the door—"

"Late!" Zach nods.

"Yeah, and not just five or ten minutes late, but forty-five minutes late," I say, emphasizing the point with an outstretched finger. "And the first thing he'll do is ask to use my bathroom, where he'll spend another fifteen suspicious minutes, and I'll hear him snooping in my medicine cabinet, and things dropping into the toilet."

"He'll come out eventually," Zach continues, "and tell you he's starving, then ask if there are any good macrobiotic restaurants in the neighborhood. Of course he doesn't eat anything animal or gluten-based since losing the 275 pounds last year. When you marvel at the weight loss—which you will, because you're being scrupulously kind—he'll show you the hanging folds of skin around his upper torso that were once his breasts.

"At dinner," Zach goes on, "you'll find only one thing on the menu that doesn't completely disgust you, but then, when the hippie waitress arrives, he'll order for both of you without asking."

"I'll admit to him that I don't really eat fermented soy curds, maybe I could—"

" 'You'll learn to love curds!' he'll say, laughing maniacally. When the food comes, he'll take a heaping forkful of something bluish and marinated and shove it in your mouth. 'Mmm, just try this!' he'll say, as it's sliding down your windpipe."

I nod. "And when the bill comes, he'll divide it in half then tell me I actually owe a little more since I had the expensive *organic* tempeh appetizer. Outside the restaurant, as I'm madly trying to flag down a getaway cab, he'll grab my hand and pull me toward him."

"He'll brush your hair back with his other sweaty hand, move in for the kiss. And try as you might, you won't be able to dodge, because he has you pressed hard against his sagging man-breasts. The kiss makes a smacking noise when he finally separates from you."

" 'We'll do this again,' he'll say. 'We have amazing chemistry, huh?' And, for a brief moment, I'll actually feel flattered."

"Oh, how I miss blind dating!" Zach chuckles.

"Yeah," I say, smirking.

"But, come on, Rachel, you have to admit, there *is* one positive aspect to this."

My eyes roll skyward. "And that is what, precisely?"

"Getting to tell me the tale afterward," Zach replies, rubbing his hands together gleefully.

16

Zippo: hey, wanna see something cool?

Rach: yesyesyesyesyesyes

Zippo: ok, click on this link: www.spinyechidna.com

Rach: what the hell is that?

Zippo: act now, ask questions later!

Rach: sounds like you're trying to sell me a used car

Zippo: in the name of Saint Nike, just do it!

Rach: if this is the site of long dong silver, you are in so much
trouble

I paste the link into my browser and wait while the page
loads, expecting to see a frog dancing in a blender. Suddenly,
a webpage opens with the image of a cracking windshield, ac-

companied by the sound of shattering glass. In the center of the spreading crack it reads "Click here to open." I click, and it opens to a page displaying a half dozen cartoon superhero figures, each with a distinctly modern spin. One is a character who looks like a punk-rock version of Superman. His red cape is studded with safety pins, his blue tights are a tartan pattern, and his booties look like pull-on Doc Martens. He looks like some hilariously stunted superhero—a superman who never got over his adolescent rebellion phase. I realize that these must be some of the characters Eva was talking about last night at the opening. Another Hall of Justice knock-off is identified as the "Wonder-Who-Farted-Twins." They are Siamese twins attached at the ankle. When I run my mouse over the graphic, the Twins each do a roundhouse kick with their unattached legs, then do a vicious front kick with the conjoined one. When the shared leg pops up, a fart sound belches out of the computer. I laugh out loud and look around, wondering who else heard the farting, hoping my co-workers don't think it was me.

Zippo: you on the site yet?
Rach: yes—what the?!
Zippo: click on tab in upper-right hand corner that says What's Gnu
Rach: ok

I click on the tab and a banner pops up written in bold, shadowed comic book typeface:

INTRODUCING MARILYN MANIZER
IN
THE PROFOUNDLY DISTURBING ADVENTURES
OF MARILYN MANIZER
VOLUME I: I'LL TAKE MANHATTAN

Beneath the banner is a comic strip.

EAT MY SOY JOY!

THIS BABE IS HOTTER THAN A VEGAN TAMALE!

INSTITUTE FOR THE STUDY OF THE EFFECTS OF FORCED BEEF CONSUMPTION

Holy. Shit. Zach turned my "blind date" into a comic strip and transformed me into a castrating female superhero named Marilyn Manizer, with double-D cups and chiseled biceps. Aside from being completely horrified, I am completely in love with the way he depicted me.

Rach: you ... she ... me ... ?!?!!!!!

Zippo: she's aliiiiivvvveeee

Rach: when did you do this?!

Zippo: when we got back from the opening

Rach: no, I mean when did you launch this site?

Zippo: depends ... do you like it?

Rach: you turn me into a muscle-flexing vixen whose failed dates wind up behind bars and you ask if I like it? I ADORE IT!!!

Zippo: oh, ok, good

Rach: may I treat you to half my afternoon snack to thank you for turning me into a muse?

Zippo: meet you in the kitchen

As the kitchen door swings shut behind us, I hand Zach a box of animal crackers. He holds it up, turns it around, and scrutinizes the back, slowly tracing with his finger the tiny words printed on the label. "Well done!" he finally says, taking a cracker and handing me back the box. "Only eleven ingredients. I believe this is referred to as a 'step.'"

"So when did you create this website, and why didn't I know about it before?" I demand, ignoring his praise.

"I launched Spiny Echidna about a year ago, when I decided I wanted to start animating some of my characters." He shrugs.

"Those are awesome caricatures, Zach—so much more interesting than the regular superheroes—and I'm not just saying that because you made me a member of the Hall of Justice. I'm already impressed, and I've barely clicked beyond the home page."

"Well, keep checking back on the site. Like those moments when you begin to feel so bored with work you actually consider setting your hair on fire. Instead, just double-click and see what the latest Spiny Superhero is up to . . ." Zach adds, smiling. He reaches for the box of crackers again and unloads the remaining cookies dump-truck style into his mouth.

Suddenly the kitchen door swings open and Molly walks in holding her empty plastic water bottle. She shoots the two of us her disappointed Mother Hen look as she proceeds toward the watercooler.

"That *is* a great idea for the deforestation unit, Rachel," Zach says, spewing crumbs, as we both start turning toward the door.

"Well, I'm glad I ran that by you then," I reply, holding the door open for him as he walks out. I wait for it to swing shut.

"I see how it is. Eat a girl's cookies and then run away like a trembling peon when the boss turns up. I'm thinking Marilyn Manizer wouldn't think much of that kind of behavior."

"Hmm." Zach nods approvingly. "Sounds like the Manizer's got an axe to grind!"

17

Vlad and I are sitting at the same table in the same Starbucks where we had our first meeting. I'm as wired as a telephone pole, and given the amount of caffeine I've imbibed in the past hour, I probably won't stop peeing until tomorrow. But it's been an intense work session, and we have at least another half hour to go.

After our first meeting, I'd gone home and taken all Vlad's history and stats, digested and reprocessed them, then generated a long, bullet-pointed list of possible essay topics drawn from his personal experiences. After I was finished reorganizing Vlad's life story, it looked like he had been *predestined* to go to business school. His whole life—according to my interpretation—was a series of anecdotes that answered application questions precisely.

When I'd e-mailed him the notes a few days later, he replied that he "Would surely like to move fast forward and begin with the essays as soon as can be." I spent the following weekend writing outlines for the Yale School of Management application. I sent them to Vlad, and now here we were, slowly and painfully revising our way through his rough drafts.

Vlad is impressively fluent in English; he speaks it more articulately than most of my friends. His written English, however, has remained a lot more foreign. To wit, in response to a question about his personal credo:

The college graduation only added to my thirst for the knowledge. Just like following the words of the great man Dr. Martin Luther King, "Have a dream!" I decided to continue business classes at the School of Continuing Education of the Fordham University. My next project involves patching some gaps in my writing skills by taking a course of the business writing. Conclusively, it is my hope to follow this credo for as long as possible.

The past hour involved my pointing out some of the "weaker" turns of phrase, and suggesting a fully fleshed-out "alternative"—which I'd written while editing the essays earlier that week. I am realizing that On Target Essay's signature touch will consist of making the whole process feel like it isn't actually me writing the essay, but the customer revising his own words—with my extremely active participation.

On the positive side, Vlad seems well aware of his weaknesses and is happy for my "active participation." As we systematically work our way through my suggested changes, he nods and agrees, only a few times questioning a correction or proposing something else. When we finally reach the last paragraph of the last draft we both lean back, smile, and begin to laugh.

"It is strenuous work for me tonight," Vlad says. "I imagine what great work you must put in over the past days."

"It is pretty intense," I agree. "But we're doing things thoroughly. And I hope you're finding the end result acceptable? This system is working for you . . . ?"

I am shocked at the words coming out of my mouth. I have never actively sought feedback from an employer. I wonder for a moment if I have been possessed by some anal demon of professionalism.

"It is very much working for me." Vlad nods. "I am looking forward to moving on to the next essays."

"Great," I reply, smiling. "I'm glad."

"I must pay you tonight," he says, opening his billfold. "I am paying you full fee as we are almost done with the Yale," he explains as he begins peeling off hundred-dollar bills. When I proposed the fee over e-mail—and prayed the message wouldn't be returned with the subject line, "Are you fucking crazy?"—Vlad replied that would be fine and that he would pay me, in cash, as we finished each application.

Cash?

Mmm, cash. It's a good word. I like the way it sounds, and I like the way it feels. It's hard currency. It's control. It's power in its most primal form.

And it's so pretty!

I look down at the money on the table and notice that the bills are the same lovely green as the Starbucks logo on the white cup. As the pile of cash grows with each successive bill Vlad adds, I start feeling flush. And flushed. The first bill is going right into the bank. But the second one is taking a stroll with me downtown to try on the new Sigerson Morrison flats. The third will be devoted to updating my compact collection. And the fourth and fifth bills—God, I love the way that sounds!—I'll carry around in my wallet for a while just to see how a wad like that feels.

"Well, thank you, Vlad," I say, scooping up the wampum. "We're very glad you've been pleased with the work so far."

"Is 'we' someone else working with you in company?" Vlad asks. "It is funny, because I looked for you on the Internet after I telephoned you, but I did not find any website. Perhaps I overlooked?"

Given that every kind of business from major retail chains to Nails R Us, the musty manicure place next door to my apartment run by a bunch of Korean women who don't speak English, all have websites, this seems like a natural question. Even Amos, the homeless man who laminates documents on the corner of 9th and 52nd, has a website. He hands out small business cards with the URL on the bottom left-hand corner: www.TheLaminator.com. It's suddenly embarrassing to know Vlad found out about On Target Essay from some soggy flier taped to a lamppost, and I desperately wish I could refer him to www-dot-something.

But the idea of a website hadn't occurred to me.

"It's under construction," I lie, worried. Maybe I should just give the money back now, thank Vlad for his trust, and tell him it's not going to work out for reasons of professional conflict before he figures out that On Target Essay is actually just me and him?

"Well, it will be very helpful, I think, when you have it finished. It will be good to be able to see all at once the services and prices and such things. All the writing samples will be posted there, too?"

I nod and smile weakly.

"You are very good, I think, at explaining over the phone the things you offer, but it can be quicker for the busy applicants sometimes to visit the website, especially if they are not in New York City."

It had never occurred to me—an eBay junkie—that busy applicants outside of New York could use my services. Vlad has just multiplied my potential client base by the global population of all people applying to American business school all over the world. I wonder if he should get a cut of my massive future profits.

"For me," Vlad continues, "the Internet is where I take care of all my business these days—pay the bills, find services, order the gifts." He smiles as he stands up to put on his long camel-colored coat and readjust the wallet he just returned to his back pocket. There's something in the gesture that reminds me of Andy, the recent ex. I don't know whether it's the physical motion itself—the pushing back of his overcoat and suit jacket—or whether it's simply his facility with money that seems familiar. Vlad has the confidence of those who are casual with cash, the ease of someone who has enough money not to worry about it. It's an attractive sense of self-possession. Hot.

I get up to put on my own coat. "I'll e-mail you the final revisions for the Yale app by the end of the day tomorrow for your approval, and then over the weekend we can start outlining Dartmouth and Wharton?" I ask.

"That sounds good. It is good to keep up the pace. The due date will come before we know. I will look for your e-mail tomorrow. Thank you, Rachel."

The way Vlad carefully enunciates both syllables of my name gives it a funny formal quality I'm not used to. It sounds far more sophisticated than I ever think of myself, and I realize I'm grinning when I walk out of the coffee shop.

*   *   *

Rach: Dr. Zach?

Zippo: yes my nubile assistant, is Mission Dupe the Estonian still proceeding successfully?

Rach: ohhhhh, that depends . . . what does ten times one hundred equal, when the one hundred takes the form of a green paper with the face of Ben Franklin?

Zippo: SCORE!!!!

Rach: what do you think of escalating the operation?

Zippo: spy-ops? sabotaging the competition?

Rach: multimedia global domination via digital interfacing

Zippo: huh???

Rach: i was thinking of a website for On Target Essay

Zippo: great idea. why didn't I think of that?

Rach: we've been wondering the same thing

Zippo: how many pitchers of brew do i get if i come up with something snazzy?

Rach: i can't even count that high, and how about some chili cheese fries with that beer?

Zippo: deal. www.FakeEssaysForSale.com coming up

Zippo: or maybe www.TurnYourShitToGold.org?

Rach: um...

Zippo: humorless as Marilyn Manizer without sleep or meat. fine, www.EssayCheaters.com it is

Rach: you're a dreamboat, Dr. Zach! thank you!! even the Manizer might learn to like someone like you

18

As I walk up the stairs to Kate's brownstone, I can see inside the brightly lit first-floor bay windows, and it looks like most of the dinner guests have already arrived. I open the unlocked front door and walk into the rich smell of chopped basil that is Kate's pesto fusilli, wafting into the entrance from the kitchen in the back. Kate asked me to pick up some pine nuts for the dish, so I head straight to the kitchen to deliver the package, dashing by the arched doorway to the living room and avoiding the other guests for now.

"Mmmmmmm," I sigh, as the kitchen's swinging door shuts behind me. "When do we get to devour this deliciousness?"

Kate is grating Parmesan, her back to me. "So did you see who's here? Say hello to everyone?"

"No, not yet," I answer brightly. "Came straight back here to deliver the nuts. Besides, I need the advance dirt on everyone in attendance tonight."

Kate continues to scrape the cheese against the grater. "Well, there'll be eight of us, not including the girls. Judy and Daniel. Did you know Judy's pregnant? She just told us last week." She dumps the growing mound of cheese crumbs into the food processor and continues to grate more. "Denise and her new guy, although I guess he's not so new anymore. But I don't think you've ever met him. And David, an architect friend of Michael's from the office.

"Here." She turns around and reaches for a container of black olives, dumps them into an empty ceramic bowl and hands them to me. "Can you take these? I should be out in a minute."

I walk toward the living room, pausing to check myself in the bevel-edged hall mirror. It is one of the house's many flea market finds, with the muted grayish sheen of all old mirrors. I like the way it gives my reflection a faded look, as though it were an old photograph. I'm wearing a fitted scoop-neck sweater top over a wool pencil skirt, with a choker-length necklace and low kitten heels. The sepia-toned reflection of a feminine girl in vintage clothes makes me flash briefly to my mother. I smile, thinking of her dinner parties and how she was always so casually elegant, a stay-at-home mom wearing a silk foulard and Ferragamo pumps, who served imported cheeses that no one bought back then, a little out of place in suburban Minneapolis. She would have loved her daughter's Brooklyn dinner parties, with Kate and Michael's arty neighborhood friends sitting around their dark-wood living room, talking about their design projects or the local Montessouri school, nibbling on crackers and the same goat cheese and Roquefort that had confused her Minneapolis friends twenty years ago.

"Hello!" I say to everyone in general, as I walk in and set down the olive bowl on the Moroccan-tiled coffee table. There's a chorus of hellos in response, and Michael asks Lola to move to the window seat to make room for me on the couch next to Judy. I squeeze Judy's arm and smile as I sit. "Congratulations!" I say. "Kate told me about the baby— that's wonderful news!"

She beams back at me. As Judy lifts her shirt to show me the slight swell in her stomach, I can see the edge of a tattoo near her hip from her rocker chick days. She's a theater set de- signer now. I think of Kate's tattoo in the same place, and how when she was pregnant with Sophie she was terrified it would expand monstrously. Michael, who is sitting in a chair on my other side, touches my elbow lightly, and I turn toward him.

"Rachel, this is David, a colleague of mine from the firm," he says, gesturing to the slightly graying guy in a loose V-neck sweater sitting on the couch. "And this is Rachel, Kate's younger sister." David stands up and extends his arm over the coffee table to shake my hand.

"Nice to meet you," I say, getting up.

"And you," he answers, nodding his head.

"And this is Carl," Denise says, putting her arm on the shoulder of the attractive guy with coffee-colored skin and long braids sitting next to her. Denise still makes her living as a musician and hasn't yet settled down with anyone seriously. Carl, like all her boyfriends, is beautiful and makes a sexy first impression. "Hi, Carl," I say, raising my hand in a little wave.

"So tell me everything, Rachel," Denise says, when I've sat down again. "I haven't seen you in forever. What's going on with that import company you work for?"

"Actually I'm not with Byzantium anymore. I'm editing content for this other Internet company on a freelance basis now."

"But I thought you liked that Byzantium job?"

"I did. But I've moved on. Trying something new." I smile placidly at Denise and Carl. "In fact, Denise, I've started a little business on the side as well, along with the freelance work."

"*Really?* A business? What is it?"

"It's a writing consultancy." I congratulate myself on how inspired that sounds. I haven't yet described On Target Essay to anyone without telling its creation story first, and I'm pleased at how easy it is to give the thing a sheen of legitimacy with just a few corporate-sounding words.

"Wow, that sounds cool," replies Denise with enthusiasm. She clearly has no idea what I mean.

"That sounds like something new for you, Rach," Judy pipes in. "How did you get into that?"

"Well, I was writing and editing promotional copy at Byzantium, and then I started working with a few people applying to business school, drafting and editing their essays—

which are essentially self-promotional pieces—so it wasn't that big of a leap." It's actually the first time I've thought about it like this. And I think it even sounds plausible.

"Sure, I see what you mean. It's all about selling a product. What a great idea." Judy nods. "Are you going to be doing this full-time?"

My eyebrows shoot up, and I try not to laugh out loud. She may as well have asked an eight-year-old running a lemonade stand when she'll be quitting school to take her product global. "Oh no, I don't think so," I reply, looking especially pensive. "Things aren't quite at that stage yet. I'm still just getting the business off the ground, trying to manage my clients and bring in some new ones, too."

David chuckles. "Ah, so it's not really so much a business at this point as a . . ." he pauses, still smiling, gesturing with his hands as though searching for something to grasp, "a hobby."

"No, it's a business," I fire back quickly in reply. "I just don't know yet how intense the . . . client flow is going to be."

"I bet you'll be overrun with clients, Rach," Michael comments. "Where were you when *I* was applying to grad school? Those essays were like this hulking barrier between me and the rest of my career. I would have loved some professional help—if," he pauses, "I could have afforded you!"

I raise my shoulders in a slow shrug and smile with coy mystery. "I'm not sure you could, Michael. But you're cute, so I might have taken you on pro bono."

Sophie runs into the living and then stops abruptly. "Mommy says dinner's ready, so everybody needs to go sit down at the table right away!" She gestures for emphasis with both of her index fingers, effectively bringing conversation to a halt.

"Yes, ma'am," I say, getting up and putting my hands on her shoulders and turning her in the direction of the dining room. "You lead the way." As I follow behind Sophie, conga-line-style, walking through the wide doorframe that connects the living room to the dining room, Kate enters from the kitchen doorway carrying a huge plate of steaming pasta decorated with basil leaves and pine nuts.

"You sit down, honey," Michael says, taking the dish from her and placing it on a ceramic hot plate in the center of the long oak table. "Rachel and I will bring in the rest. Why don't you help everybody figure out where to sit—Sophie, sweetie, that's Daddy's chair, let Mommy tell you where to sit. Maybe next to Aunt Judy?"

I experience a twinge of envy hearing Michael call Judy 'aunt.' What am I, if Judy is 'aunt'? Number One aunt? Auntier? I had been hoping to sit next to Sophie myself, to throw myself fully into Distraction and Entertainment Duty—the ultimate shield against prying adult conversation.

The door swings shut behind Michael and me. I reach for the big wooden bowl of mixed greens then start walking back into the dining room.

"Hold on a second, Rachel, while we have a quick minute," Michael says, taking down the serving plate of tomato and mozzarella slices that Kate had put on top of the fridge so the dog wouldn't get to it. He turns around and puts it on the other side of the counter, facing me. "I just wanted to ask you . . . how are you? Really?"

I used to tease Kate about Michael's nurturing instinct before they were married.

"I know your dad's illness is so unexpected—and hard to deal with," he continues, "And this has been such a blow to Kate. I mean, she's a total mess."

I shouldn't be surprised to hear this, but it feels like a shock. *Kate? A mess?*

"She's sleeping badly, and I think that trying to hide her worry from the girls only makes it harder to manage," Michael says, walking over to my side of the counter. "There's not much the girls and I can do, except try to distract you guys a little. We're here for Kate, and I want to make sure you know we're here for you, too."

I smile weakly at Michael and raise my hand to squeeze the back of his, nodding. Then I lean in to give him a hug, because I think I might burst into tears and I don't want him to see my face. I am picturing Kate sobbing, her shoulders shaking, and I am horrified. I hadn't realized until now how much I had been relying on her to conceal her grief and comfort me. When our mother was dying of breast cancer, the only steady mooring in what seemed like an endless blur of awfulness had been Kate's promise that things would be normal again, that the two of us would be okay.

"Thank you, Michael," I finally say. "You and Sophie and Lola make getting through this a lot easier for Kate and me. Thank you."

Only a few minutes have elapsed, and when we come back through the swinging kitchen door carrying the rest of the food, everyone is seated. Kate is serving up plates of pasta,

Michael sits down at the head of the table, and I see that Sophie is in fact placed next to Judy. The only empty seat is next to David, and I sense my sister's hand at work. Kate has always loved playing matchmaker.

As the food and bread get passed around the table and David hands me the salad bowl and then a platter, I notice with relief that he doesn't make eye contact. Which means he probably has no idea that anyone's hand is at work at all, and I don't have to sustain any pretense of flirty small talk. I'm still too preoccupied with the image of Kate's shoulders shaking. But as soon as the plates have stopped circulating, and we all start eating, David shifts in his chair to turn his shoulders toward me. I notice that although his hair is thick on the sides and in the front, he has an unfortunate thinning round patch toward the back. I imagine how he might appear in one of Zach's strips, as a fat monk in a brown cassock and Jesus sandals.

"Tell me a little bit more about how you got into this business of yours, Rachel," David asks and then gives me a small, sly grin, as though we share a secret. "Surely there's more to it than just going from copy girl at an import business to getting people into business school?"

I return the smile. "Not really, no."

"Well, how did you get your first client?" He leans even closer, dipping his head toward me.

"It was actually my former boss. I edited his business school application essays while I was working for him."

"And where did he get into school?"

"I don't know," I say, pausing briefly, trying to figure out a good reason why I don't, "because acceptances haven't been mailed out yet."

"So you don't exactly have a proven track record," he replies, with a wink.

"Or you could say I have a perfect record at this point."

As we speak, David is occasionally lowering his face toward his plate to scoop in big knotted forkfuls of pesto-slathered rotini and then turning back to look at me as he chews slowly. "And how did you find your other clients?" he asks, continuing the interrogation. I flash to the image of a fat monk as grand inquisitor, shaking a turkey leg at the damned.

"I advertised," I reply succinctly.

"Where?"

"On fliers. All over Manhattan."

"On fliers?" David asks with a surprised laugh. He chuckles a little before scooping in another forkful of pasta. "How charming!"

"Charming. And efficient," I reply briskly. "I already have as many clients as I can handle right now." This is almost entirely true. I have Vlad, and Jessica Tucker, and Jordan Brill-stein—a friend of Andy's from Morgan Stanley—and I'm waiting to hear back from two other Morgan Stanley people. I wouldn't mind actually getting positive replies from a few more applicants.

As David is putting on his coat later, getting ready to leave with Denise and Carl who are driving back to Manhattan, he suggests that maybe I'd like to check out that gnocchi place we'd talked about, and would I have time next week? I paste a large understanding smile across my face and wrinkle my brows sympathetically. "Ooh, the next few weeks are really deadline-heavy for On Target Essay," I lie. "So why don't I give you a call when I'm a little less busy?" Which, for you, you condescending glutton, will be never.

While helping Kate wash and dry the dishes after everyone's left, I barely wait for her to ask me what I thought of David before announcing that single does not mean desperate.

"But he's—" Kate begins to protest.

"Not even worth a free meal," I say witheringly.

The front door has hardly shut behind me before I take out my cell phone and dial Zach's number.

"You will *never* believe the nightmare date I just barely avoided!" I announce triumphantly, as soon as he answers.

"Tell me everything!" Zach commands. "Spare no detail!"

＊　　＊　　＊

When I reach my desk the next morning, there is a Day-Glo orange Post-it stuck to my monitor, which reads:

The Dark Ages just got a little bit brighter...see www.spinyechidna.com/marilynmanizer for enlightment.

I immediately log on and click to Zach's website, then to the Adventures of Marilyn Manizer, where I discover that Zach has already drawn his own creative interpretation of my encounter with David.

In the first box, Zach has drawn Marilyn attached to a medieval torture machine, being interrogated by an evil-looking monk. The monk's holding a torch perilously close to her face, making her sweat and look askance at the approaching flames. In box number two, Marilyn, looking stony-faced, is now tied to a stake, and the evil monk posts a long scroll next to her entitled: "Top Ten Reasons Your Business is a FRAUD!" Only the last two reasons are legible, but they are: #10 Too charming to be taken seriously . . . #9 Too cute to do your own accounting . . . In the third box, while the evil monk is distracted by the scent of a maidservant walking past with steaming meat pies, Marilyn escapes from her bonds. And in the final box the evil monk is now seated and chained to a desk, holding a quill pen above a scroll. A triumphant, smirking Marilyn stands behind him, torch in hand, dictating: "I believe that my many years of service as a condescending, know-it-all glutton have prepared me well for the MBA program at . . ."

19

"I'll be out in a minute," I yell. If Carlos really has to pee that badly, he'll just water one of my houseplants as I suspect he's done before.

"Rachel." Carlos knocks again. "Can I come in?"

Can he *come in?* Is he kidding? *I'm showering!*

"I'm sorry," he says, opening the door.

"Carlos!" I yell from behind the translucent curtain, turning to face the tile and no doubt giving him an eyeful of silhouette. "I will be out in one minute, can't you wait?"

"I'm sorry," he repeats, "but I thought it must be important. Your sister just called."

I turn the water off and shiver. "Kate called?"

"Yes. She says you must call her right away. It's your father." He pauses. "It's an emergency."

*   *   *

Kate tells me to meet her at LaGuardia, she's already made our flight reservations to Minneapolis. She explained things very quickly over the phone: Dad was just admitted to the hospital; he couldn't breathe. I call Aunt Barbara from a cab on my way to the airport and all she says is, "Get here soon."

When I get to the gate, Kate is waiting for me, slumped into a large leather airport chair, talking on her cell phone. She's biting her nails, something I haven't seen her do in years. When she sees me, she nods and moves her carry-on from the seat next to her so I can sit down. She's talking to Sophie and Lola and doing her best to maintain her composure.

"Okay, honey," she says, "you know who just got here? Aunt Rachel. That's right. Do you want to say hello? Okay, hang on, sweetheart." Kate hands me the phone.

"Hello, who's there?" I ask. "Are these my favorite nieces, Sophie and Lola?"

"It's just me, Aunt Rachel," Sophie says, "Lola didn't want to talk."

I know how the kid feels. "What did you do in school today, Sophie?" I can't think of anything else to say.

"We did some arts and crafts, and I drew a turtle."

"A turtle! Wow, that's great. I didn't know you liked turtles," I reply, looking at Kate. She rolls her eyes and shakes her head.

"Yeah! And *youknowwhat?* We're going to get one. Hey,

Aunt Rachel?" Sophie says. "When are you and Mommy coming back?"

"When are we coming back?" I repeat, hoping Kate will have an answer for this. But Kate doesn't respond. She just presses her lips together and looks away. "Well," I say, "you know we're going to visit Grandpa Bernie, and he's not feeling well, so we're going to stay until he's all better. You want Grandpa to feel better, right?"

"Yes," she says enthusiastically, and I picture her nodding her little head.

"And you know what? I think if Grandpa can have his daughters near him he's going to feel much better really soon. Just like your daddy feels better when you and Lola are around."

"Can you put Mommy back on?" she asks.

"Sure. I'll talk to you soon, Soph. I love you," I say, as I hand the phone back to Kate.

"Okay, baby. Listen, Mommy has to go now, and you have to go to bed . . . Okay, tell Daddy I said you can have ten more minutes. Okay, I love you, puddin'. I'll call you first thing tomorrow morning." When Kate closes her cell phone, she tears up immediately, and I put my hand on her knee.

"Don't cry, Kate," I say. "There is some good news: You're getting a turtle."

She laughs and wipes her eyes. "Did you talk to Barbara?"

"On my way here, but there's nothing new to report."

"I didn't even know this could happen," Kate says. "The treatments were supposed to make him better, not worse."

*   *   *

When we land we go directly to the hospital, even though visiting hours are over. We meet Aunt Barbara, who's been keeping vigil by the snack machine in the waiting room, and she fills us in as much as she can. She says the resident is still around, and he'll be able to explain things better, so she rises from her chair, stretches her back a little, then goes padding down the hall toward the nurses' station. I sit down in the chair she occupied and instantly regret it.

"It's like the woman's buns were on fire," I say, quickly standing up. Kate smiles weakly, then takes a seat in the next chair over.

"This is so weird." She shakes her head, looking exhausted and scared.

"I know."

"I mean, when I was here a few weeks ago the doctor never mentioned something like this could happen . . ." she trails off.

Barbara returns and says a doctor will be coming over in a minute to talk to us. She sinks into a chair and lets her legs go slack.

"Barbara," I say, "what made you finally bring Dad in today?"

She shakes her head. "I'm so angry at myself for listening to him when he said he'd be fine—you know your father, never likes to make a big deal out of things. He said he was just a little short of breath, and he tried to make a joke out of it." Barbara exhales and straightens up. "Then he got feverish and his breathing became even more difficult, so finally I just said to him, 'Bernie, we're checking you into the hospital.' When he said he thought that was a good idea, that's when I knew something must be terribly wrong."

I look at Barbara and appreciate her now more than I ever have before. She and my father had never been friends exactly— she finds him too passive, he thinks she's too clingy—but they've always been extremely supportive of each other. When my mother died, Barbara moved in with us for a while.

A doctor approaches, and we all rise immediately. "I'm Dr. Amin," he says, "please have a seat."

"How is he?" Kate asks.

"Well, when your father came in this afternoon with short-ness of breath, we took a chest X ray and at first we thought he just had a run-of-the-mill pneumonia. But he didn't have any fever and his white blood count was normal, so we de-cided that it was likely he had radiation pneumonitis. That's like a bad sunburn of the lung tissue, which is actually caused by the radiation therapy he received."

"But if this could make him even more ill," I say, "why did he have to have it?"

"Because the cancer was spreading," Dr. Amin replies. Bar-bara nods vigorously and we look at her, then back to the doc-tor, the twin authorities on our father's life at this point.

"So how does this radiation pneumonitis get treated?" I ask.

Dr. Amin nods his head. "We've started him on a course of high-dose corticosteroids, which should decrease the inflam-mation in his lung. And now we just have to wait to make sure it's doing the job."

"Dr. Amin," Kate says abruptly, "could he die from this?"

Barbara glares at her.

"Well," he replies, "prednisone is a very effective therapy for this type of problem, and it generally works very well."

"Can we see him?" I ask.

"Your dad could use some rest from the illness and the events of the day—"

"Please," Kate says, "we just flew in from New York."

The doctor bristles. "Why don't we come back first thing in the morning?" I suggest.

*　　*　　*

"I should warn you," Barbara says as she unlocks the door to the house we grew up in, "I had to move things around a little to make your father more comfortable after he had his treatments." She pushes open the door, and I see that a bed has been moved to the center of the living room, and a port-a-potty chair stands next to it where Dad's favorite recliner used to be. The house smells different, too. It's antiseptic.

"It's hot in here," Kate says, taking it all in.

"Your father gets cold a lot so I keep the temperature as high as I can stand it," Barbara replies.

It's incredibly strange to be in the house without Dad.

"You girls are probably tired," Barbara says, "why don't you hit the hay?"

"Come on," I say to Kate, grabbing both of our bags and heading up the stairs.

Kate follows me, and I let her use the bathroom first, enjoying the few minutes I have alone to look around the room that was once my whole world. Unlike the living room, everything in my room seems to be in the precise place I left it when I moved to New York. The beat-up posters of The Pixies and The Simpsons are starting to curl at the edges where the yellowing tape no longer holds them in place, and the curtains are starting to fade. My bureau is still crowded with the makeup I wore in high school. I flop down on the bed and look up at the defining decorating flourish of my elementary school years: glow-in-the-dark stars stuck to my ceiling.

When Kate comes out of the bathroom, she sees me lying on the bed and sits down next to me. "I'm glad you're here with me. It's a little less tough this way," she says.

"I wanted to come last time, too. I would have moved back here to be with Dad."

"I know, and I'm sorry. I guess I was pretending that if I didn't make a big deal out of it then it wouldn't be a big deal. God, I'm more like Dad than I ever thought. I don't know whether to laugh or cry."

"You want to cry?" I say. "Look in that closet and check out the jeans size I used to fit into in high school." I give my rump a slap and Kate laughs.

"You wouldn't want to wear them today anyway," she replies. "You had terrible taste when you were in high school. It was totally embarrassing."

*   *   *

The next morning Kate and I use Dad's car to drive the ninety miles back to St. Mary's. Aunt Barbara tells us she's sure Dad will want some time alone with us, so she'll come later in the afternoon. We're to call her if there's been any change. I'm sure she can use the break. Aunt Barbara's been Dad's primary caregiver for the past few months, and no doubt she's relieved to get a few hours to herself.

Kate and I drive most of the distance in silence. She has a surprisingly heavy foot for a mother with two young daughters, and we make frighteningly good time to the hospital.

Dad looks pale and thin, with an oxygen mask covering his nose and mouth. He must have lost fifteen pounds since I've seen him last, as well as the rest of his hair. For some reason I'd been expecting him to be sedated, but when we approach him on either side of the bed, he reaches for both of our hands and squeezes. Then he lets go and takes off the oxygen mask.

"If I knew this is all I had to do to get a visit from my two beautiful daughters," he says, his voice weak and hoarse, "I would have come up with this scheme a long time ago."

"Yeah, well don't go trying this again," I reply. "Because next time we won't believe you're sick at all. You don't even look all that bad to me," I lie.

"How do you feel, Dad?" Kate asks, pulling up a chair.

"You remember when I taught Rachel how to drive and she ran over that squirrel while she was backing up, then she put the car in forward and accidentally ran over it again? Well," he pauses, "I think I feel slightly worse than that squirrel."

"Excuse me," I say, working overtime to lift the mood, "running that squirrel over the second time was no accident. I wanted to finish what I'd started."

"I thought you were trying to hide the evidence under the tire," Kate replies.

"I tell you what," Dad says, "yesterday afternoon I was hoping someone would run me over and finish the job, too."

I don't think he intends for it to come out sounding as awful as it does. "Maybe I can ask the doctors to give you something for the pain," Kate says, standing.

"Thanks, honey," Dad says. "But I really don't have any pain, I'm just exhausted. Chasing around nurses . . ." He stops short, unable to catch his breath. Kate quickly moves to help him put the oxygen mask back on.

"Maybe you want to try to sleep, Dad," I say. He nods. "And I promise Katie and I aren't going anywhere. We're just going to sit here and have a silent contest for the next few hours. I got a couple bucks riding on this, so don't screw it up for me by blabbing on and on, okay?"

My father looks at me and smiles weakly. When he closes his eyes, I realize how tired I am, too. Dad goes in and out of sleep for the next hour, but when the doctors come by to do their rounds and examine him, he tells Kate and me to get something at the cafeteria and to put it on his tab. The silly joke is a comfort at this point.

Kate and I spend the next forty-eight hours between Dad's hospital bed, the cafeteria, and the antiseptic-smelling house. Neither of us talks very much during those two days, staying focused on the back and forth between home and hospital and the routine updates throughout the day. By Tuesday afternoon the doctor tells us that Dad can go home the following day if he remains on supplemental oxygen. He has enough strength to stay awake and talk a little that afternoon, and Kate and I begin exchanging hopeful looks. Dad informs us that when he goes home, so do we. We protest, but he insists. "No discussion, Katie. No discussion, Rach," he says to each of us in turn. "Please. It means the world to me that you came . . ." he trails off for a moment, taking a breath. "And you know I love you both so much. But you have your lives waiting for you in New York, and I'll be fine now. Go home." He smiles at us and repeats, "Please."

Before we leave for the airport, Dad gives us each a surprisingly strong hug. "Now go back and give my regards to Broadway," he says, and Kate and I groan, then laugh at the corniest joke we couldn't be happier to hear from him.

20

I arrive at the office very early the morning after Kate and I get back from Minnesota, wanting to catch up on some of my lost hours. It's 8:15 A.M., and I'd been hoping to be alone in the dark, empty office. But as I walk in, I see a desk lamp glowing in a cubicle a few rows from mine. I presume someone must have forgotten to turn off the light, but since the darkness suits my mood, I drop my things at my desk and walk the few rows to go shut off the lamp. I stop short and yelp when I see an actual body sitting in the lit cubicle. It's Zach. He's wearing earphones and facing his computer screen, but he jumps, too, when he hears my shriek. He quickly pulls off the earphones and swivels around to face me.

"What are you doing here?" I ask, my hand still on my thumping chest.

"Me? I come in early every once in a while to work on my own stuff. The Spiny Echidna stuff. Some of my animation stuff. You know, all that stuff stuff." I nod in reply. I had always thought he was just punctual, because he was invariably already installed at his desk when I arrived in the mornings. "How about you? Wassup?" Zach asks. "Where ya been?" He fires these questions as he pulls out the rolling chair from the cubicle behind him and gestures for me to sit down.

I sit down and pause for a moment, shoring myself up before responding. "My father got really ill, so my sister and I went out to Minneapolis to be with him."

"Oh no," Zach responds. "I'm really sorry to hear that." He pauses and adds, "But things are better now, I hope?"

"I don't know. He seemed to have stabilized by the time we left yesterday, but . . ." I shrug my shoulders and trail off, unable to say things are better because I don't really think they are.

"This must have been a tough weekend for you."

"Wasn't much fun. But it was good to have been out there. Sometimes it helps just to be close by."

"If there's anything I can do to make things easier for you, like pick up your mail when you're away, take you to the airport, anything, just let me know." Zach nods.

"Thanks," I reply, touched by his thoughtfulness. "I didn't even realize you had a car."

"Well, I don't actually. But I do hail a taxi really well. Sometimes it's just nice to have the company, I think." He smiles.

"That's really nice of you, Zach," I say, touching his hand.

"Sure, of course," he replies. "Oh, and Rachel, you do know that this place effectively stopped functioning while you were gone? The whole place came to a screeching halt." He makes a screeching halt sound.

I smile and stand up, briefly placing a hand on Zach's shoulder as I walk by. "I figured. When it comes to saving the environment, a copyeditor's job is never done."

Later that morning, an e-mail from Zach arrives in my Inbox.

To: rchambers@trees.org
Subject: world wide wonder

It has come to our attention—as we monitor these things obsessively—that it has been some time since you visited www.spinyechidna.com. Though we are not persuaded that the exploration of said site has the same salutary effect on all visitors, we are in a position to believe that there is one link in particular which might be of interest to you. Should you wish to click over there immediately, we'd think that a damn good idea.

He has provided a hyperlink to his site and I click on it, smiling in anticipation. I'm guessing he may have created a new character, maybe a new super-antihero—a brooding literary type—a Mr. Write for Marilyn! When the page materializes, my eyebrows leap up in surprise. A full-page banner

covering the usual homepage displays a gigantic arrow pointing to a small icon in the bottom right-hand corner of the
screen. Inside the arrow, in massive-fifty-two-point-font-size
letters, is scrawled: "Rachel Click Here!" The tip of the arrow
in the bottom right-hand corner of the screen touches a tiny
picture of an arrow piercing a rolled-up diploma—the On
Target Essay icon from my original fliers.

I click on the icon, and it takes me to another website. As
soon as I see it, I burst into a giant grin. The website is
www.OnTargetEssay.com, and I am overwhelmed by a rush
of gratitude. The homepage looks incredibly cool, the whole
thing is done in black and white and red, with a big old-
fashioned typewriter font, and a red and black target smack
in the middle of the page, covered with a white scroll nailed
to the heart of the target with an arrow. Zach has created
links for "Services," "About Us," "Contact Us," "Rates,"
"Package Deals," and "Press Links," each marked with a
rolled-diploma icon. I click on a few, but they're not active
yet. I sit there staring and grinning and clicking on all the
links.

I get up and walk over to his cubicle, still grinning. He sees
me coming but feigns not knowing me. "Wow, hey, Ethan,"
he says, spinning his chair around to face Ethan, who is sitting
in a cubicle behind him. "Is this that girl, Chambers? The one
who used to mainline spray cheese in the bathroom?"

Ethan turns to face me, raising his eyebrows and nodding.
"Dude, I *think* it is that girl. We don't see her much around
these parts . . ."

"I don't believe I've ever seen her in this latitude of the office at all," Zach replies.

I realize that, except for this morning, it *is* the first time I've ever come over to his desk to visit. I would like to give him a hug and say thank you, but I don't want to embarrass him, so I just sit down in the chair next to his desk and smile wryly. Then I reach for a Post-it notepad and a pen from Zach's desk. I write "THANK YOU" and stick it on his screen. "Gentlemen," I say, standing up, "I'll be leaving now." I nod at them both and return to my desk.

Zippo: routine staff check making sure no employees are operating above capacity

We haven't communicated at all since this morning's unveiling of the On Target website, so I respond right away.

Rach: definitely doing sub-par work here, thanks
Zippo: excellent. keep conserving energy. you may need it for special downtown secret mission later if you're up for it
Rach: a secret mission downtown?
Zippo: go along with me, and there's some guaranteed fun and a free six-pack in it for you
Rach: not like I don't already owe you a lifetime supply of free six-packs since clicking on a certain personalized link this morning. but do I get to choose the brand of beer?
Zippo: sure thing
Rach: okay, I'm in . . . you had me at 'free'

At 6 o'clock Zach stops by my desk. "Time to blow this taco stand," he says, lifting my tote bag and hurling it over his shoulder. I'm touched by the gallantry of the gesture.

"Okay, and thanks," I say, nodding at my bag.

"Ah, don't thank me. You're going to be needing your hands free for some heavy lifting in a little while!"

"Ha ha," I deadpan, putting on my coat as we head to the elevator. Whatever Zach has planned, I'm looking forward to the distraction. I lost sense of time during the weekend in Minneapolis, in all the backing and forthing between home and the hospital, and it feels like weeks have passed since I had fun last.

We hop in a cab and head downtown, getting out where the Lower East Side meets Chinatown, not far from where we'd gone to buy my glasses. We approach an unmarked white box truck, and Zach tells me to wait at the back of it. I see him approach the driver's side and he chats briefly with the men inside the cab. A few minutes later, the guy in the passenger seat hops out and comes to the back, opens the huge padlock, and pushes up the retractable door. Zach gives an impish grin as big cardboard boxes come into view.

"What are these?" I ask with a sinking feeling.

"Look like heavy boxes, don't they?" Zach nods.

"They do."

"Bet you're glad your arms aren't all tuckered out from carrying this heavy tote bag of yours."

"You're shitting me?" I reply.

"I believe Confucius said it best when he stated: I shit you not." This amuses Zach and he laughs along with the truck driver, who heard him. "But don't worry, I don't see you merely as cheap labor with powerful arms."

"You don't?" I say as the guy from the truck starts pushing some of the boxes toward us.

"Nope, I've got you pegged as a 'sit in the driver's seat and make sure we don't get a ticket when I double-park outside my studio' type of a girl."

"Oh, in that case you got me right," I answer, making a show of relief.

Zach staggers with a box toward a U-Haul that's parked directly across the street. "Crap," he says, arms trembling. "I forgot to get the keys out of my pocket."

"Which pocket?"

"Pants," Zach replies, his face red, though it's hard to tell if it's from strain or embarrassment.

I reach around and burrow my hand into the right pocket of his jeans. If Zach weren't in a serious amount of discomfort and about to drop the box, this gesture could have flustered us both. As it was, it still flustered me. "There's nothing in there," I say.

"Hey, no man appreciates hearing that!" Zach replies, causing us both to break into nervous laughter. Zach drops the box.

"There wasn't anything fragile in there, was there?" I ask.

"Just my grandmother's china." Zach smiles and takes a box cutter out of his bag. "No, actually I'll show you," he says. He slices through the tape holding the box closed and opens the panels. Inside are two rows of T-shirts, stacked several-dozen deep. Zach picks one of them up, shakes it open, and and holds it against his chest. It's a red T with a big airbrushed illustration of the Wonder-Who-Farted-Twins delivering a powerful kick of their conjoined front leg, and underneath it in gothic print, the address of his website, www.spinyechidna.com. Zach flips the T-shirt around and there's a mushroom cloud. Below the cloud it reads: "Smell Our Dust!"

He takes a blue T-shirt from the other pile and holds it up in front of me. This one has a female superhero on it who I haven't seen before. She looks like a cross between Xena the Warrior Princess and Aunt Jemima. She wears a breastplate and a do-rag. Her thought bubble reads, "You trying to lick my spoon?" Zach flips the shirt over, and on the back the character stands with her arms raised above her head wielding a menacing spatula. She says, " 'Cuz I'll flip your fat head, short stack!" I'd completely forgotten that Zach mentioned he designed T-shirts.

"Zach, these are awesome!" I say, taking the Jemima Warrior Princess from him and holding it up again. "Are there more?"

"About twelve gross."

"How many is that exactly?"

"I wish I knew."

I take another one of the T-shirts off the pile and look at it more carefully. These T-shirts are incredibly cool, and cool in that truly downtown sense of coveted cool. The kind of cool that normally you can't buy, that you see hipster kids wearing in dive bars in uncharted parts of the Lower East Side. Zach has created T-shirts with that ultimate marketing tool—authenticity. "Seriously, these are incredible. Where do you sell them?"

"I've been selling them on the Spiny Echidna website for a few months already. I take it this means you havn't noticed the link that says: 'Own It!' "

"Er . . ." I fumble, busted. I only check out the new Marilyn installments.

"Well, fortunately, my dear Rachel, you're in the minority on that one. The hardcore fans have actually been clamoring for apparel—I've been getting crazy numbers of e-mails—and I had to increase the orders. I'll be honest, I still can't get over it myself." Zach smiles and looks down, folding up the T-shirts.

After getting all the boxes loaded into the truck, we drive to Zach's studio on Water Street, which is a few dozen blocks farther into a more remote part of the neighborhood. We double-park in front of the building, and I sit in the cab while Zach unloads the boxes into the building's freight elevator. After finding a semi-legal spot to park the U-Haul, Zach walks back toward the studio to take the load upstairs in the elevator, and I stop in the pizza place on the corner to get a pie for us to share.

"It's studio twelve on the sixth floor," Zach yells at me as he walks back up the block, "I'll buzz you in and then just walk up the stairs and knock on the door to your right."

Twenty minutes later, I reach the sixth-floor landing breathless and hungry and knock on the door on the right.

"Pizza delivery! Open up or the whole thing's gonna disappear faster than the Warrior Princess can flip your fat head."

"Come on in, the door's unlocked," I hear a voice echo from inside.

I push open the door and walk into a big unfinished loft space, with cement-block walls, a beaten-up linoleum floor, and huge windows at the far end overlooking the street. The space is the size of a large studio apartment, but crowded with stacked boxes on one side and a huge angled drawing desk and easels on the other side. That entire wall, from floor to ceiling, and from left to right, is covered with taped-up pencil and ink sketches of graphic characters and comic strips. On the floor, leaning against the wall, are stretched canvases, stacked two or three deep. A few paintings that look like they're still in progress are propped on two tall easels pushed back into a corner.

Zach reaches down into a mini-fridge next to the desk and takes out two beers.

"Heineken?"

"Yes, please."

He clears off clothes and papers and an empty bag of chips from a ratty, torn couch that's wedged into the corner by the windows, opposite the desk, and gestures for me to sit down. He pulls over a small stool for himself and opens the pizza box. He lowers his face over the hot pizza and breathes in.

"Mmmm . . . you don't mind if I just go ahead and start, do ya?"

"Go right ahead, I'd say you've earned it." I'm still standing, leaning in over the stacked paintings on the floor to get a closer look at the details on some of the drawings on the wall. "Zach, this is an unbelievable amount of work," I say, stepping slowly to my right without taking my eyes off the wall. "You must have hundreds of characters here!"

"Well, I don't want anybody to get lonely out there in the Cosmos of Zach."

"How long have you been working in this space?"

"Pretty much since I moved to New York."

I walk over and sit down on the couch, leaning back with a slice of pizza, and then peer around me again. Zach had made it seem like it was all just a bunch of cartoon characters and a website for kicks, but it's actually years of work, and he's created a whole world. We chew in silence for a moment as I continue taking in all the characters, attitudes, and cityscapes on the opposite wall. It feels like I've stumbled into a fantastic bubble, into some small, parallel universe.

"Hello?" a voice calls out from down the hallway. "Zach—you in there?" After a single knock on the door, it opens. "Hey there," Eva says poking her head in, smiling when she sees Zach perched on the stool by his drafting board.

"Eva, hey." Zach stands quickly and wipes pizza from his mouth.

"I was nearby, checking out this new gallery, so I thought I'd stop by," she answers, closing the door behind her and sauntering in.

"You remember Rachel, right?" Zach says quickly, tilting his head in my direction on the couch, then adds, "From work?"

Clearly surprised, Eva says, "Oh," as if I were the one who'd just walked in.

"Hi," I answer, hoping I don't have pizza grease on my face.

"Sorry, I didn't know you guys were working."

"No, no, we're just hanging out. Rachel was helping me with the T-shirts. I got a new shipment tonight," Zach says turning from Eva to clear another spot on the couch next to me. He reaches for the pizza box on the drafting table and extends it toward Eva, opening it. "Pizza?" He holds the box open as she stands there appearing to contemplate what to do next. "Take off your coat, sit," he tells her.

Eva narrows her eyes at Zach, as if weighing her options, then slips out of her coat and reaches for a slice. She then sits down next to me on the couch, crossing her legs Indian style, and takes a bite, leaning forward to avoid getting any pizza mess on her expensive-looking knit top. "Mmm," she says, "Is this from Mario's?"

Zach nods. "Where else?"

Eva eats half of her slice and then holds it out to Zach. "Please," she says, "finish this for me."

"Happy to oblige." Zach takes the half-eaten slice and shakes his head. "Do you believe she leaves the best part?" he asks, chomping into the crust like he's Cookie Monster. Eva chuckles.

I finish my slice in silence as Eva gets up to examine the drawings on Zach's board. "This one," she says, tapping her finger against the paper then looking at him, "doesn't belong with the rest."

Zach closes his eyes and nods. "I know."

"I mean, it's not *bad*," she continues, not at all reassuringly, "it's just not as developed as the rest of that series. The character looks too much like characters I've seen before, too common."

"You're right," he replies, looking at her seriously.

The need to flee washes over me like a whitecap. The parallel-universe bubble has burst. I stand and brush the crumbs off my lap. "I think I'm gonna get going," I say.

Zach stops in mid-swig of his Heineken and points to mine. "You sure?" he asks, "There's still half a pizza and a whole beer. It was part of the deal—I promised." He smiles at me encouragingly. Eva is standing with her back to us in the same position I was standing before, leaning over the canvases on the floor, examining the wall.

"Thanks, but I think things are catching up with me now. I'm suddenly just exhausted."

"Oh, okay," Zach replies, standing, and reaching for my coat that he's hung on a nail in the corner. "Thanks so much for your help tonight."

"It was fun," I say, and he nods. "Well, um, okay then, I'll see you tomorrow."

"Bye, Rachel." Eva waves, turning from the drawings. "You know how to find your way out?"

"Oh, yeah, definitely." I grab my tote bag and wave to both of them as Zach walks over to where Eva is examining a sketch. "Bye," I say again as I shut the studio door behind me, muffling Eva's laugher.

21

Zach and I arrive at the bookstore and part ways, heading to our respective sections, business for me and magazines for him. For weeks I had been meaning to look at some of the how-to-get-into-business-school books. I wanted to be sure I wasn't off the mark with the advice I'd been giving clients—or that at least I wasn't making them worse off. But in the flurry of client meetings and Trees work and dealing with Dad, I still hadn't gotten around to it. So when Zach told me this afternoon that he was sneaking out early to go to the big Barnes & Noble downtown, I invited myself along.

After browsing through some b-school guidebooks and picking out a few to buy as reference guides, I squeeze my way through other browsers at the magazine rack and practically trip over Zach. He's sitting on the ground with a tall stack of art magazines piled next to him.

"Are there nudie photos of you in there?" I say as I kick the sole of his shoe.

"Yes and no," he replies, looking up. "Yes, there are pictures of me in here, but they won't be nudes until I finish scratching off the bathing suits."

I put my books on the ground, preparing to plunk myself down next to him.

"Wait—could you go and get me a pile of *I-D* magazines before you sit down?"

"Sure, but what gives? Why are you sitting on the floor of a bookstore behind a fortress of magazines?"

"Everything shall be revealed in due time."

"Is due time in like a minute?"

"Yes, it is."

"Okay."

I go find a batch of *I-D*s and scoop them up, and for good measure, I also take a pile of another obscure arty magazine, *Bomb*. I bring the pile back to Zach and stand before him, awaiting instructions.

"Act very natural," he says, standing up and lifting his own large stack of magazines. He points his chin toward a wall in the back of the store, and I follow him.

"Are you trying to get me to steal magazines I don't even read?"

"Oh, Rachel." he replies. "Young, naive Rachel."

"Is that a yes?"

"We are not going to be stealing. In fact, we are going to be *adding* to the newsstand value of these publications." He leads me on a zigzag path through the biography and essay sections.

"What the hell are you talking about?" I ask as Zach sits down in an out-of-the-way nook in the children's section. I sit down next to him, dropping my business books on my other side and the pile of magazines in front of him.

He opens his messenger bag and takes out a stack of folded, lavender-colored fliers. "Wa-la," he says. "The plan is to stick as many of *these*," he waves fliers, "into the centerfold of as many of these," he holds up a magazine, "as possible."

"And this is some sort of conceptual art?" I ask, while taking a closer look. On both sides of the folded paper, there's a black arrow along with the words "OPEN Here," written graffiti-style. I follow the directions and open the flier.

The Caseborough Gallery
Cordially Invites You to an Opening Featuring
Our Emerging Artists:

ZACH STEVENSON
ANDRE WACHILESKI
SHIRIN NASSERI

January 17th at 7 P.M.

On the bottom of the flier is the gallery's address and phone number.

"A gallery show?" I exclaim. "Zach, that's amazing!"

"Well, it's with two other artists, and it's just a small space in Brooklyn, so—"

"Don't poo-poo this!"

"I'm not poo-pooing—"

"Because, Zach, holy moly, this is great!"

"Yes, but it would be greater if I could be sure anyone was coming. Caseborough is run by this very cool couple, but they don't have much of a promotional budget. And they've not-so-subtly encouraged us to try to bring in as many people as we can."

"Hence fliers in pretentious art magazines?"

"Hence. The people interested in these sorts of publications might also be into checking out an obscure gallery in Brooklyn—if only to tell their arty friends they rode the G-train."

Zach starts stuffing the folded fliers into the centers of the magazines.

"This is such a good idea!" I say, thoroughly impressed. "This is a genius stealth tactic!"

"Thanks."

As Zach continues stuffing, I bend and crease the pile of unfolded fliers and hand them to him one by one. The wheels in my mind are turning. *Anyone applying to business school has to take the GMAT . . . If they buy a book to help them study, they are willing to admit they need help . . . If they are admitting they need help, there's some latent anxiety. If there's latent anxiety, and a flier offering further assistance—customized, deadline-sensitive, On Target assistance—suddenly materializes, they might be willing to pony up the dollars for that, too.* I decide I'll photocopy some more On Target Essay fliers this week and then, during lunch, I'll hit all the bookstores near the office, scope out the test-prep sections, and discreetly slip On Target Essay ads into every single GMAT review book the stores sell.

"Chambers? Hello, Chambers?" Zach says, waving his hand in front of my glazed eyes.

"This is *such* a good idea!" I say again, snapping to and resuming my folding.

"Uh, thanks," he says, evidently taken aback by my repeat enthusiasm.

When we finish "upgrading" the appropriate magazines, we stuff a few of the books displayed on tables in front of the visual arts section. Zach thinks it's not worth stuffing shelved books because his show is a limited run and it's hard to predict when, if ever, any of those tomes will be opened. I follow his lead, and when we've stuffed to his satisfaction, he nods at me.

"In the time-honored art world system of patronage, it is now appropriate to thank the master," he says.

"And this means what?" I ask.

Zach takes me by the arm and guides me toward the café. At the sight of the jumbo lemon bars and the toffee-chip brownies, my mouth starts watering. "In celebration of your opening," I say, pulling out my wallet.

"Oh, no, this one's on me." Zach shakes his finger and motions for me to put my money away. "With these purchases, I am thanking the Barnes & Noble Foundation for their generous help. So go ahead, get yourself anything you want. Just make it under two bucks fifty."

I opt for a cappuccino and a blondie, which brings my total well beyond the suggested dollar limit, but Zach tells me he'll add the rest to my tab. He gets himself a cup of hot chocolate and a slice of cake. We walk over to one of the few empty tables, and I slide into a chair, grateful to be sitting on an elevated piece of furniture instead of the industrially carpeted floor. "So when were you going to tell me about this show?" I ask, breaking off a chunk of blondie.

"Eventually."

"Why so secretive?"

"I wasn't being secretive, I just don't like making a big deal. Plus, you never know if these things are going to work out, and basically I'm a coward."

"What? Why are you a coward?"

"Because I get spooked into thinking if I start talking about things they won't happen. Or thinking that if I admit I really want something, I'm destined for disappointment." He looks down and swirls his hot chocolate.

"I guess that puts a damper on my next question," I reply, licking foam from my cappuccino.

"What's your next question?"

"Is your own gallery show something you've always dreamed about?"

Zach smiles. "Yeah, it's something I've really been working hard for. It's not like opening in Chelsea like Jim did, but for someone who does graphic art, this is a pretty big deal."

"Of course it is!" I say, excited. "Who cares where your first show is—you're *being shown*. People are taking you and your work seriously. It's wonderful."

Zach takes a sip of his hot chocolate, not realizing he's given himself a chocolate-colored froth moustache on top of his chocolate-colored actual moustache. "A lot of times it feels like everything I'm doing just gets sent out into this cosmic void. But I think this confirms that at least people have been noticing that I have been littering in that void."

I beckon his face closer to me with my index finger.

Zach slowly leans in across the table.

"Hold still," I say, taking hold of his chin with my left hand and tracing my right index finger over the edge of his upper lip. His body tenses.

"What?" he says, not understanding what I am doing.

"Milk moustache."

"Oh." He laughs uneasily.

"Well, I declare! Miss 'Merit Girl' Chambers as I live and breathe," I hear a familiar voice saying behind me. I turn and see Ben.

"Ben! Hey!" I jump up to greet him. "What are you doing here?"

"I understand they've got these things here called *books*, and I've heard so much about them," he replies. "I want to see what all the fuss is about before they go out of fashion." Zach laughs and Ben smiles at him.

"Sit! Sit down with us," I say, looking for a spare chair.

"Here you go," Zach says, and reaches for a chair that is behind him, pulling it around to our table.

"Thanks, man." Ben nods and plops himself down. He is wearing his Hugo Boss peacoat with a striped wool scarf and looks very stylish. "I'm Ben," he says, holding his hand out to Zach.

"Zach," Zach replies, smiling and shaking his hand. "I hear your fiancée throws quite an engagement party."

"Uh, yeah." Ben looks at me quizzically for a moment. "Didn't know you'd started a blog, Rach."

"No, Ben," I reply quickly, putting my hand on his arm. "I was telling Zach how amazing the whole thing was." I nod my head and smile, just to emphasize the point.

"Yeah. Rachel said it was a really incredible event," Zach adds.

Zach's choice of words makes me smile, reminding me of the comic strip he drew after I'd told him about that "really incredible event."

Catching my smile, Zach smiles back. Ben sees the exchange, and his expression changes.

"So," Ben says, cocking his head toward Zach, "did you and Rachel just meet?"

"No, no," I answer. "Zach and I are friends from work."

"From work, you mean Byzantium?" Ben asks.

"No, from Trees," Zach answers, "I made her drop those losers from Byzantium as soon as she came onboard."

"I'm sure I've mentioned Zach to you," I say, interrupting.

"Nope. You've never mentioned anyone named Zach," Ben replies.

"Really?" I ask feebly. "Well, so now you've met! Zach is the amazing art director at Trees," I add.

"No come on, seriously. You guys met online. This is your first date, right?"

"Ha ha," I play along.

"You're right, bad joke. He's totally not your type, is he, Rach? She prefers the Ken dolls with cash."

Zach says nothing and appears to be concentrating on cutting into his cake.

"Anyway," Ben announces a little loudly, and then stands up before I can add anything else. "The new ball and chain is browsing downstairs in modern fiction, and if I don't stop her, she's likely to purchase something in an attempt to educate me. So I should go. Nice meeting you, Zach."

Zach reaches up and shakes Ben's hand again, "Yeah, likewise."

"Tell Leigh hello," I say, rising as well.

"Adios," Ben says, waving good-bye.

Zach looks at his watch. "I'm gonna head out, too."

"Already? You sure?" Neither of us has finished our pastries.

"Yeah, I'm supposed to meet up with someone later, and I need to run a quick errand first, so . . ." he trails off and reaches for his bag. "Thanks for your help with all this."

"Sure, of course," I answer. "You okay?" I ask after a few moments of watching Zach buttoning his coat.

"Absolutely. I just didn't realize how late it got."

"You meeting up with Eva?" I ask cheerfully.

"No, I'm not. I'm meeting someone at a bar around the corner."

"Oh," I say, "okay." I reach for my coat and slip it on, then gather the garbage.

We head down the escalator together in silence, and when we get to the exit, Zach pauses and bows to me. "See ya tomorrow," he says and walks off in the direction of the subway.

"See ya," I say, wishing I had the power to grab him, drag him back to the café, and take us all back in time, twenty minutes ago, when things had seemed a lot friendlier.

22

"You must be Sanjay," I say, standing up and extending my hand.

"I am," my newest client replies with a firm handshake, "and you're Rachel Chambers?"

I gesture to the chair behind him. "Please, have a seat. Would you like a cup of coffee or a cappuccino, something else to drink?" I ask as I sit down, smoothing my skirt under me and crossing my legs. "I think I'll have a cappuccino." Moving these orientation meetings from Starbucks to a hotel lobby was an excellent idea on my part. We're just a few blocks from Sanjay's office, and the plush carpet and table service lend a distinctly more up-market feel to the On Target orientation meeting.

Sanjay had only recently responded to my Morgan Stanley

mass e-mail of many weeks ago. In his note to me, he'd written that he'd barely started his applications but wanted to get
them out of the way ASAP so he didn't have to think about
them again after January 10. He didn't ask about prices, credentials, or references and only wondered how fast I could get
them done. *How fast?* I thought. *As fast as On Target Essay's
Express Editing rates are high, my broker friend!* Sanjay's big
fat hurry made me realize that high speed was a marketable
product and so On Target Essay's "rush rates" were born.
Zach had created a new link on the On Target Essay website
called "Express Editing," and Sanjay agreed to the 50 percent
fee hike without flinching.

"I could definitely use a shot of espresso," he replies now,
taking off his jacket and relaxing back into his chair, "I've
had some late nights at work this week." The waitress comes
over, and I order the coffees.

It's lunchtime on a Thursday, and as I get the session underway, I keep a sharp eye on the clock on my computer
screen. Excluding the time it takes me to get to the Trees office in upper midtown and back, I have exactly forty-five minutes to devote to Sanjay. In the trusting spirit typical of Trees,
the understanding is that we'll take an hour for lunch, without
any required punching in and out. But with On Target really
taking off now, my lunch hour every day for the past week has
been much closer to a very padded hour and a half. I'm worried Molly has started noticing the consistent midday void in
my cubicle.

Things have changed since that first orientation session

with Vlad. Now I send prospective clients an e-mail the day before our meeting, attaching a numbered, step-by-step explanation of the editing process, including a description of exactly what will take place in the—now officially timed—forty-five-minute orientation session.

"So, Sanjay, tell me," I begin, "is there one aspect of your personality that you would never trade? Something that really makes you *you*?" I sit up straight, hands poised over my keyboard.

He looks up at the ceiling briefly and then back at me. "Well, I'd have to say I'm really good with people. You know, I mean I can talk to anybody, from the top guys in my department down to the secretaries. Like the assistants? They all love me—"

"Let's reframe this in a slightly different way, Sanjay," I interrupt, because if I actually hear him use the phrase, 'I'm a people person,' I might commit hara kari. "What we're going to want to focus on is what makes you stand out from the pack a little more. A very particular point of view, maybe some specific experience that really affected you, or somebody who changed your thinking."

"Whew," he replies, exhaling and drumming his fingers on the chair. "That's hard."

I'm tempted to tell Sanjay to hurry up and think harder, because we have only forty-one minutes and thirty-seven seconds left. But he's right, this is hard. Okay, baby steps. "Well then, Sanjay." I smile, shifting tacks. "Let me ask you something else. You and every other guy in every bullpen on Wall

Street are applying to the Harvard Business School *right* now. But there's only one spot left at HBS. What do you got that Tom or Dick or Janie don't?"

"Well that," he shakes his pointer finger at me and returns my smile, "is easy."

And finally, our session gets underway.

As I wrap up the meeting, Sanjay and I agree on an expedited timetable for exchanging outlines and drafts and a schedule for follow-up meetings.

"So, I really look forward to working on all this with you," Sanjay says as he stands up to put his suit jacket back on. "You're making it much less painful already."

"My pleasure," I reply, standing up and extending my hand to shake his good-bye, meeting his eye. "We'll be in touch again soon."

* * *

I press the elevator call button in the marbled lobby of the Trees building. Every second it doesn't come is another ounce added to the guilty side of the scale of justice weighing my tardiness. There's no way around it. I'm egregiously late. And I have no excuse.

I walk out of the elevator and toward my desk. Maybe Molly won't have noticed? I make it to my cube without anyone looking up. *Sigh of relief.* As I open the material on fossil fuels I've been copyediting, a new e-mail pops up in my inbox. It's from Molly, asking me to stop by when I have a chance. *Shit.* I get up immediately and walk straight back to her office. I knock lightly on her door, which is slightly ajar.

"Molly?"

"Rachel, hi, come on in," I hear her say.

I walk in and sit down in the chair next to her desk. She clicks a window shut on her computer, gets up and walks to the door, pushes it shut, and then comes back and leans against the edge of her desk, close to me.

"I know we've been giving you a lot of work to do recently, and it looks like you've been doing a good job of staying on top of the timing and the deadlines—and I appreciate that," Molly says, her hands resting in her lap. "But it seems like this week in particular, you've been gone for a long time in the middle of the day?" She says this as though it were a question.

"I know, I . . . really have . . . it's . . ." It's mortifying, but I am speechless. I have nothing to say in my own defense.

"Deadlines are pretty tight, as you know," Molly says. "And so it's really tough if people are out of the office for a long time. Of course if something comes up, you should let me know, and we can work something out. But otherwise, I really do need you in the office as much as possible."

Here is the saint who gave me all the time I needed to deal with my father without asking a single question, and I have completely abused her goodwill. "You're absolutely right," I say, nodding emphatically. "I apologize. I'm . . . sorry."

"Okay, great," she says, walking around her desk. "I did want to clear that up."

"Yes, absolutely," I say, standing, "absolutely, you're right. Okay. Back to work!"

I've blushed so deeply red I'm probably verging on purple,

and I hope no one sees me as I walk back to my cubicle. As I pass Zach's row, I steal a sidelong glance at his desk and thankfully, it's empty. Zach and I haven't spoken or messaged since awkwardly parting last night at Barnes & Noble. But it turns out Zach's not sitting in his cubicle because he's standing right in front of me, where he's caught me peering at his empty desk. I stop short, and if it's possible to continue blushing, then I've probably just turned from purple to black.

"So did you have a good night out after the bookstore last night?" I blurt out with too much enthusiasm.

"Yeah, it was fine," Zach replies, furrowing his brow slightly, as though uncertain as to why I've chosen to ask him about this now. He seems to be waiting for me to move out of the way.

"So who'd you meet up with? You seemed like you were in such a rush to go," I continue brightly, and just as clumsily, not moving out of the way.

"A friend." It looks like he's about to stop with that. "Actually, it was the friend of a friend, a girl I met recently at a party."

"A friend of Eva's?" I ask, knowing the question sounds silly.

"No, it wasn't a friend of Eva's," he adds, pausing briefly. "Eva and I broke up a little while ago."

"Oh." *Oh?* "I didn't have any idea, you guys seemed fine—"

"Right, well, we are fine. We're friends," Zach replies briefly and crosses in front of me to go back to his desk.

I walk back to my own desk and stare at the screen for a

while, wondering what to say to Zach. I know I've only made things more awkward than they were when we parted yesterday. And of course I want to ask about his breakup with Eva—if only to be sure he's okay—but I obviously can't now. The whole thing feels like a gnarled mess, and I'm not sure how to untie the uncomfortable knot I just pulled tighter.

So I decide not to deal with it at all. I send Zach an instant message.

> Rach: you didn't ask me why I was standing in your row, beet
>   red and staring at your desk

I wait for a moment, but there is no reply. I get back to work on the fossil fuels, trying to put all the afternoon's varied unpleasantness out of my mind. Twenty minutes later a reply pops up.

> Zippo: no i did not

I reply immediately.

> Rach: you weren't wondering?
> Zippo: i was
> Rach: would you like to know?
> Zippo: if you feel the need to tell me
> Rach: first, I was feeling badly about yesterday at B&N

There is no immediate reply. I wait a few more minutes and then message him again.

Rach: second, i was reeling from my dressing down by Molly Mother Hen, and was worried you'd bust me on my walk of shame back to my desk

Still no reply.

Rach: which you did

There's no response, and I'm presuming Zach's just not interested in being mollified. I'm about to write this off as yet another of the day's failed attempts to set things right when he finally replies.

Zippo: you got dressed down today? but it's not even casual Friday

Rach: it was more like today, yesterday, and every day this week, when i've helped myself to an executive-length lunch hour. Molly seems to have noticed

Zippo: did you explain that since you don't do any work when you're here anyway, that not being here really doesn't matter?

Rach: that did not strike me as the best tack

Zippo: how bad was the hen pecking?

Rach: let's just say the woman's got a big pecker

Zippo: so dijoo learn your lesson?

Rach: i think I did

Zippo: what did you learn?

Rach: though shalt not take work and all the good things it offers for granted

Zippo: like your selfless brilliant co-workers?

Rach: more like the free Fanta and legal pads

Zippo: good to see you contrite. but no more walking out of
molly's office acting like a big bumbling tomato, right?

Big bumbling tomato? So glad to know the moment was
even more awkward than I thought.

I devote the rest of the afternoon to a purifying spurt of
unadulterated Trees work, barely even pausing to check my
e-mail, and completely ignoring my vibrating cell-phone. I
stay late until I finish the entire fifty-page fossil fuel document.

At 8:30, I feel I've hardly begun my penance, but it's a
start, and I can't stay later than Molly does because that
would too obviously look like ass kissing. I also can't stay
much later, because I have four essay outlines due in the next
two days and I am supposed to be finishing two of them tonight. Right before shutting down my computer for the night,
a new e-mail message pops up. It's a message Zach has sent
from home.

To: rchambers@trees.org

Subject: Peckers

Manizer: The Fumble, Bumble & (Eventual) Breakthrough click
on http://www.spinyechidna.com/marilyn

BOK! WHERE IS MARILYN MANIZER WHEN I NEED HER!

LATER...

23

The MBA was just another sports league to me a few months ago.

It is 7:20 A.M. on Saturday morning, and this is what I'm thinking as I press snooze one more time. Eventually, I hurl myself out of bed, bundle up in my terry-cloth bathrobe, and boot up my computer. While I'm sitting in the kitchen staring dumbly at the coffeemaker percolating, I decide it's probably a good time to call my father, before getting sucked into the morning's work. It's 6 o'clock in Minnesota now, and I assume he's been up sleepless for a few hours already. The doctors told us lung cancer patients can suffer from insomnia, and unfortunately, Dad is not atypical. I figure he'll probably be happy to hear the phone ring. But at first, when he answers, he's just shocked.

"Rachel! Hey, chicken—everything okay? You're calling early for a Saturday."

I laugh out loud. His concern feels good to hear, as though our roles have been reversed back to normal again. "Everything's fine," I reply. "I guess it has been a while since we've spoken this early in the morning. Maybe since high school, when I had to get up for homeroom, which I believe started around dawn."

"Actually, Rach, I'm not sure we ever spoke then either, because I wouldn't have described you as fully awake." He chuckles. "Sometimes you'd be sitting at the kitchen table sleeping on top of a bowl of cereal. Remember?"

"That's not true! That was Kate!" I flash back to those bitterly cold winter mornings, when every extra minute of sleep I could steal felt as delicious as the whole previous night. "How are you, Dad?" I ask. "How are you feeling?"

"I'm okay, sweetheart. I've been up since pretty early this morning. Barbara makes me get up at sunrise to scrub the floors, peel the potatoes, and shovel the walk—it's ridiculous how she exploits me, even on the weekends."

This time I chuckle.

"Honestly, Rachel," he continues, changing the subject, "what are you doing up this early? I didn't know you could operate a phone before noon on weekends."

"I know, I know," I say, pouring steaming coffee into a mug. "I've been getting up early on Saturdays and Sundays for the past few weeks now to work on the On Target Essay stuff—and even earlier during the week. It's shocking, actually, how quickly I've been able to acquire all these new morning skills."

"It's getting to be that much work, huh? And how are you managing with that Tucker woman, the one who always seems to want her drafts yesterday?"

"Oh, right, Jessica. She still wants everything to have been done five minutes ago, but I'm getting used to her." I nod, having a hard time believing this myself. "I've discovered she's very predictable, so it's just a question of anticipating her complaints. It's actually much more of a challenge managing the Express Edit clients—and I have a few of them now—because although they're more hands-off, they're also less accessible," I explain, as I carry the full mug and the cordless phone back to my room. "I really have my hands full."

"Sure, it's good to stay busy . . ." Dad sounds like he's trailing off.

"True, *and* it's also starting to feel like a real business, Dad. So what if I'm the CEO, CFO, the head of HR, too—and also my own assistant. That's actually not bad for a girl who got pink slipped a few months ago." I want to pull his attention back. "You wanna be my head counsel? With this kind of management leading the company, you should really think about getting stock. I'm talking *blue chip,* Dad."

"That's a great idea!" he says, with surprising vigor in his voice, more than I've heard in weeks. "I'll do it. Let me be your first investor." I can hear his slippers shuffling on the wooden floor as he walks down the hall in the house. "I'm getting my checkbook now. How does $4,000 sound?"

"Wait, Dad, hold on, I—" *Is he joking?* "—what do you mean?"

"I mean I'd like to help you out a little. Let's take advantage of your momentum. I know that getting a business off the ground is a real challenge, even in the best of economies. It seems like a long time ago, but I remember how skin-of-the-teeth it was for me getting the firm going," he says, laughing a little. "Yeah, I recall many days when I wasn't sure it was going to stay afloat at all, when I wouldn't have any clients for weeks on end. Sometimes your mom would stop by my tiny office, with you and Kate, just so I would have some human contact during the day. Your mom believed in it, though. That helped."

"I had no idea!" I reply. He's never told me anything about the early days of the firm, and I realize I've never asked. All I ever knew was that when we were still very little, he'd quit a big Minneapolis firm to practice solo. And I do remember visiting him in his little office and clacking on the typewriter. I also have memories of my mother scouring the paper and cutting coupons, and volunteering at the consignment shop so she could get first dibs on whatever children's clothes came in. But I had thought that's what all mothers did.

"Well, it's not exactly the kind of thing you want your child to be worrying about," he says. "But still, you did your part to help out."

"What do you mean?"

"In that first year, before I got any of my first big clients, we ate *a lot* of cheap mac and cheese dinners. But every time I'd come home and say it looked like we'd be having it again, you'd get so excited, you'd start jumping up and down. It was enough to cheer me up every time."

"I do love my mac and cheese." I laugh.

"Those days seem very far away." Dad laughs, and I can picture him shaking his head and pushing up his glasses as he rubs his thumb and forefinger across his brow.

I lean back in my chair, amazed. "Dad, I can't believe I never knew this. It must have been really hard for you starting your own firm *and* supporting a family. That was quite a risk you took." I've never considered my father a risk-taker before.

"Well, sure, starting any venture on your own is a risk, and that's part of the reason I'd like to help you out," he replies. "I can tell you from experience, it's important just knowing you have support, that you have someone who believes in you. I'm not exactly in the position to help you put up your fliers, but I'd still like to do something. I'm sure On Target Essay could use a little cash infusion, right? Maybe buy some advertising somewhere . . . or maybe you need a new computer—how old is your computer, Rachel? Use the money however you think you need to." He pauses, and I don't say anything, unsure what to make of his offer.

"It would make me feel good," he adds.

"That's really sweet," I manage to reply. "I don't know what to say, Dad," I finally add. "That's a lot of money."

"Say yes!"

"But I don't know if and when I'd be able to pay you back, and—"

"I don't want you to pay me back," he interrupts. "It's an *investment*. Just like you said. I'm becoming a shareholder."

"I'm not even sure what I'd do with the money," I say, although about ten million ideas are already coming to mind.

"You'll figure it out. Don't tell me you wouldn't know how

to spend some money, Rachel." I suppose he does know who he's dealing with, although I also hope he's thinking I would invest the money in a more profit-focused fashion than he's known me to spend it in the past.

"Well, sure, but . . ." I answer, searching for another objection.

"Look, I've written the check, and I'm putting it in an envelope right now. Please accept it and use it," he says. "It's not a loan, Rachel, it's an investment. I've known you too long just to *give* you all that money, sweetie. You'd probably buy Lola and Sophie baby guitars, and you'd get me more of those patterned silk ties I never wear but that Barbara says are very expensive, and then you'd stick the rest in the bank and forget about it."

I laugh out loud into the phone now as he continues making fun of what would very likely be my wish list. Maybe he has been paying more attention all these years than I thought.

"Okay, Dad. Thank you then," I reply. "I would love to accept your investment in On Target Essay. Please consider yourself an equity shareholder—bet you didn't know I knew that term—with full voting rights. To be honest, I'm not exactly sure what an equity shareholder is or does, but I'm trying to give things a little veneer of formality."

He laughs this time. "I'm really proud to be the first investor, and I'm proud of you," he says, sounding more like before he was sick, but also more like a dad I don't really know. "And where one investor goes, others will follow—rule of the market. You're just going to have to be regular in coming out with your quarterly reports now that there's more than just the CEO and CFO on the board."

"Of *course*," I reply with gravity, but still grinning. "This is no business built on fantasy. I'm running a company with a plan here." I get an idea. "In fact, Mr. Chambers, I'd like you to be the chairman of the board. You know, a powerless head honcho, no profits, but lots of prestige. Do you accept, Dad?"

"I'd be honored, chief."

"Then a corporation is born. On Target Essay, privately held company controlled principally and pretty exclusively by two shareholders. Managed by Rachel Chambers, bachelorette of the arts, chief executive, and executive assistant. Advised by Bernie Chambers, chief counsel, chairman of the board, and possibly a close relation of the CEO—but do you think we need to disclose that?"

"Well, because we are the only two shareholders so far, and we already know it—no."

"Then it's nice to have you onboard."

He pauses for a moment, as though letting the negotiations settle. "Rach," he says. "There is one thing I'd like you to do for me though."

"Sure," I say, still feeling energized by the conversation, curious as to what he'll come up with as fair trade for these start-up funds.

"I need you to keep an eye on Katie for me. I'm worried about her."

This is so far from what I'm expecting him to say, that it takes me a moment to find my words. "You want me to keep an eye on Kate?" I question slowly, as though I might have heard him wrong. "Why? What's wrong?" I can feel the alarm rising in my throat.

"I want you to help her get through all this. I think she's having a really hard time."

"Dad, it's tough for all us, *you* most of all, but—"

"No, listen, Rach," he interrupts, and then pauses. "Katie's much more the nurturer than we are. We crack jokes, but she takes care of things. She's always been a great support to both of us." It is the first time I've heard him actually say these things, and although it's nothing I haven't realized before, it gives me a chill. "But this time, I think she's having a really hard time . . . I can hear it in her voice. This cancer is scaring the hell out of her. That's why I need you to be there for her."

"Dad," I say, my stomach clenching, "is there something I need to know?"

"No, sweetheart," he replies.

"You promise?" I ask.

"Really. I just needed to say this. That's all."

"Should I believe you?"

"Yes, you should. Now, look, I don't want to keep you anymore," he says. "You got up early for a reason. You probably want to get to it."

"Okay." I nod, feeling shaken and not wanting to end the conversation here at all. "I should get to work. But you know I'm up early now, so you can call me if you're up early, too."

"Will do, chicken. And be on the lookout for the check. I love you."

"I love you, too, Dad," I say as I hang up.

24

Even though I vowed to heed Molly's warning and actually do "work" work at work, when my phone rings and I reach to answer it, my eyes are focused on the three windows open on my computer monitor displaying various pages of the Kellogg Business School's website. I am trying to figure out if Vlad actually stands any chance of getting in. Technically, this is not part of my job. I'm just the essay girl. But, despite myself, I am interested.

"Okay, please tell me you haven't forgotten about our dinner reservations tonight at Ylang-Tzu," Ben says, not bothering with "Hello."

I rapidly click the windows shut on my screen. "Of course I didn't forget." I'd totally forgotten. "It's right here in my book, dinner with Ben and Leigh. Eight P.M."

"Nine P.M.," he replies. "Just wanted to be sure you weren't going to bail."

"Ben, this dinner is something I've been looking forward to all week." We haven't actually seen each other since the chance encounter with Zach at Barnes & Noble a few weeks ago. But since then, he's invited me out to dinners, brunches, drinks, and parties, and I've kept telling him I was too swamped with On Target work to go. Which was true, but which was still lame.

"Great," he says, "then we'll see you at nine. You know where it is, right?"

"Why don't you give me the address again, just to be sure."

When I get off the phone, I turn back to my computer and start working on the Pampers brief. As soon as I'm thoroughly ensconced in toxic runoff, Molly walks by. She peers over my shoulder to take a look at what I'm doing and shakes her head in disgust.

"That's just so disappointing," she says.

It takes me a moment to be absolutely certain I haven't left something incriminating on my monitor and that she's simply referring to the Pampers problem.

*   *   *

I meet Ben and Leigh in front of the hostess stand at Ylang-Tzu in the West Village at 9 o'clock sharp. It's the just-opened Asian fusion place of the moment.

"It seems there's a bit of a wait," Ben says when I walk in.

"How bad?"

"Only about two hours," he answers smiling, "So I asked

them if they'd be serving breakfast when we finally reach the table. They were not amused."

"Two hours? Do they know *who you are*?" I reply loudly.

Ben grins, but Leigh's smile looks a little tight. "My friend Cara got us these reservations," she says. "Cara *Taubman*?" she adds, saying it to the hostess.

"*Cara,*" I reiterate, impressed that Leigh is willing to play along.

"Cara *Taub*man." Ben nods.

"Leigh," I say turning up the volume, "do you want me to call *Tara*?"

"Cara," Ben whispers.

"Leigh, do you want me to call *Cara*?" I repeat, pulling out my cell phone, smiling at both of them.

"*No!*" she says quickly, sounding appalled. "I do need to make a call, though. I'll be right back, sweetie," she says, leaning in close to Ben and standing on her toes to give him a kiss.

I turn to Ben, feeling chastened. "I wasn't *really* going to call!"

"I know," he replies. "She just gets a little nervous when it comes to her people."

I wait for him to finish the joke.

"She's worked hard to cultivate all these relationships, and she can get really protective. It's kind of cute."

Kind of cute? This is definitely not the punch line I was expecting.

Leigh walks back in, shutting her phone, and stops by the hostess stand. She leans in and says a few words, then walks back over to us.

"Sorry about that," I say to Leigh, nodding in the direction of the hostess.

"Don't worry about it," she replies batting her hand at me. "There are just so many people who know Cara I didn't want it to become a thing, you know? I mean you read *Page Six,* you know how that can happen. I'd feel terrible if she wound up in the tabloids tomorrow because *we* were using her name at a hot restaurant."

This is far more of an explanation than I need.

Fortunately, the hostess strides over at this moment and tells us our table is ready.

"Why can't two hours pass like that at work?" Ben says, looking at his watch.

"Sometimes I'm certain hours have passed at Trees, and then I look at the clock and only six minutes have gone by since the last time I—"

Ben whistles. "That was literally a *twelve-minute* wait. Leigh, snaps to your girl Cara for this one."

I don't say anything else until we're seated.

Our table is next to an indoor rock-garden waterfall. There is a bowl of Asian snack mix in the center. As we sit down, and the hostess hands us the cocktail and food menus, Leigh says to me, "So, Ben tells me you've got a little project going these days?"

I'm sufficiently chuffed by my growing roster of clients to feel like boasting a little. I'm about to tell them about my father's investment when Leigh interrupts.

"Is it really true that you guys used masking tape and fliers to get the whole thingie started?" she asks, reaching for the snack mix.

"You've got to get started somehow," I reply, holding on to the bowl.

"Ben told me you *actually* put your home phone number on them." Leigh laughs. "You didn't really do that, did you, Rachel? Seriously?"

"Rachel wanted to attract as many clients as she could, hon," Ben jumps in, "even if that meant encouraging homicidal stalkers to give her a call."

"Hey," I reply, defensively, "homicidal stalkers value solid sentence construction, too." Admittedly it was a little amateurish—possibly stupid—plastering my home phone number across large swaths of the city, but it irritates me that Leigh has chosen to point this out.

A waiter comes over to the table, pen poised, and asks for our drink order.

"The lady will have that house cocktail, the Red Dragon," Ben says, looking down at the cocktail menu and then at Leigh and nodding to see if she agrees, "I'll have a Seven and Seven, and for you, Rach?"

"A Dewar's on the rocks, please." Sometimes the night calls for straight booze.

"So anyway, Rachel," Leigh continues when the waiter departs, "Ben also told me you've been meeting your clients"— she says this word while making quotation marks in the air—"in a Starbucks?"

"The first few. It seemed like a good neutral location."

"Yeah," Ben replies, "with the added bonus of extra hits to your punch card."

"When the business goes bust," Leigh giggles, "you'll be halfway to a free frappuccino!"

"That's cold, Leigh," I say, only half-joking.

"Oh, come on! Ben wrote up your business plan on a paper napkin! The whole thing's a goof, right?"

I look at the two of them, and I can feel the heat rising in my cheeks. Did she just call my business venture a "goof"? And why isn't Ben defending it, and defending me? I wonder if sliding a 2.5-carat rock on someone's finger blunts your sense of loyalty to everyone else—like your former best friend. Then it occurs to me in a slow, queasy realization, that if Leigh feels entitled to make fun of me, it's probably because Ben did, too.

"So what are we thinking of here?" Ben asks, and I'm too stunned to reply. "Let's say we split some apps then do individual entrées. How does that sound?"

"Great," Leigh says brightly, "you like spring rolls, don't you, Rachel? It says that these come with ponzu sauce . . ."

"Whatever you guys want," I answer, having a hard time thinking of anything but the knot of tension in my stomach.

"Good call," Ben replies. "And how about some of the caramelized pork skewers? The *Times* guy mentioned them in his review. They sounded awesome."

The waiter brings our cocktails, and I concentrate on the menu, trying to think of any other explanation for Leigh's attitude. *Maybe she's intimidated by the possibility of my success? Or by my closeness to Ben? Maybe she finds me threatening?* But I look at Leigh again, and all I see is a relaxed and polished-looking girl with one hand casually draped over her fiancé's leg, who really thinks the whole essay thing is a joke.

"You okay, Chambers?" Ben asks when I haven't responded.

"Yeah, fine," I say, "just a little tired."

"I bet filling in those little application boxes is exhausting," Ben says and Leigh laughs.

"Actually, no," I respond, looking Leigh in the eyes because I can't look at Ben right now. "It's managing eight clients, a nightly workload of about four or five hours, and a revenue of just about $2,200 a client that's the exhausting part, Ben." Some internal circuit breaker has snapped, and I can feel the rush of animosity rising quickly. "*You see,* my clients have important jobs and real ambitions, and make a lot of money, and they have *a lot* riding on getting into a good business school. So not only do they pay me and my goofy little company a lot of money to help them, some of them are even paying me *double* that amount to do it quickly," I say with unchecked hostility.

I have no desire to let up, either, as though I've been priming for this fight. "Let me break it down for you guys—let's see, that means that after working full-time in an office, just like you, I'm going home every night to draft and edit about ten thousand words per client. These clients have hired me to advise them in one of the most important steps in their careers. These are people who are going to go out in the world and launch businesses and create products and run companies. Frankly, these guys will probably be your bosses some day," I add, with an acid smile directed at Leigh. "They've got ideas, and they're making them happen. With *my* help. They could probably afford to hire anyone for any kind of service they need—they could probably *buy* their essays somewhere, and for cheaper, too. But they've chosen to hire me. My business will help them build theirs, and I must be doing a pretty good job, because *my* business right now is thriving."

Leigh and Ben are both looking at me aghast. I've been speaking rapidly, without giving them a chance to reply.

"Rach, listen—" Ben starts haltingly, but I stand up abruptly and he stops.

"I don't really need your support—although that would be nice," I add quietly, nodding at them both, "but I do ask for your respect. What I've tried to express is that this business is something I take seriously. I hope I've made that clear," I conclude, as I dig around in my bag for my wallet. I take out two crisp one-hundred dollar bills, part of Sanjay's recent payment, and place them neatly on the table in front of where I'd been sitting. "Good night," I say, walking toward the exit.

25

"Look at them," Zach says as we watch people streaming rapidly into NYU's Henry Kaufman Management Center Rotunda. "It's like they smell cookies baking in there."

"No," I reply. "It's not the smell of hot cookies that lures them, it's the smell of success."

"Ah." Zach nods. "See, that's why I'm not really suited for business school. I'm much more of a Toll House man myself."

While searching through some of the business school websites where my clients are applying, I had noticed most schools offer on-campus information sessions for prospective students. The purpose of the info session, according to one school, is to "discuss the program, curriculum, structure, and the admission process, and provide an opportunity for prospective students to ask questions about the program and admission. It will consist of a forty-five-minute presentation, followed by Q&A." It sounded about as exciting as chalk. I imagined a tense group of hard-charging applicants willing to do whatever it takes to gain any extra distinction that might tip the scales of admission.

And then I had a moment of inspiration.

It occurred to me that the people going out of their way to glad-hand admissions officials and ask questions would be precisely On Target Essay's target audience. I checked on the New York University website to see if the Stern School of Business was offering any sessions, and there was one scheduled for today. Zach and I—armed with a bag full of freshly photocopied fliers—are now about to infiltrate.

"So how do you think we start?" I ask. "I'm not even sure who's a student here already and who's here for this meeting."

"Watch and learn." Zach nods at me, takes a few of my fliers and walks over to a guy in a navy-blue suit flipping through a leather-bound binder. "Do you know where the information session for prospective students is being held?" he asks.

"Yeah," Navy-Blue Suit replies, glancing at his watch, "It's in C-23."

"Great, thanks. Oh, and here." Zach slips him a flier.

Navy-Blue Suit looks surprised, but doesn't want to let this show since he doesn't know who Zach is. He could be an admissions officer. A shaggy, hip-looking admissions officer, to be sure, but this *is* a school in Greenwich Village. "Thanks," the applicant says.

Zach walks back toward me, and I watch the guy fold up

the flier and slip it into his suit pocket. Ideally, he'll read it on his way home as he's examining some of the other admissions materials they'll certainly be handing out. He'll start getting stressed out as he reads about the minimum required GMAT scores, the percentage of minority and legacy candidates admitted, and the application deadlines. Then he'll get to my flier at the bottom of the stack, and it'll start him thinking.

"You are a marketing marvel," I say.

"That is hard to deny." Zach smiles, scratching his beard. "I know all the tricks of the trade. I used to hand out fliers for a tanning salon in Jersey, you know."

"Wow, classy," I say, continuing to scan the crowd.

"Yeah, never takes me long to identify my targets. Like for the tanning joint, I realized I only needed to go after people who were already tanned to a crisp, because they were the only ones who thought, 'Yeah, looking even more like weather-beaten Naugahyde would be totally hot!' It was a waste of time going after the creamy-whites like you," Zach replies, picking up my arm and pushing up my sleeve. "I mean look at this. It's like you haven't seen sun in years."

"Thanks." I frown.

"No, I mean you have beautiful skin."

Immediately the color rises in my cheeks as Zach lets my arm go.

"See that?" he says, smiling impishly. "If you were to fake-n-bake, you'd lose that furious blush of yours."

"Cut it out," I say, smiling back and putting my palms to my cheeks to cool the reddening. "I can't look like a flustered teen. I've got a job to do here."

"Right, sorry." Zach salutes. "No more compliments. Even if you *do* look especially pretty."

"That's right!" I reply sternly, my smile broadening further. I had actually put some thought into my look for today because Vlad and I are meeting later for an edit session. I'm wearing narrow-legged pants—the kind of that make the legs look longer—over heels, and a fitted cardigan. Vlad had said he would be attending an end-of-the-day meeting downtown and proposed to pick me up in his company car on his way back up to the office, where we could use the conference room to work. So I wanted to look properly dressed for our meeting.

"I mean you *are* dressed a little nicer than I would be when I handed out the tanning salon fliers," Zach adds.

"Well what would you usually wear?"

"A teeny-weeny bikini." He nods.

"Interesting, I wouldn't have thought you were the type to have a teeny weeny," I pause before adding the word "bikini." When I succeed in making Zach blush, I pump my fist in the air. "Yeah, that's right, how does it feel, cowboy?"

Fanning his face with his hand, he replies, "You have quite a mouth on you, little lady."

I spot another likely candidate, a woman angrily talking into her cell phone. I watch as she consults her wristwatch and yells into the phone. I motion to Zach that I'm going to approach.

"Jesus Christ, it's not rocket science!" the woman snaps, as she clicks off her cell.

"Excuse me," I say.

"Yes?"

"Are you applying to Stern?"

"Yes," she replies, though the tone is more, 'What's it to you?'

"I thought you might want to take a look at this." I hand her a flier.

"On Target Essay?"

"It's a company that offers consulting in the application process."

"And why do you think I'd need advice?" she says, unenthused.

I want to say, *Because clearly you're a huge bitch and it would behoove you to show an admissions committee as little of your personality as possible.* Instead, I say, "Because if you're not using a company like this, I'm sure you know that your competition will be." I walk away without waiting to see her reaction, but I hope it gives her pause. Actually, I hope it cuts like a machete to the bone and makes her beg for my help. But pause will be enough for now.

I look at my watch and decide Zach and I need to kick the operation into high gear. I split my pile of ads, load him up with half, and we begin handing them to everyone in the general vicinity. I expressly target breathless latecomers as they hurry in. If they are so rushed to get here on time, chances are they won't have much time to spend on their essays, either. My stack of fliers is nearly depleted when I see a black Town Car glide to the curb in front of the building. Its back window slides down.

"Ray-chelle!" Vlad calls out, raising his hand in a small wave. He is right on time.

"Be right there," I mouth, waving back, then turn to Zach, who is continuing to hand fliers to people entering and exiting the building. "Thank you so much for doing this."

"No problem," he replies, without breaking his rhythm.

"I kinda have to call it quits because the client is here," I say.

"A-ha, the Vladimir," he says, looking over to the black sedan. "Hence the pretty outfit today."

"No, no," I reply quickly, "I just want to look professional, you know? We're meeting in his office. I brought the TEDs, too," I add, patting my purse.

"Okay." Zach nods, with an obvious smirk. "I'll see you tomorrow then. I'll just finish handing these out"—he holds up a thin stack of papers—"and then I'll catch a ride home. My limo is parked around back," he adds.

"Thanks again," I say. "I'll see you tomorrow." As I walk toward the car, I fish around for some lip gloss in my purse and pause at the angle of the building, briefly concealed from both Zach and Vlad behind the wing of a sculpture. I don't want either of them to see me reapplying.

"So you were working with my competition," Vlad says, as I settle back into the seat and the car glides into traffic.

"I'm sorry?" I reply, turning to him with a quick head-shake.

"The people who will be applying against me at Stern," Vlad explains. "How did they look to you?"

I look at Vlad sitting there in his cashmere coat and Bally

loafers, with his air of grave expectation. He looks good. "Vlad," I say, "regardless of what any of them bring to the table, you are an extremely attractive candidate."

Vlad laughs. "Thank you, Rachel, you are very persuasive. Of course I know I am paying to hear such nice things, but I thank you anyway."

26

"Fucking F-train!" Kate yells to me as she runs across Houston Street and gives me a big hug. "I'm soooo sorry I'm late," she says, giggling. "But I'm here and very ready for a night out!"

"I already got the tickets," I reply holding them up in a V. "And they don't call it the 'F'-me train for nothing, you know."

Kate grabs the tickets out of my hand. "I can't believe Crippled Nipple is actually playing the Mercury Lounge tonight!" She pauses for dramatic effect, as if this piece of information would resonate with anyone besides the die-hard regulars who hung out at the Mercury Lounge in the early nineties. "When I think about the way my band used to jam with them—"

When we arrive at the club, the large guy at the door asks us for I.D. This makes Kate so happy I think she might lick his face. She rifles through her bag but can't find her driver's license. "I can show you a picture of my six-year-old," she offers.

"If you want to," the guy says.

"She'll show you her I.D.," Kate says, nodding in my direction. "And she can vouch for me because she's my *older* sister."

"Nah," he answers, "I don't need to see hers. She's definitely over twenty-one, right?"

"Okay, now I'm hurt," I reply.

"Show me," the man says to humor us both, and when I flash him the license, he smiles. "Minnesota?" he says, "I would have guessed Wisconsin." He stamps our hands and lets us in.

"Wizz-*kahn*-sin, *please!*" Kate laughs.

She looks down the long bar that leads to the swinging door connected to the stage area. "Man, this place looks different," she says, shaking her head.

"Really? Would this be better or worse?" I ask, as I glance at my reflection in the mirror over the bar and tousle my bangs a little.

"Well," she squints and scans the place again, "maybe not. Maybe I can just see things more clearly now with the smoking ban in effect." She pauses and does another once-over of the joint before ruffling her own hair in the bar mirror. "I used to reek of smoke for days after I left this place. God, I loved it here."

"Okay, Kate, enough small talk, what are you drinking?"

"A beer."

"Good start."

"Maybe an Amstel?"

"When did you turn into a girl?"

"You're right. In deference to the state of Wisconsin, order me a Beast."

"Got it," I say as I elbow my way up to the bar and try to catch the eye of the hot bartender wearing a vintage concert T-shirt and leather bracelets around his lanky wrists. "A Milwaukee's Best and a Heineken, please." The bartender nods at me and I look back at Kate, who's still taking in the club. I catch her smiling so unself-consciously, I can only imagine the late-night moments of revelry she must be reliving. I pay for the drinks and hand Kate her beer. She takes a long swig with her eyes closed. "God, that tastes disgusting," she says, immediately putting the bottle back up to her lips.

"Wanna go inside and hear the opening band?"

"What can they sound like if they're opening for Crippled Nipple?" Kate gives a full-body shudder then reaches into her purse. "Ta-da!" she says pulling out four neon-orange foam-rubber bullets.

"What are those?"

"Earplugs. It's the only way to listen to a concert."

"You are old."

"Are you kidding? I used to go through so many pairs when we were performing, I thought about buying stock in the company. But then I realized I didn't even know where to go to buy stock."

"Just takes a little Wall Street know-how, sister," I say with an authoritative nod.

"Oh, that's right! I forgot I was talking to the new expert consultant on all things business. Tell me what's going on with that," Kate replies, taking my arm and moving me toward the back room.

As soon as we push through the swinging doors and enter the performance space, the music begins pounding. Kate triumphantly holds up her earplugs. I watch her expertly twist each little bullet and stick it in her ear. She tosses two in my direction. "Here!" she yells, "take!" I do the same. I try talking to her while the band is playing, but I can barely hear myself yelling. When the next song is over, the musicians do an impromptu sound check, and I take out my plugs and lean over to Kate.

"So let me run this by you," I say. She doesn't turn around. "Hey," I say, grabbing her arm.

"Sorry, what?" she replies, turning to face me and popping out her plugs. "They were okay, weren't they?"

"I guess."

"It's hard for me to know the scene at this point, what's even considered good anymore."

"Kate," I say, "it really wasn't all that long ago that you were on that stage yourself. I doubt you've forgotten what sounds good or bad in the space of a few years."

"I guess it just feels like an entirely different era to me. I feel like a different person now. Who would have thought I would be posing as a Brooklyn mommy today? Things turn out so differently than you expect," she says, trailing off, and it's not hard to tell who she's thinking about. "But you were trying to ask me something?" Kate shakes off her pensive look.

"It's about Ben." I say as the band starts playing again.

"Ohhhhh." She nods. "Let's go outside and talk. I don't need to hear the end of this set anyway."

We walk back out and perch on stools at the corner of the bar. I take the seat facing the wall so Kate can people-watch. "So what's going on with you and Ben?" she asks. "You starting to wonder why you aren't the one marrying him?"

"*What*? No!" I reply defensively. "That's totally not it at all."

Kate looks at me inquisitively.

"No, it's that he's . . ." I swirl my beer for a second and concentrate on the liquid spinning inside the bottle. "He's just not himself anymore. When I talk to him, I don't see the guy I used to know."

"And this has nothing to do with the girl that guy is marrying?"

"Well, of course it does. He changes when he's with Leigh. He starts to talk like her, he laughs at things that totally aren't funny, *he* laughs just because *she's* laughing."

"Rach, he's in love with the girl, that's just what happens—"

"I know that, Kate!" I snap at her. "He's in love with Leigh, of course. I would hope so, they're getting married. But that doesn't mean you have to sell out your old friendships, does it? I found out the other night that Leigh and Ben both think that On Target is nothing but a 'goof,' " I use finger quotes on the word *goof* to illustrate my disgust. "Leigh was laughing outright at the whole thing, and Ben laughed right along. I've never seen him so distant or insensitive. It's like—"

"Rachel," Kate interrupts, taking my wrists in both her hands, as though to grasp my attention. "You have to stop this. You have to get over Ben. Move on."

"What do you mean *get over* Ben, he's my—"

"I mean you're in love with your best friend. You two have been best friends forever—how could you not love Ben? Rach, I know you know this. And now that he's marrying another woman you're beginning to think about how nice it would have been to go to sleep and wake up with your best friend next to you every day."

I pull my hands away from hers. "Kate, I can't believe you—"

"C'mon, Rach," Kate interrupts again, this time a little more gently. "Look, it sucks, I know. It sucks to feel like you missed your chance." She shrugs apologetically, as though sorry she has to be so blunt. "To lose someone you love. It especially sucks that this has to be happening now, in light of all the stuff going on with Dad."

"Okay, first of all, that's not remotely the issue with Ben— that's just absurd," I say, my voice inadvertently rising. "And second of all, Dad's been a lot more supportive of me recently than Ben has."

"What do you mean?" she says. "How has *Dad* been supportive?" I finish her unspoken thought in my head: *How has Dad been supportive as he coughs and wheezes between cancer treatments?*

"Well, like I was trying to tell you before, Ben has been totally absent from the whole On Target project, to the point that he told Leigh the whole thing was bullshit. But Dad, who's been asking about it all along, so believes in it that he even insisted on giving me some money to help."

"He did what?" Kate says, drawing her shoulders back.

"Dad gave me $4,000, and Ben—

"Dad gave you $4,000?"

"Yeah," I answer, "at first I didn't want to take it, but he was insistent, saying he really wanted to invest. So I agreed, but only on the condition that he'd be a shareholder in the company." I smile as I tell her this, picturing the next On Target Essay board meeting around our kitchen table. The shareholders would convene dressed in their jammies and ratty bathrobes.

"Rachel," Kate says, her eyes narrowing. "How can you take Dad's money?"

"What?" Of all people to be questioning a parental investment, Kate should be last on the list. She had accepted several times that sum from Dad at different points in her life, when the investment in her had more to do with credit card debt than anything else.

"What do you mean how can I take his money?" I say, sounding more defensive than I intend, but I resent Kate's implication that I'm being a sponge.

"Don't you think the timing is a little bit morbid?" she asks.

"Excuse me?"

"Taking money from our father—who is so sick—don't you think that's a little bit insensitive, Rachel?"

"What are you talking about? He wants me to have the money because he thinks what I'm doing is a really great—"

"Oh come on, Rach." Kate sniffs.

"I don't believe this! Why doesn't anyone think I can make a go of this business?"

"Look," Kate says, her voice an unfriendly whisper, "I'm happy to support whatever you do, but let's be real. Dad wants to give you this money now, in case he's not around anymore to give it to you later."

I look away, trying to prevent the tears that have spontaneously sprung to my eyes from sliding down my cheeks. Kate's logic never occurred to me; I assumed Dad had actually meant what he said. "What do you want me to do?" I ask her.

Kate shrugs. "I don't think there's anything you can do now."

"I don't have to cash the check. I can return it," I say, despite the fact that it's already been deposited.

"No," she says, "you can't do that, you've already accepted it. What would you say to him?" She pauses. "Next time, Rachel, please think first, okay?"

Kate turns and walks back through the swinging doors into the stage area.

Crippled Nipple has just come onstage, so I finish my beer and join her. But as Kate and I stand next to each another, mechanically swaying to the music, neither of us is enjoying the show.

27

"I go to cocktail bar at the St. Regis hotel now for a drink," Vlad says, as we look, unsuccessfully, for a cab to take me home on this unbearably cold winter night. "We have worked so hard this evening, and we have been very productive. Would you like to join me? It is my pleasure to offer you a drink and thank you."

The thought of a warm bar and a dirty martini actually sounds inspired, but it's almost 11 P.M. "I don't know how you do it," I say, shivering. "Why aren't you collapsing right about now?"

"Because I cannot just 'collapse' and start the next day all over all the same. It is not good for the spirit. Come and have one drink. You'll see it is the best way to sleep sound and be fresh tomorrow. It is a quite wonderful bar, perfect to take the plug out. Then the day can be over and one can go home with the closure."

I'm flattered by Vlad's offer, and I have no pressing need to go home. And maybe he's right: Why not take a few minutes to detox from the day rather than going straight home and starting all over again tomorrow? I say I'll go just as a cab materializes in front of us.

"We're going to Fifty-fifth Street, between Madison and Fifth," Vlad tells the driver as he slams the door shut behind us. I've heard of the Old King Cole bar at the St. Regis, it's one of those landmark New York watering holes. The cab pulls up to the hotel's gilded awning and a doorman in a green cape and cap opens the car door for me. We walk up the carpeted steps, and Vlad goes first through the revolving door, pausing to explain, "So I push." Inside, the hotel lobby is gleaming with polished brass and marble. Vlad comes up behind me as I'm looking around and touches my elbow.

"This way," he says, gesturing to his left toward a carpeted lounge with upholstered chairs. On the other side of the lounge I can see the wide entrance to a dimly lit room. My sharp boot heels sink into the light-blue carpet as we pass through the empty tables of what must be the hotel's breakfast and tea room. As we approach the other side, I can hear the low notes of jazz music, and through the dimness I can make out a dark wood bar; a shelf of liquor bottles; and low, round tables made of the same dark polished wood.

As we cross the threshold of the bar, it feels like we've stepped into another era, or into another city where I've never been. The bar is relatively small, and the back wall is painted with a mural of Old King Cole in the rich jewel tones of a Renaissance tableau. Polished wooden paneling covers the lower half of the walls, and upholstered brocade banquettes line several sides of the dark space. The only light seems to come from a few low-glowing brass sconces and the backlit bar area, and when I look down to see where I'm walking, I can barely make out the medallion pattern in the carpet.

"Let us take the corner table, shall we?" Vlad asks. "It is always the table I call mine." He gestures to the right-hand corner, an empty nook across from the bar. I walk over and slide onto the banquette behind the round glass-topped table. Vlad takes off his coat, tosses it onto the banquette, and sits in one of the chairs opposite me. I barely have time to look around before a waiter walks up to the table.

"Hello, Vladimir," he says, setting down an elegant silver dish divided into three sections, one filled with mixed nuts, one with small pretzels, and the other overflowing with wasabi peas. "What can I get you tonight, young man?" he asks, smiling, He has thick graying hair and a bit of a paunch beneath his black vest. He could be anywhere between forty and sixty and looks like he knows the precise nuances of a Sidecar versus a Sazerac or any other gentleman's drink.

"Hello, Jim. I shall have a Chivas on the rocks, please. Double, yes?" Jim nods. "And Rachel," Vlad turns to me. "What would you like?"

"I'd like a dirty martini—Belvedere—up, extra olives, please." Jim nods at me and I smile at him, already salivating at the prospect of how lush the martini olives must be in a bar this plush.

Vlad and I simultaneously reach to scoop up some wasabi peas and laugh at the collision of knuckles. "Go ahead," I say, picking out a fat salty cashew from the nuts, "I'll start with these. This place is great!" There are only five or six other patrons scattered throughout the bar, which isn't surprising—who likes to be out late in midtown on a chilly weeknight?

"The Belvedere martini, dirty, extra olives," says Jim as he places a brimming glass on a napkin in front of me without spilling a drop. Four obscenely large and beautiful olives are jammed onto the skewer. "And the double scotch on the rocks for you, Vladimir. Enjoy."

"Thank you, Jim," Vlad replies. "To relaxation after a very productive work evening." He raises his glass to me.

"And to your becoming the most competitive candidate you can be," I toast in return. I sound like an advertisement for the Army.

I take a few slow swallows of my martini, and I feel relaxed and warm. Neither one of us says anything for several moments. But sitting in the dim silence sipping a drink with Vlad feels nice. It feels like the proper, sophisticated end to an evening together.

"So, Rachel," Vlad finally says, "I know you must be very busy in this season, but what do you do in the spring when there are not so much applications to write?"

"I continue to do consulting with clients," I answer, lying quickly. "The application cycle never ends, because some schools have rolling admissions." I'd just learned that recently, reading the University of Chicago website.

"Yes, of course," Vlad replies nodding. "And do you have specific plans for growing the business?"

Growing the business. I look at Vlad and smile. Here's an attractive man who's clearly going places, and who seems to believe that I am, too. It's not just gratifying, it's sexy.

"Maybe new ventures that you will do in next season?" he adds. I take a gulp of my drink and tilt my head to the side. "Because with a business like this," he continues, "I think you could profit by some niche marketing. Reaching out to the kinds of clients who could use your services the most—like the foreigners such as me. Where else do you advertise?"

"Well . . ."

"Have you thought about advertising in universities abroad?" he asks. "That way you would target the foreigners directly, exactly the ones such as me and others, who have much ambition to go to the American business school, but problems with the English."

"That's a great idea." I am genuinely struck by how smart an idea it is.

"In fact, Rachel, if you would like," Vlad says, pausing briefly, as though momentarily hesitant, "I can recommend you to some Estonian friends of mine. They have been so panicked recently with the deadlines. I told them about the advice you've been giving me, and they seemed very jealous. I am sure they would be interested in your services."

"That would be terrific," I say, looking up from my drink into his eyes. "But I don't want you to feel in any way obliged to recommend me. I only want you to do it if you feel comfortable."

"I would not offer if I am not comfortable," he answers with emphasis. "Yours is valuable service, and if you have the time for a few more clients, I know people who could use the help."

"Then I would be grateful," I say. I'm feeling a little more than grateful and a lot closer to flattered, once again.

We continue chatting for a while, and I ask Vlad to tell me more about growing up in Kunda. He orders us both another round of drinks as he tells me about his insane passion for gymnastics as a kid.

"So you were really an Olympic hopeful?" I ask, glancing at what I assume must be the powerful musculature of his arms beneath his tailored shirt.

"Hopeful, yes," Vlad chuckles. "Successful, no. Sadly I was never very good, no matter how hard I tried. I was never— how did Brando say it? 'A contender?'—but gymnastics for us was like the basketball for the youth of this city. It seemed like a way out. For me, though," he smiles, "it was more a way to sustain injury."

I laugh out loud, a natural reaction that—normally—I scrupulously avoid when we're working together and he's talking about himself.

"Perhaps we are ready to leave?" Vlad asks, gesturing to our empty glasses.

"Yes, I think we have relaxed and unplugged and ended the day properly," I answer, feeling like I could still unplug some more.

Vlad signals to Jim for the check. I reach for my wallet, but Vlad closes his eyes and shakes his head.

"Please," I say.

"Please," he replies, putting an end to the conversation.

I slip into my coat, buttoning it up and then tying my scarf. Outside, the valet captain standing beneath the heat lights under the hotel awning whistles for a cab as soon as he sees us coming through the revolving door. One pulls up almost immediately. The valet opens the cab door and waits.

"This is your cab, Rachel," Vlad says, placing one hand on my back and gesturing toward the open door with the other. He takes my bag for me as I step into the cab and hands it to me once I'm seated. He leans over and says, "Call my office tomorrow, and my assistant will give you the names of the other friends who might be interested in employing On Target Essay." Then he adds, "It was very pleasant evening, Rachel. Thank you again for the good work."

The cab pulls away and I lean back savoring the overheated backseat as we speed over the now-empty streets. We seem to be hitting every green light, and I slump back and look up, letting the lights blend into a blur of green. What fantastic boyfriend material Vlad is. He's Mr. Upright and Well-Dressed, Mr. Ambitious but Relaxed, a man who knows how to drink his scotch and a guy who wouldn't dream of not honoring his commitments. I imagine taking him home to Minnesota to my father and Dad's reaction of pleasure and disbelief. Maybe Vlad and I could build a business together, maybe an empire with a stock listing and letterhead and lots of first-class travel as a power couple. When the cab lurches to a stop in front of my apartment building, I'm still smiling at the idea.

28

"Hey, it's me," Ben says. "Can I come over?"

I don't say anything for a moment, letting the loaded silence drag out. "When?" I finally reply.

"How about now?"

I look at my watch; it's 9 o'clock. Then I look at what I'm wearing and realize I'll have to peel off the sweats, comb my hair, and liberally apply concealer to my chin before I'll be fit to be seen by anyone, especially someone I am seriously angry at. Ben lives twenty minutes away when the subway is timed perfectly, thirty if the trains run normally. "Okay. If you want."

"Great, see you soon," he says.

The doorbell rings the next instant.

Ben is standing on the threshold of my apartment, holding out a small white paper bag. "This is for you. From me. 'Cause I think I was an ass. And I don't want you to think of me as someone who's an ass. I only want you to think of me as someone with a great ass." I open the bag and inside is my favorite deli goodie, a giant frosted black and white cookie, and two one-hundred dollar bills—the money I left on the table at the restaurant. "So can I come in?" he asks.

I step back from the doorway and hold open the door. "Yeah, come in," I reply, nodding.

He steps inside, and I close the door behind him. Then I walk back toward the living room. I hear Ben follow me. I don't look at him until I sit down on the couch and gesture to the other side of it. He sits down, and I place the bag with the cookie and the money on the coffee table in front of us. I draw my feet up under me and lean back and stare at Ben, a resolutely neutral look on my face. He is sitting on the edge of the couch, clasping his hands together between his legs, looking at me look at him, a distinctly unhappy look on his face.

"Rach . . ." he starts off and then sighs. "Rach, I am sorry about what happened the other night. I'm sorry if we said or did something to offend you."

I stare some more, still purposefully neutral, and say nothing, waiting for him to continue speaking, waiting for him to explain what it was they "said or did."

"We felt terrible when you just ran out like that," he goes on. "I mean, you know, I would never intentionally say anything to hurt you. And when Leigh made fun of the business,

you know she was just totally teasing . . . we really didn't realize you were taking it so seriously, you know?"

"But why, Ben? You *knew* I'd been working hard on this.
All the times I couldn't come out, the client meetings I'd told
you about, all the work I was doing. I just don't know what
you thought I *was* doing."

"I don't know, Rach," he says pleadingly, a nervous smile
breaking onto his face, "I guess I just wasn't thinking, you
know? I've just . . . I guess I've had a lot going on lately.
Maybe I haven't been so tuned in. But *honestly,* I really had
no idea."

"Well, that much has been clarified, right?" I reply, without
much inflection.

"Yes, yes, definitely, and I'm sorry if you thought that we
were—I dunno," he cuts himself off, and looks like he's trou-
bled or searching for words. "If you thought we were 'lacking
in respect,' somehow," he finishes, saying this last phrase
slowly, as though experimenting with a new idea he weren't
sure about.

"Well, I was offended. And it did hurt my feelings," I state
matter-of-factly.

"Rachel," Ben says abruptly, moving forward on the
couch, closer to me. He puts his hands on my knees. "I'm
sorry. I really am. The way I see it, we were all just laughing
and teasing, and suddenly something snapped, and then this
big misunderstanding arose. I wish it hadn't, and I feel badly."
He reaches for the cookie bag on the table and holds it up in
front of me. "This is my peace offering. Please accept it. Because I know that no matter how furious you are at me, most

of you is dying to tear the cellophane off this bad boy and inhale it immediately. I won't even ask you to share."

I look at Ben smiling at me, half-playful and half-pleading,
and I still say nothing. I don't feel like anything has been resolved, but I'm not sure what can be resolved, either. I'm still
offended and I still feel hurt. Ben reaches for my hand in my
lap, uncurls my fingers, and presses the white paper bag into
it. "Okay?"

*   *   *

"So. Where we at? What's going on? What's the 411?" Zach
asks the following morning, peering down at me, his chin
hooked over the edge of my cubicle's partition. It's the mid-
morning lull, when Molly goes out for her daily cup of anti-
oxidant green tea at the Korean deli on the corner, and the
mice start to play. Zach walks around the side of the cubicle,
sits on the edge of my desk, and crosses his legs. "So what's
going on with On Target? Any results from our promotional
bonanza at NYU the other night?"

"Things are going pretty well at the moment, actually," I
smile. "I did get a few inquiries from NYU people. Some were
even asking about the application process for *next* year. One
woman has already asked to schedule an 'informational interview'—her words—for next week. Oh, and Vlad offered—"

"Ah, yes, *Vlad,*" Zach interrupts, "otherwise known as
Baron Vladimir von Town Car, yes?"

"Yes." I smile.

"Right." Zach nods. "Carry on. What did *Vlad* offer you?"

"He offered to recommend me to some of his friends who

are applying to business school and hook me into the international community of poor essay writers. He said I should call his office this morning to get their names."

"That's really cool of him," Zach says, sounding genuinely impressed and giving me a quick squeeze on the shoulder. "And to how many people has he boasted of your priceless skills?"

"Well, I haven't called him yet to get the names."

Zach hits his palm against his forehead, then knocks it against mine. "What are you waiting for?"

Truthfully, I've been procrastinating for a reason. I'm a little uncomfortable with how the evening at the St. Regis ended a few days ago. I know it's ridiculous, but in the back of the cab on my way home, I'd momentarily—playfully—fantasized Vlad as boyfriend material. Just for fun. In my head. It seems silly in broad sober daylight—and absolutely impossible to articulate to Zach—but I have this twinge of nerves now, and that's why I haven't called.

"So, come on, lady, let your fingers do the walking," Zach says, reaching over my desk to pick up the phone for me. "Call!"

"Okay." I nod. I know this will be totally painless, anyway. It will involve a short conversation with Vlad's receptionist. As I dial, I get my pad of paper and pen ready to start jotting.

"Cherov speaking."

I'm so surprised to hear Vlad answer his own phone I almost hang up. "Vlad?" I say stupidly.

"Yes? Ray-chelle, is that you?"

I nod. Then I say "Yes!" I look over at Zach, and he gives

me the thumbs-up sign with both thumbs, then mimes the act of writing names down.

"We had some pleasant drinks at the bar the other night, no? Unfortunately I realize only too late that much of a good thing is not always a good thing," he says.

"I was hurting a little myself the next morning, too." I laugh. "But you're right, they were delicious, in that amazingly strong and regrettable sort of way." I'm acutely aware Zach is listening. "I'm calling to follow up on your friends who might be interested in On Target."

"Yes, of course. I have the list, and why don't I give it to you when we work this evening? And shall I order some Thai food?"

"Thai? I love Thai, yeah, that would be great," I reply.

Zach raises his eyebrows at me.

"And thank you for those contacts!" I say brightly, getting things back on track. I give Zach a thumbs-up. "Until tonight, then."

I hang up and Zach says, "Sooo, sounds like Marilyn Manizer's hitting the town for real tonight."

"What?" I attempt to brush off the obvious conclusion.

"I'm just saying it's been a while since our girl's gone gaming, hasn't it? Not much material at all from her lately."

"Well, excuse me but I've been busy."

"Yeah, I get that sense."

"You're not suggesting . . ." I let the unfinished question hang to indicate my profound disbelief that he could for one minute think about Vlad and me what I had been thinking about Vlad and me only a few minutes before.

"I think that's exactly what I'm suggesting, actually."

"Oh, come on, I was talking to *Vladimir*," I say, trying to convey the ridiculousness of his assumption. "Please, the man is all business all the time."

"And I'm sure that reassuring himself of your preference for Thai food is one of his most pressing financial concerns."

"Zach." I shake my head. "Vlad and I are ordering Thai tonight so we can work through dinner while going over his Wharton application. We'll be eating in the conference room of his office. We'll be using plastic forks!" I sputter, as if this revelation alone should dispel any lingering doubt. "I mean, it's not like we haven't done this before."

"Okay, whatever," Zach replies, maddeningly. "If you say nothing is going on between you and your client, I believe you." He starts walking out of my cube, but when he gets to the space where a door would be, he quickly turns, and raises his index finger as though to bring silence to the room. "But listen to me, Rachel, should anything happen with the two of you . . ." He pauses, and in the moment I have no idea how he plans to complete the sentence. "You'd better remember every last detail and then tell me *everything* tomorrow. The fate of Marilyn Manizer rests in your hands." He stares at me intensely, his finger still raised. "Is that clear?"

"Seriously, Zach—" I start to protest, but he puts up his hand, turns his head, and walks away.

At the end of the day, I race back to my desk from the bathroom, where I've just spent fifteen minutes reapplying my face and blending lipstick colors. I am simultaneously trying to slip into my coat, pack my bag, and log out of my computer, when

I notice an instant message from Zach popped up while I was away from my desk.

> Zippo: i went home, but you should check www.spineyechidna.com/marilynmanizer before you go. hope your green curry is as hot as marilyn's . . .

With a twinge of exasperation, I click on the link. And when the Marilyn strip unfurls, I see that Zach has decided not to wait for me to tell him everything tomorrow. He's gone ahead and made his own assumptions.

In the first box, Marilyn Manizer is dashing from an office building, and checking over her shoulder. She is carrying a briefcase with the On Target logo, and wearing a trench coat and dark glasses with her hair pulled back in a schoolmarm bun. In the next box, she is running fast down the street having just tossed her briefcase over her shoulder (it's still flying through the air). With one hand she is reaching to undo her bun, and with the other she reaches for the belt on her trench coat. A sexy cone-shaped bra points through the opening of her coat. Her thought bubble reads: "Never a %*$#@ cab when you need one!" In the third box Marilyn is standing inside a lavishly decorated Asian-style restaurant—a large elephant statue, palm trees, and a pagoda are in the background. Her hair cascades in waves to her shoulders, her cone boobs are heaving. One of her arms is extended behind her as she hands her trench coat to a waiter. Her other arm is extended before her, her hand being kissed by a man wearing a Russian officer's uniform with big buttons, epaulets, and a big fur hat.

Marilyn says: "Why, Baron von Town Car, what a big fur hat you have!" In the last box, Marilyn and the Baron are sitting at a table with candles and a champagne bottle, leaning in close to each other. Their eyes are closed and their lips are practically touching, as their flute glasses clink in a toast. Under the table, his hand rests on her leg and her foot is wrapped around his calf. The Baron says: "Heer eez to heeting the target, yes?"

*   *   *

"I was scattered of the brain today," Vlad explains holding the door to the restaurant open for me, "and I did not think even to check if the conference room was free tonight. It is only when I hear the directors are having dinner in the office—and getting catered from French place across the street—that I find out. And I find it unacceptable that the directors have business dinner with delicious French food and not me," he adds, smiling, "so I thought we come here instead."

We walk down the red-carpeted spiral staircase of Brasserie 8½, a chic midtown restaurant just a few blocks from Vlad's office. My phone at Trees had rung just as I was putting on my coat to leave, and it was Vlad explaining the conference room snafu, did I mind meeting here? I'd agreed right away and then looked up abruptly, half expecting Zach to be hanging over the side of my cubicle, overhearing me say, "Oh, Brasserie 8½ sounds great, Vlad!"

The whole way over to the restaurant, I tried to ignore the funny quiver of anticipation in my stomach. It strikes me as odd that Vlad wouldn't have done a routine check of the conference room schedule—he's so organized. It doesn't seem like him to have simply forgotten.

The bottom of the staircase opens into a bar area carpeted in the same red, and I see the white tablecloths of the dining room beyond that. As we sit down, I get a view of the whole restaurant, which looks full and has the palpable electricity of a room just warming up. I look up at Vlad as I smooth the napkin across my lap.

"This is a great choice of venue," I say with a smile. "Do you come here for business meetings?"

"No, I have not before come here, actually. It is so close to the office, and I have always been meaning to try. I thought tonight a good opportunity to kill the birds with one stone."

I smile again and nod, delighted—even excited—not to be sitting under the cold glare of the conference room's fluorescent lights. I haven't sat across from a man at a table with linens in a while, and I suppress the urge to giggle with pleasure. The waiter has already brought us water and bread, and he returns to ask us if we are ready to order. Vlad gestures to me and smiles. "I'll have the mixed greens to start with and then the grilled tuna," I say, closing my menu and handing it to the waiter.

"And I will have the winter squash soup and . . ." Vlad trails off, still looking down at the menu. "I am undecided between the monkfish bouillabaisse and the lamb chop." He looks up at the waiter. "The lamb comes with the saffron potatoes, which do seem so delicious to me . . . what do you think?"

"*Definitely* the lamb then," says the waiter with a conspiratorial smile.

"All right, the lamb it is."

"And would you like some wine? Have you had a chance to look at our list?"

"Just a bottle of Pellegrino, please."

"All right, then," the waiter replies with what looks like a tight smile to me, briskly removing the wine and cocktail menu and probably wondering why every other couple here tonight—even the male couples clearly here for business—is ordering drinks and not us. I'm a little disappointed, too, although it's absurd of me to have expected that we'd be drinking wine when we have two 300-word personal statements to review.

Vlad reaches into his briefcase and takes out a manila file folder marked WHARTON, opens it on the table, and sorts through some papers until he finds the edited essay draft I'd e-mailed him earlier in the day. He scans it in silence, looking absorbed, occasionally running his finger along the paper. I nibble at a strip of focaccia, peering out at the muted activity in the rest of the room. All the red carpet and heavy tablecloths lend an intimate feel to the whole space.

"Yes, I very much agree, Rachel." Vlad says eventually. "You are right when you say I must change the central focus and do more with the leadership aspect," Vlad says, still examining the paper. "But I see here you cut the paragraph where I describe the hard conditions of working in Kunda in the winter. And yet it seems to make better case for the good leadership if there are some details of the hardness of the place, the difficulty in motivating people, no?"

I am about to reply when the waiter arrives with our appetizers. He sets down a large plate with a pile of elegantly arranged arugula in front of me and a bowl of thick pumpkin-colored soup in front of Vlad.

"Those details are really evocative," I agree, "but that story about your efforts to raise money for the new docks just says it all—it's pure leadership." I think I see Vlad blushing in the dim light, although it might also be a flush from his hot soup.

"You are kind, but I think you also make good sense," Vlad says, with a nod and a small grin. "But I am very awkward. I suggest the restaurant and then I do not let you eat while I have already started. Please," he adds, gently taking the papers from me and sliding them under his plate.

"But as you saw on the other essay," I say, feeling as though I should continue to play along with the pretense of work so he can have the excuse to change the subject, "I had relatively few comments. Honestly, Vlad, it was an impressive revision."

"Yes, actually, Ray-chelle, I had a few questions about that one," Vlad replies, as he continues sipping his soup. He looks up with a pensive expression, his spoon in midair. "I am worried about the way my ambitions sound here on paper—the idea of going back to Estonia to help shape the emerging shipping industry—I am worried they have too much grandiosity, no?"

His 'no?' catches me midbite, just as I'm shoveling in a large tangle of green leaves. I keep my eyes turned down and raise my hand to my mouth, nodding gingerly and smiling a little as I chew rapidly. I can feel myself blushing. I raise my finger and look up as I swallow to indicate that I'm almost done. Vlad waits patiently for me to finish. "No, I don't think so at all. Given what you've already accomplished, and all the hard work you've done along the way, they sound like a natural next step. Ambitious, sure, impressive, yes, but also very logical." The waiter reaches in front of us to clear our plates. "To me," I add with a smile as I lean back in my chair, "it really reflects the Vlad I've come to know."

Vlad nods politely. "Thank you."

"Don't thank me, it's true." I smile, leaning forward a little and lacing my fingers together on the table.

Vlad nods again. The waiter sets down our entrées. I take a bite of the creamy asparagus risotto accompanying my tuna.

"Oh, Vlad, this is *delicious!*" I almost purr, my eyes widening.

"Yes, mine is quite excellent, too. Especially the saffron potatoes. I have made the right decision. If only these choices were as important to getting into the business school as the other ones!" He laughs, opening up the manila folder again.

An hour later, when the waiter comes back to check for the third time if we're still working on our entrées, we finally tell him to take away the plates. We've slowly made our way through my comments on both essays, and Vlad has been taking notes on a legal pad with a heavy felt-tip pen. He has put the drafts and the manila folder back into his attaché case, and he is flipping through the yellow notebook pages now, about to put that away, too.

"Would you like to look at our dessert menu?" the waiter interrupts. I look to Vlad for a cue, hoping he'll prolong the evening now that the work is done. *A little molten chocolate cake, a little after-dinner drink at the bar . . .*

"Surely you are very tired, Ray-chelle, I do not want to keep you any longer after the long day."

"Well, um . . ." I stammer, already picturing us clinking utensils over the warm chocolate dessert. "I'm up for whatever you are," I finish off, still expectant.

"Perhaps we shall call it night, then," he says, looking up at the waiter with a courteous smile. "Although I am sure the desserts are excellent like everything else this evening. Just the check, please."

Oh. Oh well. That's not the response I'd been anticipating, but I understand if he doesn't want to seem overbearing. That would be out of character. After all, earlier today, I was expecting to be home surfing eBay in my sweats by this hour, ignoring the heartburn from the Thai delivery food, and thinking ahead to the rest of the night's On Target work left to do. But instead, I had a delightful surprise of an evening out—and a surprise that I cannot believe was entirely unplanned. This meeting with Vlad felt different. There's been a different energy. But that he wouldn't want to compromise our working relationship only reaffirms everything I'm getting to know about him.

Calling it a night now just avoids blurring the lines, and it's exactly what I would expect of Vlad.

29

The phone is ringing, it's 6:27 P.M., and I know it's Sanjay
calling.

Shit.

Shit. Shit. Shit. Shit. Shit.

The worst of it? It's my fault.

In fairness, I did not miss Sanjay's deadline because I've
been slacking off. I missed Sanjay's deadline because there
simply aren't enough hours in the day. I was up editing essays
until 4:40 A.M. last night, arrived at Trees by 9 o'clock this
morning, and have been trying to figure out how to explain
why the D+ Sanjay received in junior year Econometrics
shouldn't damn his candidacy to Stanford. I've been doing this
while editing a document on the uses of a Toluene Degrader in

bioremediation. But the problem—aside from Toluene-degrading bacteria's inability to work effectively without oxygen—is that I'm so exhausted *I* am not able to work effectively, either. And before being able to get back to rationalizing Sanjay's bad grade in articulate essay form, the day slipped away.

I'd promised him the draft by 6 P.M. today, so it's actually twenty-six minutes and thirty seconds later than I expected him to call. When I answer, Sanjay says, "Rachel . . . um?"

It's the "Um . . . ?" of disappointment. The "Um . . . ?" that says, *I paid you a lot of money so that when we agreed you'd deliver an essay by 6 P.M. on a certain day, by 6 P.M. on that day, I'd have that essay.* It's the "Um . . . ?" before the storm.

"Sanjay, I'm sorry," I interject quickly. "I—"

I pause, wondering what the best explanation is in this situation. Should I say that I've asked my partner to take a look at the essay and he hasn't gotten back to me yet? Should I tell him I broke both of my arms and haven't been able to type as quickly as I expected? "I'm simply not finished with it yet," I admit, too tired to come up with anything more ornate yet plausible.

"Rachel, I thought we agreed—"

"I know, I know," I interrupt. There's still a fair amount of time before the application is actually due at the school, but he has every right to be angry. "I promised you this essay tonight, and I feel terrible that I wasn't able to deliver. It will only be a short delay, but I understand that it's not what we agreed," I add, thinking quickly, "so, I'd like to refund you $200 and get that essay to you first thing tomorrow morning if that's acceptable to you."

"Well," Sanjay replies, not sounding all that pleased, "I guess that's okay. I mean I probably couldn't have looked at it before then anyway. I'm getting slammed here at work," he says.

"I can imagine," I reply, imagining easily.

"I appreciate your wanting to make things right, Rachel."

"That's how we like to handle things at On Target," I say, breathing for what feels like the first time in the entire conversation.

When I hang up with Sanjay, I put my head down on my desk. *I am in such deep doo-doo.* Obviously I'll stay awake as late as necessary tonight to finish the job for Sanjay, but I just don't know how I'm going to be able to keep up this pace for the rest of my clients. I'm so worn out I'm feeling nauseous, and the bulk of the final application deadlines is now rapidly approaching. Missing *any* of these deadlines would be— scratch that, IS—utterly and completely not even conceivable. Not only would that spell the quick death of On Target Essay, but if I were the cause of anyone missing a school's final due date, thus disqualifying them from admission before they've even applied, I might have to flee for Brazil. I have no idea how I'm going to get everything done.

I open a new e-mail to write a message to Zach, and I've just typed LANDSLIDE in the subject line when I hear my name spoken behind me.

"Rachel?" Molly says. "Can I speak to you for a moment?"

"Sure, of course, what's up?" I spin around in my chair to face her.

"Let's take a walk." She nods. When Molly forces a smile a beat later, I know that what awaits me is not going to be a surprise party in the conference room.

As we start walking down the hall toward her office, I can almost hear the opera soundtrack playing in the background. This is the cinematic moment when the deep baritone voice and the wailing violins build up to a terrifying crescendo, right before the spray of bullets, the shattering of glass, and the slow-motion pan over the gaping mouths silently shrieking the word "NOOOOOOOOOOOOO!"

Molly holds open the door of her office, and I sit in the chair by her desk, the same chair where I sat as she greeted and indoctrinated me on my first day at Trees. She doesn't speak until she sits down, and it gives me a moment to look out at the brilliant Manhattan skyline for what I know is going to be the last time from this viewpoint. I can see through the bare tree branches to the top of Central Park and the barely visible miniature skaters gliding around Wollman Rink. All along the western and eastern edges of the park, the flickering evening lights make the rows of tall residential buildings glitter like necklaces.

"Rachel," Molly finally says, "I know from the work you've done that you're a very intelligent, curious young woman."

Oh, that's nice, I think. *Now get to it. I've got work to do.*

"But it seems like you haven't been able to give Trees your full attention recently." She folds her hands together.

Nope, can't argue with that. Which reminds me, on Sanjay's essay, I still haven't figured out how I'm going to explain—

"And because what we do here is so personal to many of us, we really do hope that the people working here will come to feel as personally invested in the projects as we do, that attention to every detail comes to matter to you as much as it does to us. I know that's a lot to ask, but we really feel strongly that it's indispensable. So I think it's probably best for all concerned if you start looking for another job—"

Even though Molly continues talking, I've stopped processing. Because what she's just said has given me the way into Sanjay's essay: *Because I was intellectually curious in college, I often took on too many challenges. I was not as focused as I should have been, and in indulging my curiosity, I occasionally sacrificed efficiency. In the ensuing years however, I've realized the value of taking on professional and intellectual pursuits more selectively and investing myself in every detail as fully and personally as the founders of the company themselves.*

I smile at Molly when she gives a final nod. "I understand," I say. The truth is, I don't blame her. "I'm only sorry it didn't work out better." I stand to leave, raring to run back to my computer and transcribe my inspiration for Sanjay's essay before it dissipates.

But Molly rises as well, blocking my exit. "You know, Rachel, we'd love it if you kept in touch with us."

"Okay, sure," I reply, but *get real* is what I'm thinking. I walk back to my desk and quickly type an e-mail to Zach.

To: Zippo@trees.org
Subject: How are you?

I'm fired. Just got canned like charlie tuna. Molly was nice—am doing fine—honestly I think it's a blessing. Leaving the office now, drowning in On Target stuff, call you when I come up for air. xox, R

I assume Zach has already left for the day, so I don't bother waiting for a reply. The last thing I intend to do right now is sit around and mull the fact that I've just lost another job. I need to keep moving. I need to stay productive. I need to finish Sanjay's fucking essay on why he was such a dumbass in college before I wind up refunding him any more money.

When I get home, I close my bedroom door and get down to business. First, I finish Sanjay's work and e-mail it to him. Then, I prioritize my other clients' individual deadlines, create a timetable for the evening's must-complete-by-tonight list, draft another must-complete-by-tomorrow-night list, and a third can-push-it-to-next-Wednesday list.

It turns out that not having to go to Trees the next morning is a godsend. I didn't have the courage to quit the job myself, because I was simply too scared to let go. Who knows what will happen with On Target after all these clients? Who knows if all these clients will even pay me? Who knows if I *won't* break both arms and both legs and be unable to type with either my fingers or my toes? But by being *let* go, the problem was solved for me. With last night's seven glorious hours of sleep, I'm already feeling immensely better and finally firing on all cylinders. I can give my clients the full attention they deserve. By 2 P.M. I've checked off a substantial number of items on today's to-do list. And by 3 o'clock, feeling a little bit like a rock star, I take a break. I pick up the phone and dial Zach's number at the office.

"Zach Stevenson," he answers.

"Hello, Zach Stevenson, Rachel Chambers."

"Rachel! How *are* you? I got your e-mail this morning when I came in and wanted to call you right away to see how you were doing, but it sounded like you're crazy busy—and I know you have deadlines—so I didn't want to bother you, even though I wanted to see how you're holding up and tell you that I fully intend to graffitti Molly's entire office tonight with those aerosol cans of spray cheese." He says all this without taking a breath.

"It's okay." I laugh, envisioning Zach on the anti-Molly anti-eco-terrorist caper. "You don't have to destroy the ozone layer for me. Although it would be a lovely gesture."

"Seriously, though, are you okay?"

"Yeah." I nod. "I'm honestly and truly okay with it."

"Truly?"

"Honestly."

Zach seems to take this in for a moment. "Because I'd be more than happy to march into Molly's office right now and demand she give you your job back," he says. "Or, if that didn't work, I'd also be happy to beg, plead, or cajole. I'm very good in the cajoling department."

I know Zach would actually do it, too. "Yes, I see you as an expert cajoler. But really," I reply, "the timing of this is actually perfect. Right now I need the time for On Target clients, so it's completely for the best. And how frequently in life do you get the chance to say that, huh?"

"Okay," he says. "Is there anything I can do, though?"

"Hmm," I pause, considering his offer. "Yes, actually there is."

"Name it."

"See if you can do something about this space-time continuum business, would you? My deadlines are approaching *way* too fast, and being bound by this whole time thing is seriously cramping my style."

"Yeah, okay, I'll get right to work on that." Zach laughs. "In fact, I can almost see it now, 'Marilyn Manizer in *A Girl for All Time: Adventures in Slo-Lo-Comotion.*"

*   *   *

By the end of the evening, I've managed to complete all the day's deadlines and send out all the expected drafts and edits, so when the phone rings at 9 p.m., I know the caller isn't phoning to yell at me. I even feel a quick flash of hope that it might be Vlad calling to inquire if I'd like to unplug with him again this evening. Because the answer to that would be, "Why yes, comrade, I'd love to unplug together."

I look at myself in the mirror for a moment then dive for the phone. "Hello?" I say, trying to maintain a professional yet sultry tone.

"Rachel," Kate replies, her voice sounding congested. "Barbara just called me—Dad." She pauses, and I hear three rapid, sharp breaths. "Rachel, Dad passed away about an hour ago."

*   *   *

The funeral takes place a few days later at the same site where my mother was buried more than fifteen years ago. Dad always took us there on Mom's birthday and on Christmas Eve, so the sight of the large headstone feels familiar. Her name and dates are inscribed on one side of it, the other side remains blank. I know the next time I come to visit, Dad's name will be inscribed on the headstone, too, and that's the small detail I focus on during the funeral. It's remarkably odd to be standing here without Dad standing next to me, and during the burial I keep having the urge to look around for him, even as I stare at the headstone awaiting his name.

Ultimately, Dad died quickly and unexpectedly. Barbara had taken him to the hospital because his leg had become swollen and red and was causing him unbearable pain. In the emergency room, he became short of breath and suddenly started having severe chest pain. It turned out to be a pulmonary embolism, and in just a few minutes, he was gone. The pain in his legs had been caused by blood clots, which broke apart and traveled to his lungs. Barbara didn't even have time to call us before it was over.

Kate, Michael, the girls, and I stay in Dad's house for the week. In between greeting Dad's friends and colleagues who stop by, helping Barbara get rid of the home hospice equipment, and the unpredictable breakdowns that sweep over me as I wash dishes, or climb the stairs, or check the mail, I sit at my computer and I work.

I channel my energy into other people's lives, and with my red editing pen I make their lives better. I restructure years of their experience, and I fine-tuned their stories. The work is mind-numbing, and I don't know how I would have gotten through the days without it. It gives me something to focus on outside myself. It's work I feel certain I'll always equate with my father and with this miserable time, and I just need to get through it. I owe it to my angel investor.

*   *   *

When I land in New York, Zach is waiting for me at the airport.

"Hey," I say, when I see him standing in the baggage claim area. I'd called him on my way to Minnesota and told him what happened. He asked me to keep in touch—told me to call anytime—and said I should let him know when I was coming back to New York.

"C'mere," he says, opening his arms and encircling me in a bear hug. "How are you?"

"I'm okay," I say, nodding, desperately trying to prevent myself from crying. "Thanks for coming." It's a line I've been saying all week, but it's the first time I really mean it.

"Of course," Zach replies, picking up and shouldering the

garment bag I point to that's making its way around the bag-gage carousel.

"That one's actually not mine. I just thought it might have some cool stuff in it," I say and smile, letting Zach know it's okay for him to smile, too.

"I'm glad you're back," he says.

"Yeah." I nod. "Me, too."

30

"Hello?" I answer fearfully. I roll over and look at the clock—it's 12:25 A.M. It's been two weeks since Dad died, and I'm still expecting bad news every time the phone rings late at night.

"Hi, is this Rachel?" a woman's voice asks pleasantly.

"Yes it is—who's this?"

"Hi there, Rachel, it's Jessica Tucker. Am I catching you at a bad time?" Jessica Tucker, the asset management twit from Bear Stearns.

"Hello, Jessica," I reply in a low, controlled voice, "it is a little late. Is something wrong?"

"Well, actually, yes," Jessica responds matter-of-factly, not sounding remotely apologetic. "It's about this most recent essay that we've been working on for the Harvard app. I thought your edits were insightful, and your suggestions for tweaking the structure were fine. The essay, as such, was really quite passable. But, you know, I've actually rethought the whole focus of the question, and I've completely rewritten it. So it's essentially a whole new essay, and I think it's *much* better. You'll see. I wanted to let you know that I've just e-mailed it to you and I'd like you to take a look at it, if you could." Her last sentence is clearly not a question.

Jessica is applying to only three business schools, Wharton, Harvard, and Stanford—the Holy Trinity. She treats every single essay as a religious rite of perfectionism, as though the very effort of fiddling with every sentence of every paragraph at least three or four times would imbue the essay with all the fervor she brings to her mission to get into business school. Whatever changes I make, she'll change them again. She has been my most high-maintenance client from the start—Dad and I used to call her my girlfriend—and I'm silently gnashing my teeth as she speaks.

"I'll be *happy* to take a look at it tomorrow, Jessica," I say with the forced politeness owed to a Full-Service Package, Express Rate–paying client.

"Well, I know it is late, and I do apologize about that. But I'm leaving tomorrow afternoon for a business trip to Kansas City, and as you and I planned," she replies with a forced laugh, "we *would* like to get this Harvard application mailed out by January 3rd, which is tomorrow."

"Yes, that was the original plan," I acknowledge, making silent sneering faces.

"So maybe you could have a quick look at this last essay tonight, and do a little editing, although I do feel confident that it's in good shape. I'd like to be able to review it first thing when I get in tomorrow morning—I don't get in before eight-thirty, as you know—and then I can have my assistant do all that formatting, and I can drop the whole application in the mail myself, on my way to the airport," Jessica explains. I can practically hear her grinning with the anticipation of person-ally licking, sealing, and mailing her completed application, delivering it to the postmaster general, like some spiritual of-fering. There is no point in proposing any alternative options to the Jessica Tucker Plan.

"I understand," I reply. "I'll be sure to have a look at it, note any comments, and send it back to you by tomorrow morning at eight. Have a safe trip, Jessica, and get in touch if you have any other concerns." No doubt she'll take me at my word.

"Thank you, Rachel, I will. Good night. We'll be in touch tomorrow!" she says, signing off with a little high-pitched cheer. Rah-rah.

I sigh with exaggerated exasperation purely for my own benefit and then throw off the covers. Resisting the tempta-tion to punch my monitor, I turn on the computer as I tie my bathrobe and wait for the machine to churn to life. I don't blame it, I don't want to start up, either. I retrieve Jessica's new essay and start reading it, trying not to let resentment cloud my editorial judgment. The previous one, excruciat-ingly reworked multiple times, was a lot better. But if she wants to use this new essay, then I'll make it the most work-able it can be.

About an hour and a half later, I've finished. But I'm also wide awake. While I'm up, I figure I may as well get some other tasks out of the way. A lot of work has accumulated since I returned from Minnesota. Work had been my numbing solace while I was there, but since getting back, I've had a hard time concentrating. My daily spreadsheets—Zach taught me how to use Excel, so my handwritten checklists are now computer-generated grids—never look like they're any closer to completion.

I get a bowl of Froot Loops and a Coke from the kitchen and set up shop. I draw up a bill for Sergei Malakoff—one of Vlad's friends, who opted for a Full-Service Package for his five applications, which means I've been heavily rewriting the fifteen or so essays involved in the process. Like Jessica, I'm charging him what looks like a lot of money but also investing a huge amount of time. I send an e-mail to Daniel Curtiss, a client acquired from the NYU marketing session, proposing a few possible meeting times this week. Then I get online to find out more about a school in California I've never heard of where another client is applying. When I glance at the time, it's 3:15. I sigh again, this time just from fatigue.

*   *   *

The next morning, I begin an endless On Target Essay endurance test. I complete one assignment after another, moving methodically through the ocean of tasks like a giant tanker cutting through water. I answer only On Target Essay–related calls and e-mails and emerge from my room only to refill my cereal bowl, brew some more coffee, and occasionally shower if I have a meeting with a client. But even those have diminished, because nearly every client has at least a few applications with a January 10 deadline, so that by this phase of the application process, the discussion sessions are done and the rewriting and editing takes place electronically. I can hear Christy walking by and pausing in front of my room, probably putting her ear to the door and listening, probably wondering if I haven't been handcuffed to the bed. *Hey, it happens,* I can almost see her saying.

In the early evening of the fourth day of the work marathon, I'm about to pick up the phone and order a turkey sandwich to be delivered from the deli across the street when my cell phone rings. I've been screening, taking only calls from Kate, Aunt Barbara, or numbers that belong to On Target clients. This number's area code is not familiar, so I assume it's from a client's cell phone.

"Hello, this is Rachel," I answer.

"Ray-chelle, hello. It is Vladimir."

"Vlad! Hi!" I say, completely thrown. "I guess you're still in Houston?" Vlad's applications had been all finished, polished, and posted before I'd even gone to Minnesota for the funeral. We had structured our deadlines specifically to finish Vlad's work well before he left on an extended business trip in January. I had completely forgotten he was out of town. In fact, I hadn't thought much about him at all since Dad died.

"Yes. We are still in negotiations here. Perhaps the cowboys do not understand my accent, for it is clear that we have not reached understanding. It looks like we will be here through the weekend, too."

"It's probably the reverse, Vlad—it's the cowboys who talk with that silly accent that no one from up north can understand. And Estonia *is* pretty far up north." I hear him chuckle softly.

"I have good news. I called in to my secretary this morning to get my messages. She has been opening the mail while I am gone, and there was a response from INSEAD which arrived today," he says. "And I have been accepted!"

INSEAD is a business school just outside of Paris I hadn't even known existed before helping Vlad apply. It is a mecca for the ambitious Euroset and one of his top choices.

"That's fantastic! Congratulations!" I exclaim, feeling a real rush of pleasure, the first in I can't remember how long. I'm proud of Vlad. And excited for me: This is On Target Essay's first acceptance!

Vlad doesn't miss a beat. "Thank you, and congratulations to the On Target Essay, Rachel. Does this mean I get the prize for being the company's first acceptance of the year?"

How about the prize for the first acceptance ever?

"You certainly do, Vlad! You've been a model client, and I'm so pleased for all of us—for you and for On Target."

"And I am very grateful to you, Rachel. Your help has been of the invaluable. It has made all the difference, and I am calling to thank you. But I would also like to show thank you, so perhaps we can have glass of champagne to celebrate, when I return?"

"That would be lovely, Vlad. I'd be honored."

"I hope to conclude here soon and return to New York over the weekend. How is the Sunday evening for a toast?"

"Let me check . . ." I say, flipping through my spreadsheets for the next few days. This reminds me of Vlad's first phone call, that day just a few months ago when I was standing out on the terrace at Trees, pretending to flip through an imaginary Filofax before scheduling an orientation meeting. It was a lifetime ago. I glance over the grid of tasks scheduled for the next few days, and it looks like an endless expanse of boxes still to check off. Sunday is January 8, two days before applications are due for most of my other clients. Theoretically, I should have the bulk of the big editorial work done by the 7th, with the 8th and 9th reserved for final adjustments and any unexpected complications. I should actually be able to take a break on the 8th. If things stay on schedule. Which has rarely been the case, if you factor in Jessica Tucker special requests, Sergei Malakoff's ineptitude, and the general run of my luck.

But I desperately need something to look forward to, an oasis at the end of the crossing. And I suddenly find myself really wanting to see Vlad, as though some buried urge has resurfaced all at once. I will make it work.

"Sunday evening looks great, Vlad . . . I really look forward to it."

*   *   *

Vlad e-mails on Sunday morning and suggests meeting at the Bubble Lounge, a champagne bar in Tribeca, at 9 o'clock. When I get the e-mail, I'm wearing the same clothes I slept in the night before, which are also the same sweatshirt and leggings I wore the day before that. My hair, in its ponytail, is limp with desperation, and at some point in the past few days, I'd quit returning the coffee mugs to the kitchen, so I have a collection of dirty cups scattered around my computer, on my night table, on the dresser. The wrinkled and ink-marked spreadsheets for the past ten days are tacked up on the wall above my desk, covering the whole surface of one side of the room, and I'm still checking boxes off on the last one, posted on the far right, above my dresser. The finish line is in sight, but I've hit the wall. I'm struggling. Since early this morning, when I first woke up, I've been checking my watch spasmodically, every five minutes, hyper-conscious of the passing time. I'm restless and on edge. But when I see Vlad's e-mail address pop up in my inbox, my stomach flutters, and I can feel a grin spreading across my tired face.

Glancing at my clock later, at 7:40 P.M., I feel another little thrill of anticipation. I'd promised myself I would shut down my computer and close shop for the evening at 7:45, which would leave me forty-five minutes to shower and get ready before leaving the house. The hot water in the shower feels more reviving than a shower's felt in weeks. I put on and take off two entire outfits and then discover the perfect dress in the back of my closet. I take the iridescent de-puffing eye gel from the fridge and dab it under my eyes and then go rooting in my makeup case for a new Benefit liquid blush I'd bought weeks ago and never opened. Finally, as I run out of the apartment, I stop briefly in front of the hall mirror. Despite the winter gloom and the cumulative stress of the past several weeks, I seem to have created something approximating the dewy cheeks and bright eyes that had sold me on the blush and the gel.

The wood-and-glass door of the Bubble Lounge swings shut behind me, and I paw at the heavy velvet curtain hanging on the other side of the entrance that keeps out the blasting cold. I am walking in a pair of teetering pumps, the obvious choice for an icy December night with a wind chill factor of ten below. Underneath my heavy shearling coat, I'm wearing a wraparound dress in a black silk knit. I'd bought it last summer at a Diane von Furstenberg sample sale, but only cut the tags off tonight as I slipped it over my shoulders, pulling, wrapping, and tying practically at the same time.

I walk through the parted fabric into a lofty space of exposed brick walls and vintage-looking chairs and sofas upholstered in velvet. The high ceilings are made of pressed tin, and the parquet floor is covered with fraying rugs strewn here and there. The light is dim and comes mostly from the flickering candles on the low wooden coffee tables. The lounge is close to Wall Street and attracts a moneyed thirty-something date crowd. It's a warm, shabby-chic vibe, carried by the music of a jazz trio playing softly in a far corner. I scan the small crowd, looking for Vlad's wavy blond hair. When I spot him in a corner, I can feel the color rising in my cheeks.

I walk across the glowing room toward the low-slung easy chair where Vlad is sitting comfortably, a champagne bottle resting in a silver ice bucket set on the coffee table before him. As I approach his corner, I think about all the weeks of drudgery and deadlines, of sadness and stress. But tonight is a celebration of a job well done. It's also the conclusion of our working relationship, and hopefully an evening when our professional formalities can finally be abandoned.

"Ray-chelle, hello! It is so wonderful to see you," he says, standing.

"Hey, Vlad!" I reply, leaning in to give him a congratulatory kiss on the cheek. I peel off my scarf and coat and sit down in the easy chair next to his. The air feels chilly against the skin exposed by the deep V-neckline of the dress.

"You look very elegant tonight, Ray-chelle. It is so nice of you to come and have the celebration."

"Of course!" I say, touching my hand to my chest, making sure the knit dress is still wrapped where it should be. "I wouldn't miss the chance to toast you—and us. I was so excited when you called—I've been looking forward to this evening ever since!"

Whoa, easy princess.

I reach for one of the champagne flutes Vlad's just filled and take a gulp. Then I look up and smile sheepishly, realizing I should have waited to make a toast before drinking.

Vlad doesn't seem to have noticed or is pretending not to. He holds up his glass, and I follow suit. "I wish to make a toast to you, Ray-chelle, for your hard work and your astute comments. Always, you were at the ready to assist me with the bad English and the clumsy ideas. Without your help I could not have done such good applications. This INSEAD success is our success together," he concludes, smiling broadly. I smile back. We clink glasses and take a sip. The dense champagne bubbles feel velvety gliding down my throat. I take a few more sips and then Vlad reaches over with the bottle to top off my glass.

"And there is something else I would like to tell you, Ray-chelle—and to toast to," Vlad says, putting the bottle back in the ice bucket. I look Vlad in the eyes, raising my eyebrows and blinking once slowly, a deliberately demure reaction that completely belies the racing in my chest. "Ray-chelle," he begins, "perhaps you suspect this, or perhaps you do not . . ." He pauses and peers into his champagne.

"What's that?" I ask with excruciating calm that demands all my self-restraint.

"Well," he goes on, looking up again, "from the beginning with On Target Essay I have felt that . . . that we have quite a special relationship, yes?"

I nod.

"I have felt that perhaps I was not quite like the other clients, that there was something different."

"I think that's true," I say encouragingly, with a bright look. My heart may as well have fists, it's pounding so impatiently against my chest. And even as the words are coming out of Vlad's mouth, I try hard not to let myself anticipate what he's going to say. I keep myself restrained in the moment, I concentrate on reigning in my racing thoughts. I am trying to suspend all expectation even though I know exactly what I would like to hear him say.

"Well, I want *you* to know that *I* have known from the beginning—and you must correct me if I am wrong . . ." He looks at me and smiles, trailing off as though trying to gauge his timing. "I have known from the beginning that I was the On Target Essay first client ever."

My heart suddenly stops pounding, and I can feel my face go slack. Prickles of heat explode under my arms and in between my breasts like hundreds of hot needles. I try not to let any of this show, but I doubt I'm successful and I don't really care. I don't care if Vlad sees that I'm embarrassed, I just don't want him to know what I'm embarrassed—mortified and upset—about. I put down my champagne glass, force a little smile, and reach up to brush my bangs out of my eyes. My fingers feel cold and clammy against my flushed forehead.

"You did? You knew?"

"Yes, I did," Vlad replies, chuckling. "I did suspect, yes. The posters on the street, the uncertainty with the prices for the services." He laughs out loud and shakes his head, as though reminiscing about a fond memory.

"But then why? Why did you stick with me if you knew?"

"At first I was simply curious, yes? On the posters, it seems to offer all that I was looking for. And I was so impressed after the first interview and with how you understand the things I was trying to say from the very beginning."

I'm just staring at him now, my face blank, my eyes occasionally blinking.

"I could see that you were trying hard, so very hard, and it seems clear to me that things were going to grow quickly for you. Sometimes I felt as though I saw opportunities in you and the On Target that perhaps you even did not see."

"That's probably true," I say in a low voice, trying hard

not to think about other things Vlad might have seen through.

"I felt as though it was almost my secret, to know of this potential. Perhaps to help it a little bit. And to have been the first!" Vlad adds triumphantly, holding up his glass as though to toast again. "It is the hope of every businessman to discover valuable resource first."

"Well, you've been a true friend then, Vlad," I say, holding up my glass, too, making an excruciating effort not to sound as deflated as I feel.

"No, no, I did no favors, Ray-chelle—I have merely been wise consumer. It was about making good business decision. And we are here tonight to celebrate the payoff of this smart investment." He smiles broadly, like a proud papa, and reaches for the bottle to top off our glasses again.

Here, here.

I spend the rest of the evening getting drunk. I feel utterly hollowed out and exhausted, too spent to do anything but continue to raise my glass to my lips and swallow. The view has changed dramatically, the oasis on the horizon has disappeared. I know what it must feel like to experience the dashed hope brought on by the delusions of fatigue and desert conditions: As bad off as you were before, it was better than the misery that follows the evaporation of your mirage. In the cab on the way home, as I think about what I have to do tomorrow, it looks just like today and yesterday, just as flat and arid and pointless.

31

I wake up the next morning just before noon and feel like I still need nine more hours of sleep. When I finally swing my legs out of bed, I discover my whole body is sore. Post-moving-day sore. That feeling of exhaustion in which every muscle aches separately and then in concert. I am trying hard not to focus on the embarrassment of last night, but it feels like it's registered in my body.

Tomorrow is January 10, which, since September I've been thinking of as D-Day, the climactic invasion and victory day. At this point, though, everything is surprisingly under control—the work, for the most part, has been delivered. As I shuffle to the kitchen for some orange juice, I'm not feeling the same feverish rush as the past few weeks, or even yesterday. Now I'm just waiting for the deadline to come and be done with.

I return from the kitchen with the morning's first dose of cereal and coffee and sit down at my desk to check my On Target e-mail to be sure no crises have arisen overnight. As I wait for the machine to awaken, I sort through the pile of opened mail by the side of the keyboard, to check—like I do every morning—if there's anything important that I can no longer put off dealing with. I see the invitation to Zach's gallery show that he sent last week. The invitation I keep meaning to respond to. I berate myself for the hundreth time for having still not RSVP'd. He sketched a caricature of my head on the envelope with a speech bubble reading, "I'll be there!" Since dropping me off at home from the airport, he's also been leaving regular messages on my voicemail and sending "Non-Urgent Just Checking In" e-mails that I read, smile at, then promise myself to find the time, as soon as possible, to write the reply that they deserve. But in the frenzied work routine that's overwhelmed the past two weeks, I still haven't yet. And with each successive voicemail and e-mail I feel even worse for not having replied, and even less inclined to deal with my snowballing guilt.

But now that the work-stream has finally abated, it's time to buy my way back into favor with Zach: blame it on the insanity of the past few weeks, beg forgiveness, and take him to lunch.

To: zippo@trees.org
Subject: wanna

have lunch? Yes, you'll be pleased to know that the swamp thing has finally resurfaced from her self-imposed exile. And perhaps you'll be pleasantly surprised to learn that despite certain stresses of late, and contrary to every natural instinct, she has *still* not sprayed, spread, or nuked any processed foods recently (excluding Kraft products). These days, she's eating by color group—this week is red—and she's wondering if you would care to join her for lunch tomorrow for a meager repast of radishes, marinara sauce, and Twizzlers. If you wish, you may bring a different color food. The possible answers are:

(a) I'll be there!

(b) I'll be there, but I'm bringing orange food!

(c) I'll be there with spray cheese on!

A few minutes later, he sends a reply.

To: rchambers@trees.org
Subject: RE: wanna

(c) I'll be there! But I'm bringing black food—red makes me look fat.

We agree to meet the next day at a small gourmet deli a block away from Trees, and Zach is already inside when I arrive.

"Hey, kid," he says with a smile as I approach. The last time I saw him, when I'd just returned from Minnesota, I'd been a fragile wreck, and the hug he'd given me at the airport had seemed like the obvious gesture. But today, with the weeks that have passed since we've seen each other, and under the harsh florescent lights of the deli, the right greeting seems a little less clear.

I'm no longer quite certain how I'm supposed to act around people anymore. Normal interaction just feels bizarre. And most people who've heard about Dad can't quite figure out how they're supposed to respond to me, either.

"Hey," I reply, opting for a quick nod, squeezing his elbow lightly. "I'm starving. Let's eat."

"Right," Zach says, pulling out his wallet. "And this one is on Trees, so feel free to order at least ten pounds of fancy lettuce from the salad bar."

I smile at Zach, thankful to him for replying with his usual Zach-like indifference to awkwardness. "I appreciate that," I say, "but now that I'm no longer an employee of Trees, I no longer feel morally compelled to consume vegetables."

"Yeah, good call. Veggies are for losers," he says, as we make our way over to the deli counter.

When we get to the seating section upstairs, I unwrap my sandwich and discover that the smoked turkey and pesto I thought I was getting is actually a grilled vegetable. "Awww man!" I exclaim. "It's been that kind of month, you know?"

"Here," Zach says, handing me his unwrapped roast beef sandwich and taking mine. "Trade ya."

"No, that's okay—I was just kidding about the moratorium on veggies. One should learn to love roasted peppers. It's a sign of maturity."

"Too late," he mumbles, taking a gigantic bite of the grilled vegetable sandwich and then grinning at me with bulging cheeks.

"Thank you." I nod at him. I unwrap his sandwich and take a bite out of the center of the thick stack of sliced rare meat. I can feel the sharp tang of horseradish tingling in my nose. "Zach, that invitation you sent me was fantastic," I say, after swallowing. "I feel bad that I've done such a terrible job of keeping up with things recently."

"Totally understood," he says, batting the question away with his hand.

"So how are preparations going for the show?"

"Pretty well. Most of the work has been hung, but there are still some details to take care of, and a few things might change as the other artists' work goes up."

"So are you excited? This is such a big moment," I say. I'm feeling oddly frustrated, trying to get beyond all his calmness and get at some nervous anticipation.

Zach makes a face and takes a bite of his sandwich. "I am excited. It's nice exposure for stuff I never thought would be seen anywhere outside my studio. Just being cautious, though. I don't want to count on any big breaks coming from all this, that's all."

"Okay," I reply. "But is there anything I can do to help to get the word out? I'm very good at putting up fliers, you know."

"Thanks, I think things are under control at this point. And I know you're really busy right now—it's that time of the year for all your clients, right?"

"Well, actually, things are finally winding down. All but a few of the applications I've taken on are pretty much done. If all goes according to plan, I'll be hitting Send on the final revision of the application season tomorrow, and I *can't wait*." I linger on the last two words lovingly, as a broad grin spreads across my face.

"And what happens after that?"

"I'll be taking down the shingle and calling it a season. In fact, I've decided I'm going to be taking it down for good."

"What do you mean?"

"I mean I'm done. Finished. Spent. On Target Essay will officially go out of business."

"What?" Zach asks, putting down his sandwich.

"It's not worth it to me to keep up this whole front of a business for the sake of a couple bucks," I reply.

"But *that's* not why you've been doing this. I mean that's not really what you mean, is it?"

"Zach, this whole thing has been crazy! It started on a lark, then before I knew it clients came gushing in and I just started swimming as fast as I could to keep up with it. And I don't know exactly how it happened, but now it's at the point where I've started getting e-mails from people looking to apply to business school next year, who want to book an editing package *now*. They want advice about when to get started and where to apply—as though I have any idea what the difference is between . . ." I pause, searching for two random business school names. "Kellogg and Tuck," I finally add, laughing. "Which, before a few months ago, I only knew as cereal and hemorrhoid pads. Frankly." I pause for a moment and then shrug. "Frankly, I just don't care."

"Are you kidding me?"

"Look, it was dumb luck that started this, and now I realize the smart move is to *stop* doing it before anyone actually gets wise to the scam. I'm just tired of the whole thing."

Zach looks unconvinced, as though waiting for an explanation. "Do you really believe you've just been some kind of master scammer this whole time? That it's just been a big game?" he finally asks. "Rachel, I designed your website, and I check it all the time. I see the number of hits you get every day. People you've done work for recommend you to other people. Those people come check it out. They're impressed by what they see and then they shell out big chunks of change to get in on it. That's not a scam, Rachel. That's a fully functional business."

"Oh, *please!*" I reply. "What would I really be giving up here by closing up shop? A 'business' consisting of marketing stunts, stressful deadlines, and a *lot* of hard work for a bunch of schmos with shitty syntax. I don't think I'm interested in pursuing this any further," I conclude, regaining my cool. "I just don't see the point."

"Okay." Zach nods, sounding clipped and businesslike. "But at least admit that if you're going to ditch this venture, you do so knowing that you're quitting a business that you launched and that took off. You supplied a product, people saw it, bought it, and then sold their friends on it, and now they're clamoring for more. That's called a success story."

"Well, thank you for this lecture on supply and demand, Professor Stevenson. It's been riveting, but I've never been a big fan of economics."

Zach ignores my interruption. "I don't get your attitude,

Rachel—maybe you just don't want to acknowledge your own potential. Or you're scared that this will turn you into something you don't envision yourself being, like a success."

"What are you talking about?" I ask, putting down my sandwich.

"I'm talking about how you've lost sight of something, Rachel. You've lost sight of yourself, and how you felt about this whole venture. Who cares where the initial idea for this business came from? The truth is that it's been something you've cared about from the minute you got that first phone call. And you've loved every minute of success. I know you've had a really rough time recently, and you have every right to take a break at this point, but don't pretend like you never cared. You *did*. And so did your father. Don't lie to yourself."

I cannot believe what I'm hearing. "I'm getting this speech from you? *You*?" I ask again. "Who are *you* to be giving me advice? Who are *you* to tell me how I think and what I *really* care about? What makes you think you have any idea what's right for me?"

"Because, Rachel, I see you for who you are. I see you as the person who took an initiative and ran with it. You've had some really terrible luck along the way, and things *have* been really tough. But don't let yourself be misled by a bad turn. Giving up is the easy way out, Rachel, and you'd be a fool to do it. You've got to quit quitting. Just look at what's in front of you," he adds, sounding exasperated.

"Yeah? Well what is in front of me, Zach, huh? Because all I see is some guy who lives in a world of cartoons and make-believe. If I'm not mistaken, your stock and trade is fantasy, so thanks for the condescending analysis of my situation, but if you don't mind, I'll take my advice from someone who's a little more rooted in reality."

I ball up my napkin, throw it on the table, and walk out.

I'm not going to let some guy—who's been all too happy to indulge in my misadventures—suddenly tell me that I'm being a fool. That I've missed the essential, that I'm deceiving myself! Lecturing me like I'm some underachieving high school fuck-up! *Quit being a quitter?* I'll just put that one on a bumper sticker.

*   *   *

These thoughts echo in my head as I jab hangers through the neck and armholes of the collection of clothing piled at the end of my bed. As soon as my laptop becomes visible beneath the diminishing mound of clothing, I know exactly how I'll spend the rest of the night, and I can't wait to see the four letters that will spell solace: e-B-a-y.

I made a bid on an art deco compact ten days ago, and it's now the final hour of the auction, so I intend to watch the clock run out on my winning tender. I click on the image of the compact to make it larger, eager to become reacquainted. Its cloisonné cover is especially pretty, with red enamel details, although its copper bottom half looks a little damaged. But I've never seen a piece quite like this one, and it'll make a nice addition to the collection. Apparently another bidder agrees and yesterday upped my bid by five dollars, bringing the price to twenty-five dollars. It's not a fantastic piece, but it's still reasonably priced for what it is. There are only fourteen minutes left in the auction, and I raise the bid three more dollars.

As I wait for the auction to end, I open another screen and log into my On Target Essay e-mail. There are several old messages I've been needing to answer. As I'd mentioned to Zach before he chose to deliver his rant, several people had e-mailed me within the past few weeks expressing interest in hiring On Target Essay for next year's application season. I'd replied to them all immediately—it was the professional thing to do—but informed them that I wouldn't be able discuss anything until after all deadlines had been met for this year's candidates. Now it was time for me to reply that, unfortunately, On Target Essay was not going to be able to help them out at all because On Target Essay was not going to be in operation next year. Hitting reply to JenGandt83, I start composing my valedictory.

> Dear Jen:
> Thanks again for your interest in On Target Essay. Unfortunately, however, On Target is not accepting future clients because . . .

Because why? Because "I'm tired" doesn't seem quite right. Because "I just don't care anymore," doesn't sit properly, either.

> Dear Jen:
> It was gratifying to hear that your friend, Jessica Tucker, was so satisfied with On Target Essay. And I'm extremely pleased

that she thought highly enough of the service to recommend
it to you. However, On Target Essay will not be operational
next year because . . .

Because "it turns out I came out of my trance and saw the
whole thing for the inane copyediting outfit that it is. So unless you can see the greater purpose in Excel spreadsheets and
brainstorming synonyms for *success* and *leadership*, I'm
afraid you're shit out of luck." But that doesn't work, either.

I reread Jen Gandt's e-mail to me: "Since Jessica is known
around the office as the perfectionist's perfectionist, and she
spoke so highly of the work you did with her, I know you must
be the best. I also know it's early to be discussing applications
for next year's season, but I wanted to be sure your client roster
hadn't closed." When I had read that two weeks ago, I laughed.
I was so exhausted, all I could think about was that Jessica was
the most high-maintenance, borderline psychotic person I'd ever
encountered. And even if her friend was only half the detail-
obsessive "perfectionist," I wasn't interested. Reading Jen's message again now, I catch myself smiling again, but this time at
Jen's compliment. It hadn't occurred to me that Jessica would be
capable of dispensing praise, let alone praise unqualified enough
to lead her colleague to believe I "must be the best."

Dear Jen:
Thank you for your interest in On Target Essay . . .

I glance at the clock on the bottom right side of my computer screen and notice that the auction for my brilliant red

compact is officially over. I quickly click open the eBay screen to see how much the shipping cost is going to add to the purchase price. The winning bid is thirty dollars, which can't be right since I only added three dollars to the previous twenty-five dollar bid. Somehow they must have miscalculated, because I put in the winning bid for twenty-eight dollars. Then I look at the winning bidder's moniker: SassyLdy.

Did I really just lose that compact to someone named SassyLdy?

I glance back at the screen. SassyLdy has a big purple winner's star by her name. That compact was so mine it may as well have had my initials engraved on it. I already knew exactly where I would display it on the vanity. How did I lose this? I get off my bed and resist the urge to shove my laptop to the floor. I shouldn't care this much, but I do. I lurch back over to the computer, enraged and helpless, and click on the picture of the compact again to enlarge it. Scratched, yes, but now some SassyLdy will be the one who gets to see those marks every day.

I grab at the remaining pile of clothes at the end of the bed and hurl them to the ground. I'm so upset my hands are shaking. I look at the pile of crap now lying on the floor and see the two comic character T-shirts that, weeks ago, I bought from Zach for Sophie and Lola to wear to his opening. I pick one up and throw it across the room. I want to cry.

How did I just fuck things up so badly between us?

What have I done? If my stomach started to sour when I lost a discolored compact five minutes ago, that's nothing compared to the nausea I'm feeling now.

I sit back down on the bed and pick up my laptop, hoping it's not too late to retrieve something. I close the eBay page and start typing an e-mail.

Dear Jen:

Thanks for your interest in On Target Essay. The first step when getting started with new clients is to set up an orientation session, so I can get a sense of your interests, strengths, and credentials, and you can get a better idea of the On Target Essay method. I'm available to meet with you Monday through Thursday evenings of next week. Please let me know which day works best for you.

I look forward to being in touch again soon.

All best,

Rachel Chambers

On Target Essay

I hit Send.

32

When I open the door to the Caseborough Gallery on Baltic Street, I'm nervous. I hold the door open for Kate, who's pushing Lola in her stroller and holding Sophie's hand, and we're met by a loud din of voices emanating from the crowded space. I take a deep breath and walk in behind them, letting the door slam shut on the cold outside.

I'd invited Kate to the opening weeks ago, when I first found out about Zach's show. It seemed like it would be a nice distraction for both of us, and I knew she'd love the idea of discovering a new gallery in her neighborhood. Then, after the fight with Zach, I'd called Kate and told her we weren't going after all.

"Zach and I had a falling out," I told her when I called that night.

There's a pause and Kate asks, "What happened?"

"We were having lunch today and he . . . went off on me."

There's another pause. "I'm not sure I see what you mean, Rach."

I summarize Zach's sermon and my ensuing harangue. There's a much shorter pause from Kate this time before she replies, in her cut-the-bullshit way, "So what you're saying is that he told you some straight truth and it hurt your feelings? He told you something you didn't want to hear and you lashed out?"

"Well—"

"He gives you a little bit of a how-things-are talk, he touches a sore spot, and you get nasty. So now you're going to avoid him—now that you guys have finally started saying things to each other? I'm not going to say whether I think Zach is right or wrong, even though I think he's completely right. But I am going to say that this guy has been paying attention, even if you haven't. So what are you waiting for to apologize, Rachel?"

"I think it might be beyond apology, though, Kate."

I can hear her let out an annoyed sigh into the receiver. "Rach, if you didn't take away anything from his lecture, you deserve to lose him. Of course we're going to this opening."

The gallery opening started at 7, and it's only 7:30 when we arrive, but already the space looks full. Small clusters of people scattered throughout, their chatter echoing between the polished concrete floors and the high ceilings. Kate had been talking up the show to Sophie and Lola all day, so both are keyed up with little-girl energy, while Kate and I both know that she is really coming so I won't chicken out. Zach and I haven't spoken since the fight three days ago, and I'm not even sure I'm still welcome here tonight.

I'd spent the past two days with a knot in my stomach, rehearsing my apology. I thought about e-mailing Zach, but I couldn't admit how badly I was feeling in a medium of lowercase letters and emoticons. I considered calling him up and telling him how I felt over the phone, but it didn't seem like enough, and mostly it seemed like it could go all wrong. He could say nothing at all, and there could be just dead silence in response.

I help Sophie out of her coat as Kate unwraps and unzips Lola. Both little girls are wearing the T-shirts I gave them. Sophie is Jemima Warrior Princess—Kate even tied a bandana in her hair—and Lola is wearing a shirt with a punked-out Mousewoman named Maxi. Both girls are drowning in the adult-size T-shirts, wearing them belted like tunics over tights and turtlenecks.

I see Zach in the far corner of the gallery, shaking someone's hand and surrounded by a small circle of people. When the door slams shut behind us, he looks over and I know he's seen me. I watch him shake someone else's hand in the group, then I look away quickly, feeling like an intruder. I shouldn't be here at all. Zach looks as polished as I've ever seen him. Instead of his usual layered T-shirts and hooded sweatshirt, he's wearing a dark ribbed turtleneck sweater and baggy brown cords. Even his beard looks neater.

I look to Kate, who is smiling, and then I turn slightly and realize she's smiling because Zach is walking toward us. I hesitate before saying anything, no longer sure how to phrase the apology I've been repeating incessantly for three days.

"Hi," I say tentatively.

"Hi," he replies, almost mimicking my tone, and I wonder briefly if he's making fun of me.

My mouth feels too full of all the things I want to say, and the only thing that comes out is a lame, "You look really . . . nice."

"Hey, thanks. Yeah, you know, I made a little effort," he replies, grinning, and running his hands over his newly trimmed beard. I am just about to introduce Kate again, assuming he's forgotten her name since their brief encounter several months ago, when Zach leans in and kisses her cheek.

"Hi, Kate. It's really nice to see you again. And thanks so much for coming."

"Well, congratulations to you, Zach! Rachel tells me this is your first gallery show—what a wonderful space," Kate replies, gesturing to the long expanse of white walls extending back through three separate small rooms. "It's a beautiful setup."

"I think so, too. I really couldn't be happier with the way things turned out tonight. The stuff looks so much better hanging on these walls. I'm wondering if the owners didn't touch up a few of my pieces with some white-out and magic marker, because I'm definitely not as talented as the *incredible* artist who drew all these pictures."

Kate laughs. "Rumor has it, actually, that you're not untalented at all. In fact, evidence on the Internet also confirms this. The girls and I have been visiting the website a lot lately,"

Kate adds, putting her hands on the little girls' shoulders, "and I've been looking forward to seeing your stuff full-scale."

I'm listening to their exchange, a little puzzled and amused. However awkward I'm feeling, Kate and Zach are acting as if things couldn't be more normal. As if there weren't any strain to speak of, as if Zach and I hadn't hurled hurtful accusations at each other a few days ago. In fact, if it weren't my married older sister and my former partner-in-crime co-worker who'd only met once previously for about three minutes, I'd think they were trying to impress each other.

"Well it's a pleasure to welcome such informed viewers. In fact I'd love to take your very stylish friends here on a personal tour," Zach says, smiling at Sophie and Lola, clearly delighted by the newly expanded age range of his fan base.

"Girls, this is the artist who drew the superheroes on your T-shirts and all the great stuff we were looking at on the computer yesterday." They look up at Zach with the disbelieving curiosity of children who've just discovered their own belly buttons. "Zach, this is Sophie and Lola. Can you guys say hello?" Kate prompts.

Zach crouches down to talk to the girls at their eye level. "Hi. I have to say, I think your dresses are very cool! Thanks for wearing them to the show!"

Lola clings to Kate's leg, pressing her face into the back of her mother's knee.

But Sophie steps forward, twirling around in her giant T-shirt. "My name's Sophie. Are you the one who draws Jemima and the Twins and those guys?"

"Yup, that's me. I draw them and a bunch of others, too. Do you draw?"

"Yeah! We even had an art show at home the other day."

"Well, I wish I could have come to see it. What was your medium?" Zach asks very seriously, prompting Kate and me to laugh as Sophie stops and looks puzzled.

"My medium?" she laugh-yells as though suddenly getting a joke. "No, we made paintings! And when Daddy came home, we had a show."

Zach nods his head gravely and then shifts toward Lola, who is now staring at Zach's beard, fascinated, while gripping Kate's pant leg with one hand and sucking the thumb of the other hand.

"Who's that on your dress, Lola?"

Lola lowers her head to peer at her tummy and says, into her thumb, "Mackthee."

"And what kind of animal is Maxi?"

Lola takes her thumb out of her mouth and looks up. "Maxi is a mouse."

During the exchange, Kate looks at me over Zach's squatting figure, glancing down at him meaningfully with a discreet nod. "Hey, girls!" she says. "Why don't we take a look at some of the big drawings Zach has made." She doesn't wait for their response, takes them by the hand, and leads them away, leaving Zach and me alone in the middle of the gallery.

"Zach," I say, then close my eyes, trying to summon the courage to tell him how desperately afraid I was that he wouldn't ever speak to me again, and how awful that feeling was, more awful than I ever expected—

"You know what?" he says, interrupting my thoughts. I open my eyes and look at him. "There's a lot of great art here tonight. You should really take a look at some of it."

I understand his reaction—he just doesn't want to deal with the whole thing right now and I can't blame him—but I must at least get an apology out. "I just need to tell you how sorry—"

But he cuts me off again. "Seriously," he replies coolly, "we can talk later."

As if sensing the artist is being stalked by an unwanted fan, one of the gallery owners approaches. "So sorry, but can we steal him for a moment?" Merle Caseborough asks me.

Zach nods. "We'll catch up later," he says and allows himself to be escorted away.

Of course he wasn't going to want to talk about it, especially not here and now. It's a big night for him. I shouldn't have imposed this on him. I said nothing and he said nothing, but I still feel crushed. It was delusional of me to think things could be set right between us. Kate's just wrong, and I'm fooling myself if I don't get it. Standing alone in the middle of the gallery, I feel completely unmoored. I want to leave. I look to the wall to my left, which has Zach's name stenciled in black letters and seems to serve as a literal and figurative rebuke. Just to the right of his name hangs the first of a dozen large black and white comic strips, each about two feet by four feet and matted behind glass. I wait for the two people standing in front of the first strip to walk on and then I move closer.

I'm already awed by the size of the strips. I'd seen sketches of Zach's characters in his studio, in the notebook-size pencil drawings covering the wall, but the only completed strips I've seen are the ones on the website. The sheer scale of the strips, the actions blown up in stark black against white, in big, sixteen-inch squares, makes them seem even more grandiose. The first panel of this strip shows a female character with cone breasts and busting biceps, wearing a beauty-queen sash across her chest. My jaw drops, and I wheel around: It's Marilyn Manizer.

"Oh my God!" I say, much too loudly. "Marilyn!" I take a few quick steps to the other side of the gallery and spot Zach in the next room standing in a group of people with the gallery owner. I spin back around to look at the panel. And then I look at the next one, also featuring my alter ego. I get closer and then quickly walk around the whole room, looking at each of the framed strips hanging on all four walls. Marilyn. Marilyn. Marilyn. Marilyn. My eyes get wider and my grin keeps broadening as I barge through small groups of people to examine each of the familiar strips. I'm on the opposite side of the room when I look back over at Zach. He is still standing in the group, but he's now looking at me looking at the strips. Our eyes meet and we both smile broadly, as though sharing a hilarious private joke—even though the joke is hanging on every wall surrounding us. I start laughing, and the couple passing nearby stares at me, then in the direction I'm looking, trying to figure out what they're missing.

I begin walking toward Zach, and I'm just approaching the cluster of people surrounding him when Anita Caseborough, Merle's wife and the other gallery owner, takes him by the arm.

"I want to introduce you to some friends of ours, Zach," she says, "Helene and Gareth Davis, that couple I was telling you about. They're very interested in cartoon and outsider art—they collect Crumb and Henry Darger—and Helene just *loves* your stuff," Anita adds, lowering her voice. "I think she's really interested in a couple of pieces, but doesn't know which to choose."

Zach sneaks a glace my way as Anita guides him past me and toward a forty-something couple in the corner who are standing in front of a strip—the one in which Marilyn barely escapes being barbecued by a fat monk. I give him an encouraging smile and turn back to continue looking where I left off.

I wander around slowly from strip to strip, each panel reminding me of the instant messages and phone calls in which I'd embellished for Zach my ridiculous misadventures. I chuckle softly, remembering some exact phrase I used, Zach's melodramatic reaction, and, of course, the silly exploit itself. All these banal events, now transformed into the baroque adventures of a larger-than-life superheroine, framed and hanging on gallery walls. Who could have imagined such an awesome ending to any of it?

I look around for Kate and the girls and spot them standing in front of the first Marilyn strip, the one of her imaginary nightmarish blind date. I see Sophie pointing at the box where the hippie date spoons macrobiotic goop down a funnel lodged in Marilyn's mouth, and she screws up her face and makes an "Ew" shape with her mouth. I wonder what Kate would think if she knew that before her transformation into a superconqueror of the city, Marilyn Manizer started out as Rachel Chambers. And that Zach, the mild-mannered, scruffy nice guy, is responsible for that transformation. I'm not even sure what to think, except that I still can't stop laughing, can't stop wishing I could tell Kate and everyone else here that I'm the improbable inspiration for these works of art.

Zach has played the confidante and the alchemist, listening to my stories, getting at the good parts, and then turning them into something much bigger and more meaningful. I had no idea Marilyn was anything more than an illustrated extension of our little game at work. I wonder how long Zach has been making these blown-up renderings of the strip, and how long he's been planning to show them. As I walk around the gallery rereading the caricatures of my own maudlin life, I marvel at what Zach has made of me. I've been the commonplace muse to a cartoonist who's fashioned me into something much more inspiring than I ever was. He took my everyday disasters and fuck-ups and self-deprecation, and laughed with me as I laughed at myself. And it wasn't simply that he got the joke, it was that we shared it. I guess the whole point of it was that we shared it.

I feel a tap on my shoulder and turn to see Zach standing next to me. He's smiling sheepishly.

"So, do I owe you an apology?" he asks, gesturing to the walls around him. "A cut of the profits? A credit for all the hard work you put in being yourself?"

"You don't owe me anything. Except for the right to thank you." I finally give him the hug I've been wanting to give him. I hug him long enough to embarrass him, probably, in front of everyone in the gallery, although most people seem too busy with the Marilyn adventures to see the artist and his completely blind and anonymous muse embracing in the middle of the room.

"I'd love to take my esteemed collaborator here on a personal tour of the show, if she'd like?"

"I'd be delighted. I'm not familiar with the work at all—and I have a lot of questions," I say as we go back to begin at the first panel. We stop in front of the framed strip and I gesture broadly, pointing. "I've been wondering, for example . . . do you draw your material from your own life?"

Zach chuckles. "Unlike the heroine, I wouldn't ever kiss and tell. Unless, of course, I survived a date with Marilyn," he replies, turning toward me and bowing slightly.

"Maybe you should give it a try." I laugh again and smile stupidly.

We wander from panel to panel, and Zach makes as if to give me a moment of silence in front of the strip of Marilyn being henpecked by Molly, acknowledging what had been a particularly mortifying episode. I stop at the Guerrilla Marketing strip and give Zach's hand an exaggerated squeeze, thanking him for making me look *much* more powerful and savvy than even the most generous distortion of reality would allow. We get to the last strip in the series, and I realize that it's a new one that I've never seen before.

In the first panel, Marilyn Manizer is hanging off a

precipice, one muscular, trembling arm hanging on, the other dangling toward the ground far below. In the second panel, an unidentified hand reaches out to her over the ledge. But the third panel—the final panel—is blank.

"What? Zach?" I say, turning to face him. "What's happens to Marilyn now?"

"I don't know," Zach replies. "What do you think?"

EPILOGUE

The day the *Business Week* issue ranking the top business schools arrives on newsstands, On Target Essay's website gets more hits in twenty-four hours than all the hits combined since it launched—thanks to one little blurb tucked away in a side-box in the magazine. And if only one-half of 1 percent of the 73,012 unique viewers who visit the site that day sign on for my service, I'll still have approximately one new client for every day of the year.

When traffic peaks and the overwhelmed website crashes, I smile and call Zach, still the de facto webmaster. Then I start planning the party. If I've learned anything, it's that the truly savvy businesswoman knows the importance of seizing a moment and celebrating properly.

BUSINESSWEEK

When you've only got one shot to impress, you need to make a killer impression. That's not only the slogan of On Target Essay, a new writing consultancy for the business school set, that's precisely what Rachel Chambers, the young entrepreneur who founded the company, has been doing herself.

Chambers, a 27-year-old writer originally from Minnesota, claims that she never expected the company to take off so explosively. But with a roster of clients from all the biggest investment banks and consulting firms, she has created one of this year's most successful new business school services.

Her low-key but professional style, and uncanny ability to spin a flaw into a mark of character, have made her a sought-after player in the application industry. A killer impression, indeed. Business school applicants could learn a lot from Chambers, a businesswoman who saw a market, found her niche, and cashed in.

ROBIN EPSTEIN received her MFA from Columbia, and is a freelance writer who has written for sitcoms, magazines, and has contributed to *This American Life*. RENÉE KAPLAN is a television producer, and a former writer and editor for the *New York Observer*. They met in college and both live in New York. Visit their website at www.shakingherassets.com.